Starlight

Gary Weston

*To Frank & Betty
Love Sue
x x*

Copyright © 2010 Gary Weston

All rights reserved.

ISBN:1479187127
ISBN-13: 978-1479187126

DEDICATION

Dedicated my family, to Su Kane, the Bike Doc, Cerbarus the unstoppable and the Revolting Animal Motorcycle Club, Bluesdog, Smiley, Oddball, Surf, Scrubber, Shadow, Bumblebee, Mandy, the irrepressible Frances Hartshorne and to all the fantastic people who do what they do for the animals that share our planet. To Paul Butterworth for his advice on motorcycle training. To Kevin Couling as Lord of Little Neston cum Hargrave. It is also dedicated to the people around the world who spend their lives trying to make a difference for the welfare of animals, both wild and domestic. To Anna Scott Graham, chief typo basher and Suzy Stewart Dubot for promoting this project.

Also a special thank you to the readers who have purchased this book who by doing so have made a donation the the Peoples Dispensary for Sick Animals.

Come and Join the Revolting Animals M C C on one of their many charity bike runs on youtube.

http://www.youtube.com/watch?v=ysiabNggZ8c

ACKNOWLEDGMENTS

To Su Kane and the Starlight Army and the Revolting Animals Motorcycle Club

CHAPTER 1

Twenty years ago, in the West Midlands of England, UK.

The park was a handy short-cut between home and school. Eleven year old Su Kane always went this way, taking her time, because her mother wouldn't be home from work for another twenty minutes. Su had her own key of course, but she had something to do before going home. She had walked with Frances Hartshorne, her cousin who was in the same class as her, but parted at the gates on the south side of the park. Where Fran lived didn't require a walk through the park, so, Su said bye to her cousin and walked along the path that followed the banks of the small lake. Between the bandstand, playground and lake was a small picnic area with a wooden table and benches concreted into the ground.

Su dropped her school-bag on the table and took out her lunch-box. It was covered in pictures of horses and dogs which she had glued onto the box herself. She opened the box and took out the half sandwich and leaving her stuff on the table, went over to the water's edge, dry brown leaves crunching underfoot. The lake was man-made and she knew the first few yards all the way around were deliberately shallow, in case anyone fell in. The middle was deeper to allow the paddle boats somewhere to go.

She shivered a little, but she didn't mind the chilly weather, enjoying instead the autumnal colours of the surrounding trees and bushes. Over the years, the small islands created for bird-life had overgrown to provide natural shelter and nesting places for the ducks. From close by she heard a familiar splash and several ducks swam from behind low reeds towards her. She counted five in this particular group. There was always an anxious moment as she waited for the sixth duck. Swimming around in agitated circles, the first five quacked their impatience at her, demanding the titbits. But Su waited for Waddle, her favourite duck. A minute later, there was another splash and Waddle came out from behind the reeds.

She, for Su was sure she was a she because female ducks were usually less colourful than the male ducks, splashed awkwardly towards her, stopping shy of joining the group. One colourful male duck flapped his wings at Waddle, quacking raucously at her. Waddle knew her place in the pecking order, and held back, keeping her distance. Confident he had made his point, the male duck took up his dominant position closest to the girl. Su knew what to do. She had already broken up some of the scraps into many small pieces, apart from a few larger pieces. She sprinkled the smaller bits around the five ducks, and when they were preoccupied she threw the larger pieces at Waddle, who gobbled them up. She had eaten the morsels before the others had even noticed.

'Sorry, Waddle. That's the lot.'

Su took her box to her bag and stuffed it inside. She could see the ducks were already making their way back to their little island, Waddle keeping her normal distance from the others. Su had been there the day Waddle had been hit by the stones the little boys had been throwing at her. They were her own age, but not from her school. She had shouted at them to stop and they had laughed at her, but when she ran at them and pushed them hard, they realised she had meant business and ran away, still laughing at her and calling her names. When they had gone, she looked for Waddle, and could see she was injured. But she was eleven. What could she do?

The following day, she had hurried from school, her mind totally consumed by the thought of the injured duck and angry inside at how those stupid boys had deliberately hurt her. She had taken extra slices of bread when her mother hadn't been watching and hoped the duck was okay. When she finally saw the pretty duck, damaged but alive, she was both happy and sad at the same time. She always made sure Waddle got some of the bread.

After two more weeks, Waddle had recovered well, but not completely. Su never missed a day of bringing her scraps, including Saturday and Sunday. It was the best she could do, trying in her own way to make amends for the boys cruelty. Perhaps Waddle would survive. Looping the handle of her bag over her shoulder, she started for home.

Su had only gone a few yards when she heard a splash. If it was those boys again throwing at the ducks, she would soon sort them out. But there were no boys; just a man walking away. She slowed down, pleased it wasn't the boys. Then through a gap in the trees and bushes, she could see something in the lake. It was a plastic shopping bag. It was what the man had thrown into the water, she decided. Not much of an example to set, throwing rubbish in the lake.

The bag was tied up at the top and air had been trapped inside, keeping it afloat. It was about ten yards off shore, just where the shallow part ended. She sighed and was about to move on, when she noticed the bag was moving. There was something inside it; something alive. What on Earth could it be? Then she heard the cry that kittens make. She couldn't believe it. The man had tossed in a bag of live kittens as if they were garbage, so that they would sink and drown.

Su looked for the man, but he had gone. There was nobody around, only her. She felt tears of anger running down her cheeks. The bag moved about as the kittens struggled inside. She *had* to do something. She dropped her bag on the bank and began wading into the bitter cold water. It came up to her chest. Her feet were sticking in the thick mud on the bottom, and she could hardly move. She could hear the kittens as she slowly got closer, and she could see the bag was beginning to sink. On she moved, the water over her chest. She could swim a little, but not well. The only way she could reach the kittens was to try to swim over to them. She took a deep breath and lunged forwards, the bag only two yards away, but it was into the deeper water now. Her clothes made the swimming difficult, but she made progress.

She was almost on top of them, when the bag started to sink below the surface. Almost in reach, Su made a final desperate few strokes and she had it, but the bag was full of water. She knew she had to get the kittens out of there, otherwise they would drown before she made it back to the bank. Treading water, she ripped open the bag and could see the tiny kittens, three of them, and she could tell she was too late. And then one of them moved.

One was still alive. She took hold of the kitten, wet and cold in her hands. She could feel it breathing in her hands, its heart barely beating, its eyes still closed. Perhaps the others were still alive, too? But she couldn't get back to the bank with both the kitten and the bag. She took another look at the two in the bag. She was sure they were dead. She had to let them go. She let go of the bag and sadly watched it sink.

It was awkward making it back to the bank trying to hold the kitten out of the water. She was exhausted from the effort as she eventually managed to scramble out of the lake, freezing and covered in mud. She shivered with the cold, and tried to catch her breath as she lay on the grass. The kitten looked as if it too had died, but she saw it move slightly. She knew that if she didn't get it home, it wouldn't survive much longer. It took all her resolve to get to her feet and pick up the kitten and her bag. Tucking the kitten inside her dripping coat, she looked around for help. She was completely alone. She ran as fast as she could to get to the warmth and sanctuary of her home. Running towards her, she could see her mother.

'My, God. Su. I've been frantic. What the hell happened to you?'

From under her coat, Su took out the kitten.

Su's mother tried to make sense of it all. 'Why me, Lord, why me?' She took off her own coat and wrapped it around her daughter. 'Come on. Let's get you home.'

CHAPTER 2

'What ever possessed you to do a thing like that?' said Barbara Kane, peeling off her daughter's wet clothes. 'Ruined, most of these. Have you any idea the cost of school uniforms?'

Su wasn't sorry for what she had done. Given the choice she would have done it all over again. 'I had to try and save them, Mum. I couldn't let them just drown. Can I keep her, Mum? Please?'

Barbara sighed and shook her head. 'How did I know that was coming? Look at these shoes. One month old and now I have to find money for another pair.'

Su *was* sorry about that. She knew how hard it had been since her father had died. It was always a struggle making ends meet.

'I'll pay for her food out of my pocket money, Mum. I'll take care of her.'

'Never mind that for now. Right. In that shower with you. I'll put a hot water-bottle in your bed. Make sure your hair is clean.'

Su got in the shower feeling the hot water thaw her freezing skin. She knew her mother wasn't really angry with her. She was just concerned, that was all. She lathered her hair and let the soapy water wash down her body. Eventually she stopped shivering as the heat did its job.

In the kitchen, Barbara opened a tin of chicken soup and emptied it into a saucepan. Su's pyjamas were warming by the fire. As she filled the kettle for the hot water bottle, she looked over at the kitchen table where the kitten was wrapped up in a towel. It was the first thing Su had done when they had got home, not thinking about herself, just the kitten.

'Be better off if you did die,' she said. 'I've no money for pets.' The kitten looked so tiny and helpless, its grey and white fur clinging to its skin it was so wet still. Briefly, the idea of finishing the job and drowning the kitten in the sink went through her mind. Su wouldn't be any the wiser. She would just tell her it hadn't survived and that was that. She picked it up, wrapped in the towel. I was just skin and bone, only hours old. But somehow, holding the kitten as if it were a baby, brought out her maternal instincts. She had no doubt that Su would do as she promised and look after it. 'You make it through the night, I guess you were meant to be.'

Putting the kitten back on the table, Barbara filled the hot water bottle and took it to Su's bedroom and put it in the middle of the bed under the sheets, covering it up with the Donald Duck duvet. Then she took the warm pyjamas into the bathroom where Su was drying herself off.

'Here. Put these on and get into bed. I've soup on for you. I have to see to it before it boils over.'

'Mum. I have to look after the kitten.'

'Bed. Don't argue.'

Barbara rescued the soup and put it on a tray with a few slices of bread then she carried it to her daughter. 'Right. Sit up. Now get this down you.'

'But...'

'I'll look after the kitten. I promise. I'll bring you hot chocolate later.'

Su sneezed, almost turning the tray over.

'I wouldn't be surprised if you caught a cold after being in that lake at this time of year. Eat up.'

Barbara left Su to eat and returned to the kitten. It was wriggling about on the table as if reaching out to her. 'And just how do you suppose I'm going to get some food inside you, you little perisher?'

Barbara knew she had to do something fast and she decided she needed expert advice. She picked up the phone book and called the number for the Peoples Dispensary for Sick Animals.

'Oh, hi. I was wondering if you could give me some advice please? My daughter rescued a little kitten and we are looking after it. I was just wondering if you could tell me what to feed it. Oh. I never knew that. Lactose intolerant. Really? Good job I called, then. I was thinking just milk. I'd go and get something else but I have to take care of my daughter. You will? Oh, thank you so much.'

Less then a half hour later she opened the front door to the local veterinarian for the P D S A. To anyone who knew him, he was just called Uncle Garf.

Barbara said, 'Come in. I was amazed when you said you'd come here.'

'I live just around the corner. I only work part-time these days. Just a volunteer to feel useful. Another vet's taking care of the surgery.' Garf walked with the aid of a stick and limped into the hallway. 'Not as agile as I used to be. So. Where's the patient?'

Barbara led him into the kitchen. 'She had been thrown in the lake in the park. My daughter jumped in and rescued her.'

'Really? Good heavens.' He placed his bag on the table and opened it as he looked down at the kitten. 'Would you mind picking her up for me please? If I bend down I might not get up again.'

Barbara picked up the kitten in the towel and put her on the table where the vet could get to her. He took out a stethoscope and listened to her heart and lungs. 'Her lungs are clear. Her heartbeat is normal.' Next he used a rectal thermometer. 'Temperature normal. Looking good so far.'

'She'll live?'

'I didn't say that. That's up to a much higher authority. All we can do is give her a fighting chance.'

They hadn't seen Su enter. 'She has to live, Doctor.'

Garf smiled at the little girl. 'I'm not a doctor. I'm a veterinarian. So. Your mother has been telling me what a brave little girl you were.'

Barbara said, 'You should be in bed, young lady.' She turned to the vet. 'She caught a cold doing what she did.'

'I needed the toilet,' said Su. 'Is she going to live?'

'Maybe,' said Garf. 'With you looking after her she stands a chance. I'll sit down if I may.' He sat on one of the dining chairs. 'Now. Kittens normally get all their nutrients from their mothers. Just giving her milk would be very bad for her indeed. I've some special formulae which is lactose free. Right. Here you are. Take some of it and stand it hot water, just to warm it up a little. Now. I've a feeding tube in here somewhere.' He rummaged in his bag. 'Here we go. Only as much as she wants to eat every couple of hours, then wash the tube out well after each feed. That's the way. Don't force it on her, let her help herself. Perfect.'

'I can do that,' said Su.

'When you're feeling better,' said Barbara.

Garf said, 'That's just stuff going into her. It also has to come out again.'

Barbara said, 'How do you mean?'

'Well, the mother cat normally stimulates the kittens rear end with her tongue. Su is now the mother, not that I'm suggesting she should use her tongue. Get hold of some of that kitchen cloth, wet it in warm water then gently rub her bottom until she poops.'

'Ugh!' said Su. Then she nodded. 'I can do that.'

'Not in your condition,' said Barbara 'I'll do it for now. Like this?"

Garf said, 'Perfect. See all that coming out of her? This needs to be done after each meal, for about a month. Now, Su. Orphaned kittens, even with the best of care, may not always develop as they would with their mothers to look after them. It is possible she could be blind or deaf. But fingers crossed that she'll be fine. Just be prepared for her not to be, right?'

Su sighed. 'Okay. Why do people do such things?'

Garf shook his head sadly. 'I've asked myself that same question for nearly fifty years and I still don't know.' He closed his bag and picked up his walking stick. 'Right. I have to be going or my wife will be sending a search party out for me.'

'Say thank you, Su.'

'Thanks.'

'Special people call me Uncle Garf. I'd say you qualify.'

Su started coughing and Barbara didn't like the look of her. She put the palm of her hand on the girl's forehead. It felt hot and clammy. 'You're burning up. Okay. Back to bed for you. I'll take care of the kitten for now.' Su went off to bed. To Garf, Barbara said, 'Thanks for your help. What do I owe you?'

'Me, nothing. Just make a donation at the clinic when you can. I'll call back in a couple of days. Good luck.'

Two hours later, it was time to feed the kitten again. She sat on a chair with the kitten in her arms, feeding her like she'd been instructed. 'Just look at you eat' she said, watching the kitten feed.

She thought of a time eleven years earlier when she would sit just the same way, breastfeeding her daughter. Eleven years. Where the hell had that time gone? A stupid industrial accident taking away her husband before Su had turned two; an insurance company refusing to pay out the full policy claiming he had been a worker acting negligently, contributing at least in some degree to his own death. Years of struggling, often working two jobs to keep a roof over their heads and food on the table. But they survived, one way or another.

Christmases were especially hard, because that's when he had died. Working an extra shift to make sure his family had the best Christmas they could afford. He never finished that last extra shift. And for the last few years Su had always asked the same question. "Can Santa bring me a puppy, Mum?"

And the answer would always be the same. "Santa knows we can't afford to keep a puppy, Su."

Barbara smiled at the irony. 'Now look at me. You are no puppy, but here you are anyway.'

The kitten had stopped suckling and was fast asleep in her arms. It was warm, now, and after one hell of a first day, her life was in the laps of the various gods. Her daughter had waded out into that freezing lake to save it and now here she was, clinging on against all the odds for the right to survive. With the kitten well fed, dry and warm, she put it on the table, emptied the laundry basket, placed the kitten in it wrapped up in the towel and left her to sleep. She went into Su's bedroom and didn't like what she saw. There was vomit on the duvet and it was obvious Su was far from right. Her forehead was really hot and her head was rolling from side to side.

'Su? Su?'

'Mum. I feel bad.'

Barbara raced to the bathroom and got the medicine box and took out the thermometer and hurried back to Su and pushed the end into her mouth. One hundred and three it went up to.

'I'm calling the doctor. I'll be right back.'

* * *

Doctor David Pottinger was old school. No youngster himself, he set about checking the little girl's condition. 'Any idea how long she was in the lake?'

'She told me she had to swim out to save the kittens. I don't know. Five, maybe ten minutes?'

'She has a mild case of pneumonia. She probably swallowed a lot of that water. God knows what that's like. You did the right thing calling me.'

'Is she...?'

'She's a strong, healthy girl. No need for the hospital. Keep her warm, give her plenty of fluids, make sure she completes the course of antibiotics.'

'Mum. Is the kitten..,?'

'She's had a feed and is fast asleep.'

'Can I see her?'

The doctor nodded. Barbara went to the kitchen and gathered up the kitten in her arms and took it to Su.

'See? Snug as a bug in a rug, thanks to you.'

Through weepy blue eyes, Su looked at the kitten, still fast asleep. She reached out and stroked the white markings on her chest.

'Look, Mum. She has a star on her chest. She's just like...starlight.'

Doctor Pottinger smiled. 'Sounds like a good name for her. I'll be on my way. I don't think you have anything to worry about. You know, not many kids her age would have done what she did. You have a very special daughter, Mrs Kane.'

Barbara looked down at her daughter who was now asleep. 'I think you're right. Thank you.'

Chapter 3

'Thanks for doing this, Joan. The last thing I need is not to be earning.'

'It's what sisters do. You get off to work and I'll look after Su.'

'She's fast asleep. I was up half the night what with Su and the damn kitten. Help yourself to anything in the house. Now you remember what I said about feeding and emptying the kitten? She'll be needing another feed by now.'

'I know what to do. Now you get off to work or you'll be late.'

'Thanks, Joan.'

Joan Hartshorne went into the kitchen and put the kettle on to make herself a cup of tea. While that was boiling, she looked in the laundry basket where Starlight was wriggling, instinctively trying to find her mother.

'Look at you. So cute. I suppose I have to feed you as well, do I?'

Joan sat with the kitten in her arms, feeding her from the tube. 'Nothing wrong with your appetite, puss. That's always a good sign.' She continued to hold the kitten after the tube was empty. After another ten minutes Joan followed the vets instructions to make Starlight empty herself. 'That stinks.' She cleaned up the mess and got a clean towel to act as a blanket and placed the kitten in a cardboard box she'd found. 'Off to sleep with you.' The kitten yawned and curled up into a ball and dozed off. Joan washed her hands and then went to see the other patient.

'How are you feeling?'

'Horrible. I've got a headache. How's Starlight?'

'Asleep, like you should be. She's had a good feed and emptied herself. I'll do it all again before your Mum gets home from work.' Joan picked up the thermometer from the bedside cabinet. 'Open wide.' She left the thermometer for a moment and checked it. 'One hundred and two. High, but coming down.'

'I'm hungry, Aunt Joan.'

'Okay. I'll get you something for your headache. Could you manage scrambled eggs and toast?'

Su nodded. 'Please.'

'You were very brave saving the kitten.'

'Only one of them, though. I wish I could have saved all of them.'

'You did your best. That's all anyone can do.'

'I hate people who hurt animals. What's wrong with people like that?'

Joan sighed and shook her head. 'I've no idea. I suppose they weren't brought up to respect other creatures and understand they have feelings and can feel pain, just as people can do. At least you've done your bit.'

Su coughed again. 'It wasn't much though. I wish I could do more.'

'Maybe when you're older. I'll get you something for your headache and something to eat.'

Chapter 4
Four Years Later.

'Starlight. Get off the table,' said Barbara Kane, wagging a finger at the cat.

The cat did what she did with most commands. She ignored them and continued preening herself. Su took charge and picked her up. 'Come on, you. Boy are you getting heavy.'

Starlight had grown into a pretty, independently minded feline, with something of an attitude. She had fully recovered from the ordeal at the start of her life, and was a pampered pet that curled up on Su's bed at night. Her coat was a smoky grey but the star shape on her chest never went away. She wriggled in Su's arms insisting on being put down. She walked with a swagger over to her food bowl, flicking her tail at the people she allowed to share her home, then she started on her biscuits.

'Su. You'll be late for school again. Get a move on.'

'Yeah. I'm going. It's only geography first period. I mean who needs that? Anyone can read a map.'

'Your dad always said women couldn't read maps. He meant me in particular. Go. And keep out of trouble. Don't forget you are going to Joan's for dinner tonight.'

'Yeah, whatever.'

Su walked through the park, not in any particular hurry. At the southern gate, Fran was waiting for her.

'I nearly gave up on you,' said Fran. 'Now we'll both be late.'

'I won't. I'm not going.'

'You are impossible,' said Fran. 'Do you really want to get expelled?'

Su shrugged. 'I don't really care. I might turn up this afternoon.'

'Well, you wouldn't wanna miss Pretty Peter's class now would you.'

Another shrug. 'He's okay.'

'That's not what you said about him the other day. Look. I'm going. Are you coming with me or not?'

'Like I said. I might go this afternoon.'

'Whatever. Are you coming over tonight?'

'Dunno. Maybe.'

With a disparaging shake of her blonde hair, Fran walked off. Su was becoming more impossible by the day. They were still best friends, but sometimes Su could be hard work. What rankled Fran the most was, even though Su fooled around more than worked, missed more school days than she actually attended, seldom did any homework, she would swat the night before any exam and still come in the top five. For herself, she would spend hours on her books, always did her homework and would be lucky to scrape a pass in her exams. Infuriating.

Su watched Fran walk off to school, fished in her pocket for her cigarettes and found two in a packet. She lit one up and headed for the shopping centre She finished the smoke before she got to the entrance of the shops and crunched up the butt, dropping it in a trash bin. The shopping centre was warm and although she hated the rubbish music, the place had a bit of a buzz to it. There was always something to look at. Su checked out the clothes shops; just looking through the windows. She really didn't get it. All that fuss over clothes and shoes and make-up, for God's sake.

She had her own style and wasn't about to follow like a sheep, just because some naff magazine said she should. Jeans, faded and frayed, and a studded leather belt, leather jacket and scuffed trainers were her attire of choice. In case she went to school, she had the regulation white shirt on, making at least some small concession to authority; forgoing her preferred long t shirts she hand dyed with the wildest colours she could find. Her make-up, when she bothered, was a little eye shadow, mascara and lip-gloss.

She did do strange things with her hair, though. Her natural blonde shoulder length hair was now a random explosion of a dozen different colours, from blue to crimson. The more her mother or teachers frowned at her, the more colours went into it. Thirteen at the last count. She checked herself in the window reflection. She grinned. She was what she wanted to be. After a couple of hours walking around, she thought about what Fran had said. "Well, you wouldn't wanna miss Pretty Peter, now would you."

Peter Giles was a trainee teacher, terrified of the kids, but was as hot as hell, as far as she was concerned. Su loved to wind him up. She would sit next to Fran at the back of the class, fluttering her eyelashes, pouting and blowing kisses at the poor, flustered young man. He taught English. He'd be annoyed with her that afternoon, because she hadn't done her homework. Again. Yeah. She'd go and wind up Pretty Peter.

* * *

'I was so embarrassed,' said Fran, hurrying out of the school gate. 'I didn't know where to look.'

'Pretty Peter did,' said Su with a laugh. 'Right here, at my boobs.' She lit up her last cigarette.

'What boobs? You haven't got any.'

'Mine are bigger than your bee stings.'

'Crap. Will you do up your shirt? I don't want my mum and dad seeing you with your boobs hanging out.'

'Don't be such a drama queen. It's only a couple of buttons,' said Su, fastening her shirt. 'He only got a flash of my bra.'

Chapter 5

'Hello, Aunty Joan.'

'Hello, Su. You two had a good day at school?'

'Suppose so,' said Fran.

'Got any homework to do?'

'No,' said Su.

'A bit,' said Fran.

'Right. Go and get that done. Su. You keep dying your hair all the time like that, you'll be as bald as your Uncle Bill.'

Su shrugged and followed Fran upstairs to her room. Fran kicked off her shoes and flopped out on the bed. Su checked her appearance in the dressing table mirror. 'Can you imagine me being as bald as your dad?'

'Knowing you, you'd still look bloody gorgeous.'

'Yeah, probably. You're not really doing your bloody homework, are you?'

'I should. Mucky will blow her noggin' if I don't.' The formidable Mrs Mucklow was particularly scathing of students not handing in their homework. 'Sod it. Put some music on, will you?'

Su put some heavy rock on, only to be told to turn it down by Fran.

Fran said, 'What do you think of your mum's new boyfriend?'

Su shrugged. 'Mick seems okay. They're probably at it already. That's why she wanted me out of the way for the night.'

'She looked happy last time I saw her.'

'She always does when she's getting some action. Yeah. Whatever makes her happy.'

Half an hour later, Bill Hartshorne called them to go downstairs.

'Hi, Uncle Bill.'

'Hi, Su. It looks like Joan's done heaps so I hope you're hungry.'

'Uncle Bill. Can I ask you something?'

'Go for it.'

'It's kind of personal.'

'Okay. I'm just going outside for a smoke.'

'Filthy habit,' said Joan.

'You smoked like a chimney when we first met,' said Bill.

'I had the good sense to stop. Dinners on the table in five minutes. Fran. Lay the table, will you?'

Bill said, 'She'd have to be one hell of a big chicken to lay a table.'

'Five minutes.'

Outside Bill said, 'What is it, Su?'

'Nothing. I just wanted to cadge a few smokes off you.'

'Joan would do her nut if she knew I gave you smokes. Come in here.'

They went into the garage at the back of the house and Bill lit up a smoke for himself and gave the packet to Su. 'You can have those. Your aunt's right you know. Filthy habit.'

Su lit up and blew out smoke. 'Thanks, Bill.' She liked Bill, always making daft jokes. She also liked his garage where he hid away from Joan occasionally. 'What's under there?'

'Take a look.'

Su lifted off an oily tarpaulin from a lumpy shape in one corner. 'A motorbike?'

'A Triumph Tiger 100. Nineteen fifty nine. Five hundred C C. Twenty seven brake horse power. Just a single Amal carburettor to tune up. One of the last of the pre-unit models. That means the gearbox and engine were separate items. After that, it was engine and gearbox combined. This was still a classic in its day. Heard of Bob Dylan?'

'Of course.'

'He had one of these beauties except he crashed it. I was a kid at the time. I remember hearing about it on the radio. Not sure why, but he retired from public life after that crash. It was years later when he started doing anything again like touring.'

'You know so much stuff. A Tiger. I like the sound of that. I never knew you were a biker, Bill.'

'Once upon a time I also had hair. Then I met Joan.'

'Is it all here?'

'Pretty much. I bought it a couple of years ago from a mate of mine. He practically gave it away. Just a collection of bits in boxes. Joan threatens me with divorce every time I go near it.'

'Not much use just a load of bits.'

'True. I just don't have time these days. Like bikes do you?'

'Yeah. I'm gonna have me one when I'm older. I bet I could put it together.'

'You?'

'Why couldn't I? Because I'm a girl?'

'Not that. I just didn't see you as being mechanically minded, that's all.'

Su picked up a couple of parts and examined them. 'I bet you I could do it.'

Bill looked at his niece and then the old bike and stubbed out his smoke. 'I tell you what. Get it together and running, it's yours.'

'No shit! Seriously?'

'It was just some silly idea I had buying it in the first place. And like you said. Not much good like that. To pass your test you would have to start on a moped or something. You can go to a bigger bike later. From memory up to a one twenty five cc, as long as it's under fourteen B H P. Pass your test on that when you are seventeen and I think you can ride the Tiger.'

Su stared at the parts. She didn't just see a collection of bits, but a complete, gleaming bike. 'I can do this.'

'Come on. Time for dinner.'

Chapter 6

It was a rare moment in the Kane household. Su sitting at the table with her mother and Mick. It was fish and chips from the local chippy. Mick had bought them. Six months her mother and Mick had been together. It amazed Su they had lasted this long. Mick was so...ordinary. He looked ordinary, he had some ordinary boring job somewhere. He hardly said anything. Dull as. But her mum was happy with him. Then she learnt just how happy.

'Mick's asked me to marry him. Pass the sauce.'

Su passed the sauce. 'Yeah?'

'Yes. He asked and I said yes. Are you going to eat that fish?'

Su passed the fish over to her mother. 'You're getting married?'

'Yes. Mick's had a promotion at work and things are going well between us. So I said yes.'

'Okay.'

'Is that it. Okay?'

Su shrugged. 'Yeah. I guess.'

'Well, don't get too enthusiastic, will you?'

'Okay. Congratulations.'

'Thanks. Mick's divorce will be final soon. It'll take a few months to organise everything.'

'What's going to happen to me?'

'I want you to be a bridesmaid. You and Fran.'

'Thanks. But I meant what happens to me after the wedding?'

'Nothing changes. Except Mick moves in here with us.'

Su looked at Mick who managed a faint smile. A very ordinary smile, she thought.

Mick finally spoke. 'You don't mind do you, Su?'

Mick stayed there most nights anyway, so it hardly mattered. 'Yeah. I'm cool about it.'

* * *

'Red to positive, black to negative,' said Bill. 'It had to happen sooner or later, Su. One of these days you'll be flying the nest and your Mum doesn't want to be on her own. Besides. Maybe she loves him, anyway.'

Su turned the headlight switch. Nothing happened. 'Bulbs blown.'

'There's a spare one somewhere. Here try this.'

'Thanks. I said I don't mind about it. It's her life.' She turned the switch and the light came on.

'Well done. With a bit of luck, we can fire her up. Su. She may be your mother, but she's still a woman.'

'Have you seen that bloody dress she wants me to wear? Pink. Bloody pink. Fran, too. We'll look like two bloody Christmas fairies. Pass me that side cover, Bill. Ta. There. That's it. Job done.'

Bill had admired the dedication Su had put into the bike. Every Saturday and Sunday, sometimes during the week if she couldn't be bothered with school, himself in an occasional advisory capacity, but in reality it had been Su who had put the hard yards in. Her natural ability to figure where everything went together, rarely consulting the Haynes manual for direction, got the bike to her former glory. It had taken six months of dedication, but like his niece said, Job done. 'Okay,' he said. 'Moment of truth. Wheel the beast outside.'

Su took hold of the handlebars and knocked the side stand with her foot and the spring snapped it in place. Then she wheeled her pride and joy out of the garage.

'Right,' said Bill. 'Keep her in neutral. Petrol tap on. Choke on. Watch she doesn't kick back. That can hurt.'

Su patted the tank. 'Come on, girl.' She followed her uncle's instructions and rammed the kick-start lever hard with her right foot. There was a healthy blast from the exhaust and the old bike came to life again after more than a decade of being a dormant machine. Su blipped the throttle and the beast responded with a throaty roar, which brought both Joan and Fran outside.

'Hey,' said Joan. 'You'll have the neighbours up in arms. Keep the noise down.'

Fran stared at her cousin, covered in oil, hair like a living rainbow, old jeans ripped and filthy, and thought she looked magnificent. Su turned the engine off, her point being proven.

Bill said, 'I'll give her a spin later on and get an M.O.T certificate for her.'

'That was bloody beautiful, Bill.'

'Yep. Now all you have to do is learn how to ride, then pass your test.'

* * *

Bill still had a full motorcycle licence, so he offered to teach Su to ride. It seemed like second best to her, riding pillion to her uncle, but it was still a thrilling, exhilarating experience to be on the open motorway, roaring along at seventy miles per hour. It meant something to her that they wouldn't be riding the bike if she hadn't worked so hard putting it all together. She knew she had to pass the test on a much smaller bike first, but she was determined to do that in the shortest time possible. After a few miles, Bill took the bike off the highway onto a disused warehouse site. He stopped the engine, dropped the side-stand and got off and took his full-face helmet off.

'This place is perfect for you to practice on,' he said. 'What they'll be looking for is that you have control of the bike. That includes slow riding speeds as well as speed limit speeds. Stall in traffic as you're riding along; some tosser not paying attention could easily plough into the back of you. Now you know how to change gears, so just take her around the car park perimeter a few times. Don't use the choke because she's all warmed up. Off you go.'

Su started the bike and blipped the throttle a couple of times. Pulling on the clutch she toed it into first, and fed the revs perfectly, getting smoothly up to twenty miles per hour. There was a bit of crunch as she took it into second, but third was as smooth as silk. There wasn't enough room on the car park to get the speed up for fourth; so she relaxed into it, getting used to the weight and feel of the machine. She used Bill as a traffic island and went around several times in a figure of eight, changing between gears as she cornered, and again going into the straights. Bill was pleased with her progress. She was a natural. After twenty minutes, she pulled up alongside him, gears in neutral, engine ticking over to a happy beat. She took off her helmet and shook her rainbow hair.

'I need a smoke.'

'Me too,' said Bill. She propped the bike on its stand and took a cigarette off her uncle. 'You did good today. Now you're getting used to the feel of the bike, you need to think like you are on the open road. Pulling out into traffic. Indicating. That sort of thing. You've a lot to take in, but you're a fast learner.'

Su drew deep into her lungs and let out the smoke in one long sigh. 'Thanks, Bill. It pisses me off waiting to take my full test.'

Bill chuckled. 'You are so like your dad. He was never patient about anything.'

'Mum said that's why he died. He couldn't wait for the machine to stop. He cut a corner once too often and paid the price.'

'Yeah. That about sums it up.'

'I don't even remember him. Did you like him?'

Bill shrugged. 'Your dad was okay. Just a regular bloke. He thought the world of you.'

Su nodded. 'Hard to miss somebody I don't remember.'

'He loved you and he loved your mother. That says it all, really. But losing him has made you what you are. A tough, independent young woman. You are brighter than your dad ever was. You can be whatever you want to be. Don't ever waste that.'

'I guess. But sometimes I get so churned up inside, I just wanna kick ass.'

'The teenagers motto. And to be honest, there's many an ass out there deserves kicking. Just make sure you kick the right ones.'

She could relate to that advice. 'I can do that, Bill.'

He pointed a warning finger at her. 'But one battle at a time, yeah?'

'I can do that. Shit. I just wanna get on my bike and ride forever.'

'You will. But you need to be patient. Study the Highway Code; practice for your test. You'll soon be riding solo.'

Su stubbed out the butt with her boot. 'I suppose. In the meantime, I gotta pretend to be the sugar plum bloody fairy at my Mum's wedding.'

Chapter 7

It was two days later when Bill paid a visit to the Kane household, armed with a pile of literature and pamphlets.

'Evening, Barbara. Hi, Mick.'

'Hi, Bill,' said Mick. 'That looks serious.'

'It's for Su. It's what she needs towards her bike test.'

Barbara wasn't smiling. 'I still don't approve of her having a bike, but stopping her doing anything she's set her mind on is just about impossible.'

'Ah!' said Bill. 'I've watched her ride and I can tell she's a natural. She's got great balance and good control. She's also a quick learner and she's a good head on her shoulders.'

'And I'd like it to stay on her shoulders.'

'Barbara. Things are a lot stricter these days. Not like in my day when you could pretty much jump on a B S A two fifty and just take off. Where is she, anyway?'

'Upstairs. I'll shout her.'

Barbara called Su who came right down.

'Uncle Bill. You wanted to see me?'

'Yes. I'd like to go over this with you. Have you eaten?'

'Yes. What is all that stuff?'

'It tells you all you need to pass your bike test. I knew things had changed, but I had no idea how much. Come on. No time like the present.'

They sat at the kitchen table away from Barbara and Mick who wanted to watch television. Bill spread the papers about. 'Right. First off, you can't ride anything until you are sixteen. That's not that far away. But that doesn't mean you can jump on a bike and take off. You have to do your off road compulsory basic training first. That has to be with qualified instructor. We can get that booked up about a month in advance and I'll still take you out on the Tiger for extra practice. You need a little put-put to take your C B T on.'

Su sighed, 'Uncle Bill. I know you mean well, but I haven't any money for all this.'

'Ah! I knew you were going to say that. My treat for your sixteenth birthday.'

'Bill...!'

'Hey. If we leave to your mother, it will never happen. Coincidentally, my neighbour Old Charlie, has a fifty cc Vespa scooter. It's been in his shed for the last ten years to my knowledge. I'll buy it off him. Charlie won't want much. You'll have to sort it all out, though.' He grinned. 'I think you'll look kinda cute and delicate on a scooter.'

'I don't do cute or delicate. Bad enough being in pink for the wedding. But it's wheels so I'll take them, thanks.'

'Actually, have you heard of John Wayne?'

'Of course.'

'John rode one of those around the film studio. Marlon Brando owned one, the king of cool, Dean Martin had one, and did you see the film Ben Hur with Charlton Heston?'

'No way. He had one?'

'Yep. If he wasn't chariot racing, he was on his scooter. I'm telling you lot's of cool people had one, so you're in good company. Right. We book you in right away for your C B T. Once you've got through that, you can go on the road on the Vespa. You'll have to stick to that for a full year then once you've hit seventeen, you can step up to a one two five cc bike. We'll worry about that when the time comes. Now according to these pamphlets, if you pass on a one two five cc bike, you can then ride your Tiger, because at twenty seven brake horse power, it's under the thirty three BHP limit. So in just over a year and a bit, you can be riding Tiger.'

'That isn't actually as bad as I thought it would be. And you'll pay for all this?'

'Yeah. But we'll keep it from your mother and aunty if we can. You need to apply for your provisional licence as soon as you can to make sure you have it in time for your C B T. You have a lot to learn and do, but I know you can do it. I'll book you on the five day super course, which means it's out of the way in a week.'

Su leaned over and kissed him. 'Uncle Bill, you are brilliant.'

'Yes. I have to agree.'

Chapter 8

It was the morning of the wedding and Su and Fran were in Su's bedroom getting ready.

'I feel stupid,' said Su.

'Well, you look lovely,' said Fran. 'I like mine.' Fran did a twirl in her pink dress.

'You would,' said Su. 'After today I'm never wearing a bloody dress ever again.'

'What about when you get married? You'll want a wedding dress then.'

'Married? Who's getting bloody married?'

'Oh, come on,' said Fran. 'Of course you want to get married.'

Su checked her appearance in the mirror and applied more lipstick. Her hair was still a crazy kaleidoscope of colours, but piled high on her head, because her mother had said it made her look more like a girl. Su hated it but it was her mother's special day, so she had reluctantly agreed to it.

'What the hell for? I'm not getting married.'

'You...you aren't gay are you?'

'Piss off. Why would I be gay? Just 'cus I don't want to spend my life looking after some bloke don't mean I'm bloody gay.'

There was a knock on the door and Barbara and Joan entered the room. Barbara was wearing a simple, pearl white ankle length dress, nipped in to show her curves and just the right amount of cleavage.

'Well. Don't you two look gorgeous,' said Barbara.

'Yeah, right,' said Su. 'You look really nice, Mum.'

'You look fantastic, Aunty Barbara. ' said Fran. 'You too, Mum.'

Joan was wearing a light blue two piece outfit that could be worn for other occasions. 'Thanks. Now the cars will be here in a few minutes, so are you two ready?'

* * *

It was a registry office wedding, and Su patiently went through the motions as a bridesmaid, standing with Fran behind the bride and groom. All the time the celebrant was droning on, Su couldn't help but think just how futile it all seemed. She was relieved when the ceremony was over and it was time for the reception in the British Legion club. As soon as the photographs had been taken, she was back into jeans and t-shirt, her hair a wild explosion of colourful profusion. She disappeared out of the back of the building, and sat with a cigarette in one hand and a bottle of red wine she'd smuggled out when nobody was looking, in the other.

'Don't you get too drunk, young lady,' said a familiar voice.

'Hi, Uncle Bill.'

'A bloody pain having to smoke outside all the time,' he said, lighting up. 'Makes me feel like some social outcast.'

'You can come around the house while Mum and Mick are on honeymoon. Smoke as much as you want.'

'I might just do that. I expect you'll be having a party or two while you've got the place to yourself.'

Su took another swig of wine. She had nearly finished the bottle off. 'It crossed my mind.'

'Why not? It's what being a teenager is all about. At least it was back in my day. Your Mum and dad knew how to party. You just be careful with boys, okay?'

'Like how?'

'You know what I'm talking about. You are still under age. Don't get too carried away. Boys your age are only after one thing.'

'Not with me they won't. And no, I'm not gay.'

'I never thought you were.'

'Fran asked me if I was. Just 'cus I said I'll never get married.'

Bill chuckled. 'It isn't compulsory. Besides. You might change your mind when you meet a boy you like.'

'Doubt it.'

'Have you done with that wine?'

'Just about,' she said, finishing it off.

'Then we'd better get back inside. Come on.'

After another couple of hours of watching the oldies dancing to Barry Manilow and throwing caution to the wind and threatening to dislocate spines and hips by doing the twist to some dude called Chubby Checker, Su was relieved to see the happy couple get into the car to take them to the airport.

'Just remember what I said, Su. No parties.'

'As if. Have a nice time, Mum.'

Fran and Su watched the car drive off. Su said, 'Thank God for that. Now we can do some serious partying.'

Chapter 9

"Wilch" was in love with Fran and would have happily jumped off the nearest cliff had she told him to. He was also eighteen. For teenage girls nudging sixteen, eighteen year old boyfriends were useful. They could usually drive, have access to their dad's car, could sneak them into pubs, but more importantly, could buy booze, dope, condoms and pretty much anything else should it be required.

Fran maxed out with Dan Wilchester by getting him to supply copious amounts of booze for the party. All it had taken was a veiled promise of sexual delight, Fran had no intention of taking beyond first base. Second if she was in the mood. That Wilch was an acne blighted, gangly, ginger haired young man with questionable breath, was redeemed by the fact he was a head burger flipper with a regular wage and could borrow his mother's Ford Mondeo whenever he wanted. So spots and halitosis apart, he was quite a catch.

Wilch carried in the fourth box of assorted booze and placed it on the kitchen table. He had spent the equivalent of three weeks burger flipping wages and had high expectations of throwing a six with the dice of love. He stared at Fran, who, in his humble opinion, was beyond doubt the hottest chick he had ever met. She made him stutter. He never stuttered normally, but when it came to talking to this goddess in blue jeans, he stuttered worse than a road drill.

'I...I ...wo wo wo wondered if this was enough?'

'I reckon it will hit the spot,' teased Fran. 'Might even be enough to get me in the mood.'

Wilch grinned a crooked teeth smile. That was a signal, right? It was all on, yeah? The double portions of fries he had bestowed upon her whenever she'd come into his place; the sneaky large cola he gave her when she'd asked for a medium; the cheeky grin and come on look she'd given him had to count for something, right? Fran had other ideas.

Su jumped in. 'Wanna stick some noise on, Wilch?'

'Yeah. Okay. Gotta get in the mood, yeah?' he said, staring at Fran's boobs, wondering if …

Wilch went into the lounge and Su pulled out the tray of sausages and jacket potatoes from the oven. It was good booze mopping up fodder. It was also cheap.

'You and Wilch...?'

'Only in his dreams,' said Fran. 'I couldn't get drunk enough.'

'Stick a bag over his head he might be okay.'

'There ain't a bag big enough to make Wilch okay. Can you listen to that crap he's put on? Shit. We'll have to dump that or lose all credibility.'

A dozen various friends had been invited, which meant they could easily end up with double that number. Su could already hear people coming in through the front door. Thinking ahead she picked up two bottles of red wine and stowed them away in the cupboard under the sink, to make sure she and Fran had something for later on.

'Come on,' she said.

The lounge already had nearly twenty teenagers milling around, only half of whom she recognised. Ejecting Wilch's choice of music she put on something a bit more wicked.

'Got a load of booze,' said Gazza Vane. Su liked Gazza. He was always nice to her.

'Nice one, Gazza. No Tania?'

'Split,' he said with an indifferent shrug. 'You with anybody?'

'Not yet. Hey, Carol. How are you doin'?'

'Cool.' Not big on conversation, cool covered most things without the need for detail. She was a plump strawberry blonde and a great guitar player. Su was pleased to see she had brought her electric guitar along.

'Gonna do a few numbers, Carol?'

She shrugged. 'Dunno. Depends how pissed I get.'

'Booze in the kitchen,' said Fran.

Half an hour later, another fifteen had arrived, the sounds were cranked up and those without partners were pairing up. Gazza had his eye on Su and Fran was doing her best to put people between herself and the always hopeful Wilch. Wilch was beginning to have some ideas that maybe he wasn't going to be as lucky with Fran as he'd hoped.

All the food was soon eaten, the booze was disappearing at an alarming rate, couples were disappearing discretely into the bedrooms, and Su was playing "swallow my tongue" with Gazza, who knew just how far to go, which wasn't as far as he'd liked. Then the music suddenly stopped and there was a blast from Carol's guitar. Man, she could play that thing. It was Gun's 'N' Roses.

'Come on, Fran,' said Su.

The three hammered out a respectable rendition of "Sweet Child Of Mine". Slash would have been impressed with Carol's guitar work. The others clapped the beat and sang along. Fran was ripping it up, well lubricated with a bottle and half of red. Su was a wild child gyrating and dancing with rainbows in her hair. The crowd demanded more and the trio belted out another three numbers.

'I need booze,' said Carol. 'Hey. You two. I wanna ask you somethin','

Needing another drink, Su led the way to the kitchen followed by Fran dodging Wilch. From under the sink, Su got the two bottles of wine and gave one to Carol who had earned it, then she shared the other one with Fran.

'Wassup?' Su asked. From the open back door, she could see smoke and smell something familiar and tempting.

'You two can push out a song,' said Carol. 'I'm puttin' a band together. My dad's got a pub. He says I can put a couple of gigs on.'

Su said, 'No shit?'

'Yeah. I got my brother on drums. I know some harmonica player called Bluesdog who said he might join in for a laugh. Wanna be in it?'

'Yeah!' said Su. Any new experience was usually a good one.

'Cool. Like the blues?'

'Dunno. Rock, yeah. Dunno.'

'Blues is good. You gotta learn the words though.'

'We can do that,' said Fran. She couldn't believe they were going to be performing live with a real band. 'What's the crack?'

'I can get it together for next Friday night,' said Carol. 'Wanna come to the pub on Wednesday for a session and learn a few numbers?'

'We'll be there,' said Su, keen to join the smokers and cadge some dope.

'Cool,' said Carol.

Chapter 10

Fran did her best to look like a rock chick; Su was a rock chick. She knew she'd got the look right when Phil Crowe, owner of the Nagging Bladder public house and father to Carol, eyed her suspiciously with her wild hair and "sod you, mate" expression.

'It's okay, Dad. They're with me.' Carol was setting up the tiny stage in the corner of the bar.

'Hi, Carol,' said Su.

'Come and meet Todd. He claims to be my brother, but I seriously doubt it.'

Todd Crowe was younger than Carol, fifteen at most. He gave a whole new meaning to weedy. It didn't stop him looking the girls over, though. 'Hi. I hope you two can sing better than Carol. She'll empty the place if she does the vocals.'

'Maybe,' said Su, 'But she's ace on the guitar.'

'Just ignore him.' said Carol. 'He's a bloke. Come over here and we'll go over the music. Wanna drink? Only soft stuff or Dad'll do his nut.'

Su said, 'Coke's fine, thanks.'

Carol went to the bar and asked her father for drinks and Todd joined Su and Fran at the table.

'She is amazing on the guitar, though,' Todd admitted. 'Writes songs, too.'

'She played at our party,' said Fran. 'You should have come along.'

'I'm not really into parties. Can you read music?'

'No,' said Su.

'No worries. You just gotta learn all the words.'

Carol brought a tray of drinks over and sat with them. 'We are only doing six songs. That's enough to get right before the big night.'

'Here. I got you a copy each,' said Todd.

'And this is blues, is it?' Su asked.

'Yeah,' said Carol. 'With a rock feel to it. Ever heard of any of them?'

'Nope. Maybe when I hear the tune,' said Fran.

'Room for a little bloke?'

They hadn't noticed a big man with a pint of beer walk up to them. He was huge, had a grey beard down to his chest and the blackest shades Su had ever seen. She could only guess at his age, but he probably would make her mother feel young again next to him.

'Bluesdog. Hi,' said Carol. 'Take a seat. This is a couple of friends of mine, Su Kane and Fran Hartshorne. They'll be singing with us.'

'So I gather. At least you'll be eye candy for the blokes.'

'Bluesdog?' Fran said.

He just shrugged. 'Just a name. Are we doing the usual set?'

Todd passed him the music and he looked them over. 'Yeah, okay. I'll go warm up. I'll do this one first, so you get the feel of it.'

Bluesdog got up on the stage, took his harmonica out of his pocket and played a few notes, then he was into the first number. This was a man as one with his musical instrument. The music filled the large room and Su and Fran were instantly into it. At the end, Bluesdog went back to the table.

'You're great,' said Fran.

The big man shrugged and emptied his glass. 'I can play a bit. I need another pint.'

By the end of the night, they had nailed the six song set.

'A bit raw,' said Bluesdog. 'But with blues, that can be a good thing.'

'We'd better be off,' said Fran. 'I've had a blast.'

'You got wheels?' Bluesdog asked.

Su said, 'We don't live far. I do have a bike, though. A Fifty Nine Tiger 100.'

'No shit. Got it here?'

'No. I gotta be seventeen then pass a test. Can't ride it until then.'

'Bummer.'

'She put it together all by herself,' said Fran, proudly.

'Yeah? I'm impressed. I gotta trike, myself. Out the front if you wanna take a look.'

Su and Fran said goodnight to Carol, Todd and Philip Crowe and followed Bluesdog outside. The trike was the coolest thing they had ever seen with metallic paintwork and a fire-breathing dragon on the tank.'

'Totally wicked,' said Su.

'I did my own paint job. It's what I do. Custom paint jobs. Bikes, trikes, hotrods. If you want your Tiger done, let me know. I'll give you a good price.'

'Thanks. Something to think about. We'll see you Friday, then.'

'Yeah. Before seven so we can warm up.'

* * *

Friday night came and Su and Fran got to the Nagging Bladder just before seven. Outside was an impressive array of motorcycles, some gleaming works of art, others day to day "rat bikes", rough as guts and leaking oil. Su felt her usual frustration about her own bike in her uncle's garage. Inside, it was wall to wall bikers. The jukebox was belting out heavy rock classics and just walking into the place made Su Kane tingle. Most of the bikers were hairy giants but they parted for the girls. Su had done what she could for Fran with make-up and hair, and she almost pulled the look off. Su was just Su and did pull it off.

'Hey,' said Carol. 'Bluesdog put the word out and half the bikers in the county turned up. Cool, yeah?'

'I love it,' said Su.

'Yeah,' said Fran.

'Learnt all the songs?'

'All in here,' said Su, tapping her forehead.

'Okay. Get a drink and we're ready to rock and roll.'

It was one of the best nights Su and Fran could ever remember. They harmonised well and hardly put a note or word out of place. It took forty minutes to get through the set with Carol, Todd and Bluesdog doing a number in the middle. Then they all did a repeat of a couple of songs for an encore. The bikers loved them and gave them a standing ovation. Drinks were on them for the rest of the night. Suddenly, it was like becoming part of one big family.

Chapter 11

The garage door was still open, and the Triumph was gone. At first Bill Hartshorne thought the garage had been broken into, then he saw the note on a nail on the inside of the door.

"Had to ride. Su X"

'Damn that girl.'

'Dad? What's happened?'

'Your bloody cousin happened, that's what happened. She must have come in early, sneaked in here and got her bike.'

'I never heard it go,' said Fran.

'Because she pushed it down the street before riding away. Bloody idiot. She'll lose her licence before she even gets it.'

Fran couldn't help but grin. This was so typical of Su. Seeing all the bikes the night before had been too much for her. 'She'll be fine, Dad.'

'Bloody well better be. Wait till I see that little minx.'

* * *

Su was happy. She had ridden her bike to the letter of the law through the town and out into the country side. The narrow winding roads were perfect for a blast on the bike. She became one with the machine, feeling the powerful engine roaring away under her control. The weather was perfect and she was on top of the world. She rode on for another half hour, then pulled up and parked the bike. She was on the brow of a hill, with a small patch of grass for her and the bike to be off the narrow lane. She checked the fuel. She had just over half a tank left. This was as far as she was going that day. A smoke and then back to get her ears chewed off by Uncle Bill.

Placing her helmet on the seat, she took out her pack of cigarettes and lit one up. She lay on the grass and watched the clouds of smoke dance in the breeze. Life was pretty good. The party. The gig at the pub, and now a ride on her beloved bike. Yeah, life was pretty bloody good. Her moment of blissful tranquillity was interrupted by noise. Just some dogs. She ignored it. But the barking and the rest of the noise didn't seem right to her. She sat up, trying to pinpoint the sounds. It was coming from somewhere behind her. She got up and tried to determine the direction the sounds were coming from. It was behind the hedge next to where she had parked the bike.

There was a small gap in the hedge and she forced the branches apart so she could see what was going on. It was just a field. The noise was coming from the field beyond that. She could hear voices, men shouting, dogs barking. Curiosity got the better of her. She squeezed through the hedge. Following the sounds, she crossed the empty field to the next hedge. Whatever was going on was just beyond that hedge, but she could find no gap. She noticed a dip in the hedge, just low enough for her to look over. She was on tiptoes and the view wasn't great, but she could see what was happening. What she saw made her feel physically ill and disgusted her. What she saw changed her view of the world and her life forever.

Chapter 12

The Triumph roared up to the garage doors. Bill Hartshorne stood with his arms folded ready to go ballistic. Fran was behind him. Su cut the engine and took off her helmet. Her make-up was smudged from her tears.

'I trusted you, Su,' Bill said. 'And this how you repay me. I've a good mind to...'

Fran tugged his arm. 'Dad. Something's wrong.'

'Damn right something's wrong. She sneaks into my garage, leaves the door wide open, takes off uninsured and without a bloody licence and...Su? What's happened?'

Su got off the bike and went to him and hugged him. 'It was horrible, Uncle Bill.'

'Don't tell me. You got pulled over by the cops. Have you any idea...'

'No, Uncle Bill. I saw something.'

'Okay. Come on inside and tell me what happened. Fran. Get the kettle on and make us all tea will you?'

'Yes, Dad.'

'Where's Aunty Joan?'

'Out doing the shopping. I didn't tell her about your little escapade.' They sat at the kitchen table and Fran brought them tea.

Su sipped her tea and started telling them what had happened. 'I was out in the middle of nowhere. I stopped for a few minutes before coming back. I heard a noise. Dogs.'

'What? Like a kennels?'

'No. I feel sick just thinking about it. I was high up but they couldn't see me. I was behind a hedge. There was like a big barn, but the doors were open and I could see inside. There were men in there and they had dogs. They set them on each other.'

Bill said, 'Shit! You mean dog fighting?'

Su nodded, her hands shaking. 'They were ripping each other to pieces. Blood...everywhere. And those bastards were cheering them on. One dog...oh, God. All his belly was ripped open and all his guts...'

Su started to cry and Fran put her arms around her. 'Dad. We have to do something. Call the police.'

'They'll be long gone by the time they got there. They need to be caught in the act. Su. Do you know where this place is? Could you find it again?'

'I...I think so.'

Fran said, 'How many men were there?'

'Hard to say. Maybe twenty?'

'Jeez,' said Bill. 'It would take a small army to sort that lot out. And my guess is those sort of men wouldn't take too kindly to have anyone interfere.'

'I gotta do something,' said Su. 'I'll never be able to sleep at night if I don't.'

Fran said, 'We'd need a bloody army to stop it.'

'Like that's going to happen,' said Su.

'Maybe we *can* raise an army,' said Fran.

'Hey,' said Bill. 'You two are not getting involved and that's the end of it. Leave it to the police.'

'A fat lot of good they've done,' said Su. 'Those men weren't bothered about the law. Who've you got in mind, Fran?'

* * *

It was Wednesday night and time for another rehearsal at the Nagging Bladder, but there was more than just music to discuss. Bluesdog had made a few calls and already a dozen of his friends had turned up.

Bluesdog sipped his beer. 'About twenty of them, you reckon?'

Su said, 'I only had a quick look, but yeah. About that many.'

'Bastards,' said a biker named Oddball. 'You can find this place again?'

'Yes. Trouble is, I got no wheels. My Uncle was livid when I took the bike.'

'Don't you worry about getting there,' said Bluesdog. 'I can take two on the back of my trike.'

Fran said, 'My dad will have a fit if I go.'

Su shrugged. 'So don't go.'

'Oh, I'm going alright. He can have his fit. He don't need to know about it.'

'One thing for sure. We need a few more of us,' said Oddball.

Bluesdog grinned through his thick beard. 'You leave that to me. Shit. This business has really depressed me. You wanna play some music and cheer us all up?'

'Come on,' said Carol. 'Todd. Get bashing those drums.'

Chapter 13

Friday night and the Nagging Bladder was full to capacity. Phil Crowe was more than happy with the crowd. Most of the riders drank only one or two pints each, but their pillions made up for them. Carol, Todd, Su, Fran and Bluesdog were belting out their routine with another two numbers added. About halfway through the set, Bluesdog called for order and got it.

'Okay. Most of you know why we are here. Last Saturday, Su Kane here, saw some pretty ugly shit going down. Anybody here think dog fighting is a good idea?' Nobody did and a few expressed their opinions about people who thought otherwise. 'That's what I think, too. Now, I don't know about you, but I like nothing better than to go for a run at the weekends. I might be inclined to head out that way and maybe have a word with those gentlemen. Anybody else fancy a run out tomorrow?' Everyone in the room put their hands up. 'I'll be here at eight in the morning. Something tells me it's gonna be interesting. Okay. Some more music, Yeah?'

* * *

'Okay, ladies. You good in the back there?'

'Yep,' said Su.

'I'm ready,' said Fran.

Bluesdog blipped the throttle and the pack was off, sixteen bikes following him, all doubled up with tough as bikers. Su guided Bluesdog and one hour later, they were where they needed to be. It was a squeeze to get all the bikes onto the grass patch off the lane but they managed it.

'I went through this gap in the hedge,' said Su.

Oddball had the ornate walking stick he always carried and got in the gap and used his body and stick to push the branches a little wider and then they all got through it, into the empty field.

'Listen to that,' said Fran.

They could all hear the noise from the dogs and the men cheering them on.

Su said, 'I could see them from over there.'

It was no problem for most of the men to see over the top of the hedge. 'That's disgusting,' said Oddball. 'How do we get down there?'

'There's a gate over there,' said Bluesdog. 'That goes onto the drive to the barn. Su, Fran. You stay put.'

'No way,' said Su. 'I'm going down there.'

Bluesdog grinned. 'I just knew you were gonna say that. Okay. But you two stay behind us lot, right?'

Su and Fran nodded.

'Right, Dudes. Time to say hello.'

Chapter 14

They went through the gate, onto the dirt track that led to the barn. All along one side were vans and utes. A few had dogs inside, waiting for their turn in arena. There was a bend on the track that had the bikers out of sight of the barn.

'Okay,' whispered Bluesdog. 'Keep the noise down. We don't want to lose the advantage. Stay put and I'll take a look and see what we're up against.'

Bluesdog kept close to the hedge and stopped when he reached the bend. He had a clear view of the barn, but this time the door was shut. He was considering a game plan when the barn door opened. A man was dragging a dog along by its hind legs and he dropped it on the ground, dead. Bluesdog could see the damage the dog had endured. Instead of going back in the barn, the man walked towards the big biker, on his way to his van. Bluesdog dodged out of sight and signalled to the others to stay back. The man casually walked along the track and turned the bend. His eyes widened when he saw the bikers. His eyes closed again when Bluesdog hit him. It was just one punch but the man dropped to his knees and fell face down in the mud.

'Have a nice day, dude.'

Bluesdog signalled the others to follow him, but he pointed a warning finger at Su and Fran and they dropped behind the pack. They went to the barn door and they all looked at the mangled dog. It was all they needed to see to know that what they were doing was totally justified. From inside the barn they could hear two more dogs fighting and the men urging them on. Bluesdog got hold of the door and yanked it open. Apart from the snarling, snapping dogs, the place went silent.

'Hey, Dudes. This a private shindig or can anyone play?'

The men charged at the bikers and it was like running into a brick wall. Fists, feet, elbows, teeth and knees all struck home. The dog fighters weren't about to go down without a fight, but they were no match for the bikers. Oddball kneed one in the groin then swung his stick into the face of another man, sending a shower of blood and teeth into the air. The man dropped to his knees and a well aimed knock on the back of his head from the stick wielding biker and his eyes crossed, closed and he was out.

Scrubber took a hit to the chin, shook his head and then poll-axed his opponent.

'Hold it,' yelled a man. The fighting instantly stopped when they saw he had grabbed Fran and held a knife to her throat. 'Back off or I slice her open.'

They backed away. Several of the dog fighters were lying in the dirt in pain, trying to get to their feet.

Su yelled, 'Hurt her, it'll be the last thing you do.'

'Keep calm,' said Bluesdog, staring at the man with the knife.

'Back off over there. Move it.'

The bikers did as they were told. The man kept Fran between him and the pack. The others were getting up and joining him.

'We're taking her with us. Follow us, you'll never see her again.'

That was his plan. It wasn't Fran's. She kicked back hard with her heel into the man's shin-bone. He didn't drop the knife, but it was away from Fran's neck. Her elbow in his guts got him to double up and drop the knife. Su raced over, smacking her knee into the man's head and then it was total mayhem. The whole fight took less than three minutes, but at the end of it, all the bikers were standing, albeit bloodied and bruised. The dog fighters were either unconscious or wondering which planet they were on.

Bluesdog went over to the man who'd threatened Fran, grabbed him by his ears and pulled him screaming to his feet.

'I don't like you much, Dude. If you ever see me again, start running.' A final punch ended the one sided conversation.

'Hey, Bluesdog,' said Su. 'These two dogs are in a bad way.' The dogs had done what their owners had intended; half killing each other. 'We have to get them to a vet.'

'Not easy on a bike,' said Oddball.

'Plenty of vans outside,' said Fran.

'Okay,' said Bluesdog. 'We use whatever vans we need to get all the animals to a vet.' He picked up one animal and carried it outside. Another biker picked up the other injured dog and they all walked out of the barn to the parked vans. Six vans had dogs in the back. The keys to the vans were still in the ignitions. The two injured dogs were carefully placed in the back of a spare van with two separate cages inside. 'Let's roll, Dudes.'

Chapter 15

They were making good time until they hit the town. The police patrol car pulled up in front of the trike. The officer got out and went up to Bluesdog.

'We still have speeding limits at the weekends, last I heard.'

'Gotta bit of an emergency,' said Bluesdog pointing a thumb at the convoy behind him.

'Somebody hurt?'

'Yeah, just a bit. But we left those behind. We got their dogs with us, bleeding to death.'

'What?'

'Dog fighting. We just put an end to it. We're trying to get the dogs to a vets.'

'Now listen and listen good. Are there people needing medical attention back there?'

'Nothing an aspirin won't cure. Can't say the same for the dogs, officer Dude.'

'So what are we hanging around here for? Come on.'

Officer Dude got back in the car and with the lights and sirens going, the convoy was going twice the speed limit until they reached the PDSA clinic. A man with a walking stick was just leaving the building when one cop car, one trike, sixteen bikes and nine vans pulled up alongside him. Su Kane and Fran Hartshorne jumped off the back of the trike.

'Uncle Garf,' said Su. 'We need your help.'

The bikers were already getting the injured dogs out of the vans; both were unconscious through loss of blood. 'Better get them inside, then,' said Uncle Garf as the patrol car drove away. 'Smiley? Bumblebee? We got customers.'

* * *

Bumblebee happened to be not just a vet nurse, but Oddball's partner. She had known that he and the others were going to sort out the dog fighting gang and was relieved to see that apart from a black eye, he was unscathed.

Smiley a veterinary nurse and a biker himself, said, 'Looks bad.'

'Hey you lot. Everybody outside,' ordered Uncle Garf. 'Not you young ladies, and you two can stay, too,' he said looking at Bluesdog and Oddball. 'Everyone else, out.'

The dogs were carried into the operating room by Bluesdog and Oddball, Oddball nodding grim faced at his partner. They carefully placed the dogs on the operating theatre tables. Uncle Garf was already putting on a gown and a mask as he looked the dogs over.

'You,' he said, snapping on gloves and looking at Su. 'You called me Uncle Garf. Do I know you?'

'You saved my cat Starlight five years ago. My name's Su Kane.'

'Got it. You jumped in the lake to save a kitten. Smiley, Bumblebee. Make a start on that one. This one's the worst.'

The two nurses started cleaning off the blood to examine the wounds. 'Going to need a drip to get some fluids into him,' said Smiley.

Without looking up from his canine patient, Uncle Garf said, 'Did Moonshine live?'

'Starlight. Good as gold thanks to you, but she has a bit of an attitude.'

Bluesdog grinned. 'She must take after you.'

'Can you save them?' Fran asked.

Garf shrugged. 'They're in a bad way, but we'll do what we can. How are you going, you two?'

'Getting there,' said Bumblebee.

'I know this gentleman. You're Oddball. The very lucky partner of this lovely Swedish lady right here. You I haven't met before. So. You are?'

'Bluesdog.'

'Of course you are. Are these your dogs?'

'Hell, no. We heard about a dog fighting outfit and we decided to have a philosophical discussion with them about their chosen recreational pastime.'

'Is that so?' said Garf, still not looking up. 'I trust they got the gist of you reasoned argument?'

'I think they saw the error of their ways, Dude.'

'Judging by the blood in your beard, I am guessing it was quite a heated exchange. I just wanted to establish who was responsible for this barbarism. Now. This is going to take a couple of hours at least, so I suggest you call back on Monday.'

Bluesdog said, 'We have several uninjured dogs outside. Any ideas?'

'All I can suggest is you take them to the RSPCA. They'll take it from there.'

'I'll do that. Thanks, Dude.'

Su said, 'Thanks, Uncle Garf.'

They went outside where the others still waited. Oddball was asked, 'Gonna be okay?'

'Maybe,' said Oddball. 'My Bumblebee's in there, and she's the best. 'These others need to go to the RSPCA.'

'I know where that is,' said Scrubber. 'Might as well get them over there now.' He got in the van and they all drove away.

Bluesdog said to Su, 'You jumped in a lake to save a kitten?'

'Yeah.'

Fran said, 'She was only eleven. She nearly died of pneumonia.'

'I bloody didn't. I was just a bit crook for few days. Nothing major.'

Bluesdog shook his head. 'Jeez. I don't know about you lot, but I need a beer.'

Chapter 16

'Hello, you. Come and give your Mum a big hug.'

'Hi, Mum. Hi, Mick. Have a good time?'

'Paris was amazing, wasn't it Mick?'

'Bloody expensive.'

Barbara shook her head. 'And they said romance is dead. God, I've missed you. We brought you some nice things back. So. What have you been up to? Trouble I expect.'

'Just working hard at school. The usual.'

'Like I believe that. What sort of things have you been studying?'

Su shrugged. 'Loads. Music. Lots about animal welfare. Lots of things.'

'Yes? Good to hear you're knuckling down with your exams coming up.' Barbara scanned the room for damage. 'No wild parties while we were away?'

'Fran came round a few times to help me with my homework. Pretty boring, really.'

Barbara smiled approvingly. 'It sounds like my little girl is growing up at last.'

* * *

'Hi, Uncle Garf.'

'Hello, Su. Come to see the patients?'

'Yeah. Just on my way home from school. Are they okay?'

'They're a tough breed. I think they'll make it. We'll keep them in here for a few days while they heal up. Come and take a look at them.'

Su followed him into the recovery room. The two dogs, mortal enemies trying to kill each other just a couple of days before, were lying next to each other in separate cages. Both looked like patchwork quilts with stitches everywhere.

'They're both still a bit doped up at the moment. Smiley and Bumblebee did a great job on this one.'

'Poor things. What's going to happen to them?'

'Like the others. They'll go to the RSPCA. They'll be assessed for behavioural problems. If they're completely antisocial, it might have to be euthanasia for them.'

'After all we've done to save them?'

Garf sighed and shook his head sadly. 'They couldn't risk putting them with homes if they are dangerous. Hopefully they can be saved.'

'Why do people do this, Uncle Garf?'

Garf chuckled. 'I remember a brave eleven year old girl asking me that very same question. Unfortunately, I have no better answer for you now than I did back then. You did what you could. You and your friends. Su. Just be careful what you get involved in, right? People capable of this kind of cruelty won't think twice about hurting anyone who stands up to them.'

Su could see with her minds eye the man holding a knife to her cousins throat. 'I know. But people need to stand up to this kind of thing.'

Uncle Garf smiled. 'You know something? I reckon you'll be doing quite a lot of that from now on. Just be careful.'

Chapter 17

Su Kane amazed everyone, especially herself. It was a month to go before her O level exams and she caught up the months of dodging classes in a matter of weeks. It wasn't that she couldn't learn; she had merely decided not to bother. Even Pretty Peter Giles was impressed with her progress.

'This is good work, Su. You haven't been replaced by some alien from space, have you?'

'I just want to do good. Prove that I can.'

'You, Su Kane, are every teachers worse nightmare. You frustrate the hell out of us. We see really bright students like you, with ability to do just about anything, and despite our best efforts, we the teachers can't get through to you.'

'But it's so bloody boring. Sorry.'

Peter smiled. 'I couldn't agree more. And most of it is a waste of time and completely futile. It's the system and we're stuck with it.'

'That makes no sense whatsoever.'

'It isn't meant to. But what are the alternatives? From generation to generation we pass on what we learn, hoping they'll do more with it than we did.'

'But we don't. People are horrible.'

'Am I horrible?'

'No. You're gorge... okay. But I've seen shit. Sorry.'

'Stop apologising. But stop swearing as well, okay? Su. Bar none, you are one of the brightest students of your year. But one of these days you'll be out of this mind distorting institution, only to find that it's ten times worse out there. Between the two of us, this place teaches you which hoops to jump through. Out in the real world, you actually have to jump through the hoops.'

Su had never heard any teacher talk like this. Suddenly, Peter Giles, as handsome as he was, had stopped becoming a teacher and had turned into a human being. Why hadn't she seen this before? More importantly, what was he really saying? Staying behind when the others had gone so she could hand in her homework was proving to be an education in itself. Lights in her mind were being turned on.

'If you know so much, why are you stuck here in the system?'

He pointed at her. 'That was the most significant question you have probably asked in your entire life. It deserves a respectful answer. You really understand what I said about you being in a system?'

'I think so, yes. People...powerful people, want to control us. Like you said. Jumping through hoops. Their hoops.'

'Ah! Did you hear that?'

'What?'

'The sound of pennies dropping. If I give you some sound advice are you mature enough to take it?'

'Time to find out, I guess.'

'Right. You asked me if I know so much, why am I stuck in this system. If you ever repeat this, I'll deny it, okay?'

'Okay.'

'Because if I can make one student, one really bright student like you truly aware each year, I'll stay in the system. This is what you should do. Do the very best you can in your exams. Work hard. To the powers that be, that will be proof enough you can jump through their hoops. Now, ninety nine out of every hundred will be content with that. They will spend their lives merrily jumping through hoops and say "Thanks, boss," each time they pick up their wages. Armed with this knowledge, you will pick your own hoops. Am I getting through to you yet?'

'You know I have a crush on you, yeah?'

'I noticed. Not going to happen between us. All your flirting with me was a waste of time. Also, it would be illegal because you're under-age. Not only that, my boyfriend wouldn't like it. That's between us, okay?'

'Damn. You burst my bubbles.'

'Sorry. Use the last ten minutes wisely. Ace your exams. Then go out and beat the bloody system.'

'Okay. You just swore.'

'Sorry.'

Su Kane walked out of the school gates both confused and enlightened at the same time.

Chapter 18

'Hello, stranger,' said Smiley, wiping down the operating table in the PDSA clinic.

'Hello, Smiley,' said Su. 'I was just passing so I thought I'd drop in and say hello.'

'Always nice to see you.'

'Uncle Garf not about?'

'Not today. He's getting old and doesn't do as much as he used to. I still learn heaps from him, though.'

'He's cool.' Su watched Smiley as he busied himself cleaning down, getting ready for the next patient, whatever that was going to be. 'You like your work?'

'Love it. I wouldn't do it for the money, though. I get great experience here, so I'll keep chipping away at it and make a career out of it.'

'I bet you need lots of brains to do your job.'

'Yeah? Damn. Nobody told me that,' said Smiley with a grin. He stopped working and leaned up against the cupboard units. 'A reasonable intelligence helps.' He nodded to a wall where several certificates were displayed in matching black frames. 'I got my diploma. That's a combination of theory and practical work. Bumblebee's certificate is next to mine. She has more experience on exotics because of her volunteer field work in other countries. Shell soon be off again I expect.'

'How long does it take to get the diploma?'

'Two years. Are you interested in doing something like that?'

'I don't know. I've my O level exams coming up. Once I have those out of the way, I'll have to think what to do for a job.'

'O levels are a good start. If you want to do something like me, do as well as you can at the sciences, English of course, and maths wouldn't hurt.'

'Okay. Makes sense.' She looked at the cages used for recuperating animals. There were only two occupied. One had a sleeping cat in it and the other had a snow white rabbit who was twitching his whiskers at her, staring with his pink eyes. 'What happened to those two dogs we brought in?'

Smiley shrugged. 'No idea. The RSPCA had them off us. I have no idea if they found homes for them. That was pretty cool what you did rescuing them.'

'I had to do something. It was the bikers who sorted the dog fighters out, though. It was one hell of a fight.'

'I bet it was. Unfortunately that case was just the tip of the iceberg.'

'What do you mean?'

'There's just so much bad shit out there. In this place we see the caring side of people, mostly. They love their pets and can't afford regular vets treatments, so they bring them here. Some people are in real states; crying because their pets are hurt or sick. Those people I've plenty of time for. Then there's the other extreme. People we don't see. They let their animals starve or be injured and do nothing about it. That just makes me mad.'

Su nodded. 'Me, too. But that's neglect, which is bloody bad enough. The one's that really make me angry are the one's who hurt their animals, like those dog fighters.'

'Yeah. You'd be amazed how much of it goes on. It isn't only domestic animals, though. Even wild animals get to suffer.'

'Yeah? Like what?'

'Badgers for one. Here we are at the end of the twentieth century and some people act like they are in the dark ages.'

'But badgers?'

Smiley sighed. 'Sadly, yes. Beautiful creatures. Nocturnal. Live in setts underground. They just go about their business, no harm to anyone. But they are tough and they have claws that could rip you to shreds. They would only attack in self defence of themselves or their cubs. It got so bad there is actually an act of parliament to try to protect them, called the Protection of Badgers Act. Looks good on paper, but it doesn't do a lot to stop it.'

This was something else for Su Kane to be thinking about.

Chapter 19

Mrs Ponsonby took her glasses off and looked at the girl sitting in front of her.

'Miss Kane. Over the last few weeks I have been actually getting good reports about you. You have no idea how refreshing that is. It is most unusual to hear the words *is working very hard* and *turning out excellent work* in the same sentence as Su Kane. As your career advisor, it is good to know, nonetheless.'

'Thanks, Mrs Ponsonby.'

'Now. The examinations start next week. Usually, I wait until we get the results in, but I thought it a good idea to have a chat in the meantime. Have you any idea of the sort of career path to follow?'

'I think something with animals.'

'Animals. Interesting. In what capacity?'

'Hmm?'

'How exactly would you see yourself working with animals?'

'I dunno, really. I got a mate who's a vet nurse with the PDSA. But that's lots of studying and I dunno if I can handle it.'

'Yes. I see where you're coming from. And to be honest, with your track record, apart from your current enthusiasm, you may well find sustained study challenging. I'm not suggesting you aren't bright enough, just a question mark over your willingness to stay the course, as it were.'

'I suppose.'

'However. We have to give you the best possible options. Lets assume you change your mind after the exams and decide you really want to pursue a career like your friend. It would be a pity not to have gone the extra mile to make it possible. In other words, concentrating on the subjects most pertinent to that particular career path. I'll have to check into the specifics, but I have a feeling what appropriate O levels are required for that, would also be relevant for many other careers.' She wagged a finger at the ceiling. 'That's not to say you should neglect any of the other subjects.'

'No, Mrs Ponsonby.'

'Good I'm glad we are clear about that. Right. Leave it with me, I'll make some enquiries. I shall also look into animal care alternatives for you. Run along and we'll have another chat in a day or two.'

'Thanks, Mrs Ponsonby.'

Chapter 20

'I was only trying to help,' said Mick, pushing his empty plate away.

'It would drive me bloody mental,' said Su. 'I mean. Can you really see me working in a bloody office?'

Her mother glared at her. 'No need for that kind of language. Mick's only making a suggestion.'

'Yeah. Sorry Mick. But me in an insurance office? I'd be screaming up the walls within a blo...within a day.'

Mick said, 'It's just something to think about. With a couple of good O level results, you'd have a foot in the door. I'd put a word in with head office. A few years from now, you could be in something managerial.'

'Mrs Ponsosnby's looking into stuff for me. I told her I would like to work with animals, somehow.'

'Animals?' said Barbara, clearing the plates. 'First I ever heard of it.'

Su had told her mother nothing about the dog fighting and going to the PDSA. If she saw the bikers, she would be calling them Hells Angels in no time. Persuading her they were nothing like that would be a waste of breath. It was best left alone. It was the same for the Friday night music sessions at the Nagging Bladder, like the one she was going to that night. As far as her mother was concerned, she was out with Fran and that's all she needed to know. The clock on the kitchen wall told her it was six thirty three and she had to hurry to get herself ready and over to the pub by seven.

Her mother optimistically asked, 'I don't suppose you'd do the washing up?'

'Sorry, Mum. I gotta go.'

* * *

It was just before seven when she met Fran outside the Nagging Bladder. There were already a few bikes parked up outside.

'I see Bluesdog's here,' said Su. 'Come on.'

Carol, Todd and Bluesdog were busy setting up the stage and testing the amplification.

'Hi,' said Su and Fran.

'Hi. Ready to let rip?' said Carol.

'Just say the word,' said Su.

'Hey. Look what the cat dragged in,' said Bluesdog as the door swung open. 'Hi, Dude.'

'Hi yourself,' said Smiley. 'I heard a rumour there was band here but then I saw you.'

Bluesdog jumped off the stage and slapped his old friend on the back. 'I'm the best harmonica player in the Nagging Bladder. Wanna pint, Dude?'

'You can twist my arm. Hi, Su. Sorry. I forgot your name.'

'Fran. Su's cousin.'

'I remember now.'

'Haven't seen you in here before,' said Su.

'Not my regular dive. Too many unsavoury characters like Bluesdog here. Thanks, mate,' said Smiley taking the pint from him.

Bluesdog said, 'I haven't seen you since we brought those ripped up dogs in. What you been up to, Dude?'

'Cats and dogs and the very odd rabbit. Usual stuff. Hey, Oddball. Hi.'

'Come and grab a seat,' said Oddball. 'The place will be packed in another half hour.'

Smiley said, 'Okay. Su. Mind if we have a chat?'

'Sure. We have a few minutes. We'll just get a drink.'

Su got a cola for herself and Fran from Phil Crowe and joined Smiley and Oddball while Bluesdog, Carol and Todd tuned up. 'What's up, Smiley?'

'You know we were talking the other day?'

'Yeah?'

'About badger baiting?'

'I remember. Bastards.'

'Pretty much. I was talking to an old pal of mine last night. He was in a bit of state, to be honest.'

'Go on.'

'My pal, Ferret...we call him that 'cus he had a couple of ferrets as pets when he was kid. Anyway, he runs a farm with his old man. A free range pig farm. But Ferret, like his old man, has a soft spot for wildlife. They kept back over twenty acres of their land just for woodland creatures. They pretty much just leave nature take its course. Anyway, there's about three badger setts in there. Some say they spread T B to cattle, but Ferret's old man don't hold with that. Live and let live, he says. A few others don't share that concept.'

'Baiters?' said Oddball.

'Looks like it. Ferret was out one night, and saw some flashlights in the woods. He decided to check it out. He didn't tell his old man, 'cus he's got got cancer and he's on the way out So Ferret went on his own. He took his twenty two he uses to keep rabbits down, and went into the woods. There were six men there. They saw him with the gun and ran for it. It was too late for the badger. The dogs had gone in, probably with radio transmitters strapped to them for location. The men had dug into the sett and let their dogs on her. They hacked her to bits with their spades for good measure.'

'Bloody unreal,' said Oddball.

'It gets worse. The badger had been protecting her young. She was badly injured, dying. Ferret put her down, out of her misery.'

'Oh, God,' said Fran. 'What about the babies?'

'Ferret got those out. They'll survive because he's got them and he's taking care of them. I've given him what advice I could over the phone. He reckons those blokes will be coming back for the other setts.'

'Not if I've anything to do with it,' said Su.

Carol called them to the stage and Todd hit the drums to time them in. They sang all eight numbers, Su and Fran trying to put the images of injured badgers out of their minds. Fran was quite distressed, unable to stop a few tears falling. Su was just very angry. After the set, Bluesdog went up to Su and Fran.

'Something's happened, Dudes. What is it?'

Su said, 'Come and have a talk with Smiley. I guarantee you won't like it.'

She was right. He didn't like what he heard. Bluesdog had a word with Phil Crowe who opened up a back room for a council of war.

* * *

A dozen bikers, all having had a hand and a fist in breaking up the dog fighting gang, sat grim faced as Smiley repeated his story. At the end, they sat fuming, unable to comprehend how evil some people could be.

'This farm's what, about sixty miles from here?' Bluesdog asked.

'About that,' said Smiley.

Oddball stated the obvious. 'How the hell will we know when they are going to strike? Seeing Ferret with a gun might mean they never come back.'

Smiley said, 'According to Ferret, there's signs of activity all over the badgers setts. All three of them. This is how these jokers get their kicks.' He sipped his pint, thoughtfully. 'I'm riding over tomorrow, to check out the cubs. I'll stay the night. See what's going on for myself.'

Bluesdog said, 'About six of the bastards, right, Dude?'

Smiley nodded. 'According to Ferret.'

'Any three of us could take them out,' said Oddball.

Bluesdog stroked his beard, thinking things through. 'My bet is they won't be back this weekend. Not after Ferret scared the crap out of them with his shooter. They might get their bottle back in the next few weekends after that. Like Oddball said. Any three of us could sort out six cowards like those creeps. If we take it in turns for three of us to stay at the farm for the next few weekends, we might nail the buggers. Any takers?'

Every hand in the room went up, including Su's and Fran's.

'No need for you two to be involved,' said Bluesdog.

'Wanna try and stop us?' said Su, jutting her chin out, defiantly.

Bluesdog roared with laughter. 'Hell, no, Dude. I ain't *that* brave.'

Chapter 21

Fortunately for Grant Mitchell, he looked nothing like a ferret. Once upon a time he had tried unsuccessfully to stop people calling him by that nickname. Eventually, realising he was fighting a losing battle, he accepted and even embraced it. When Smiley pulled up on his Yamaha Dragstar six-fifty, Ferret was wearing one of his favourite things; a pullover knitted by his mother, not long before her weak heart took her away from him.

The image of the curled up ferret had faded; there were holes all over the place and it had some rather dubious looking indelible stains on it. In order to preserve the garment, Ferret had tried to darn the holes as best his clumsy fingers could, with whatever wool that came to hand, irrespective of colour. Any self respecting charity shop would have trashed it, considering it to be unsellable, not understanding its true value to Ferret.

In times of trouble and anxiety, with no mother to turn to for advice, he would put on the ancient pullover, immediately finding solace in the warmth and feel of it, and memories of his long departed mother would flood back. Smiley understood this about his old friend and took it as a sign that although Ferret grinned on seeing him, deep down he was deeply troubled.

'Thanks for coming, Smiley,' said Ferret, grasping his pal's hand.

'It's what mates are for.' Smiley followed him into the house, and into the lounge where a fire burned in the grate. Smiley took off his gloves and warmed his hands by the flames as Ferret got two cold beers from his cold room and passed one over. 'Cheers, mate.'

'Yeah.'

'Where's your dad?'

'In bed. He's not a well man these days. He won't make Christmas.'

'Damn. I always thought he was indestructible. I thought he'd outlive everybody.'

Ferret shook his head. 'Not this time. If you see him, for God's sake don't tell him why you're here. He couldn't take it.'

'It's a bad bloody business, that's for sure.'

'Not just on our land, apparently. On the jungle drums I know of a few more have had the same problem. My neighbours down the lane. The Miller's. They put aside a few acres for conservation. They were teaching their grandkids to respect wildlife. They went to have a look one day and the badger and cubs had been ripped to pieces. They even left one of their dead dogs behind, what was left of it. The kids were devastated.'

'I bet. Those scumbags want putting down. You told the police about what went on here?'

'Yeah, for what good it did. They sent a token plod to take a look. Told me the chances of catching them were between zero and nil and that they had other priorities.'

'Sounds about right.'

'He was more concerned about the trespassing than the butchery. He just didn't get it.'

Smiley could see the anguish in his friends face. 'Okay, pal. You got friends that want to help. And I mean really help. About a month ago, they stopped a dog fighting gang. Left them minus a few teeth.'

Ferret smiled. He liked the sound of that. 'Take a look at the orphans?'

'Yeah. I got all sorts in my bag. Lead on.'

Ferret led the way outside and Smiley grabbed his bag from his top box. The cubs were together in one cage in a large shed. Smiley opened it and took out one sleepy cub. 'Tried feeding them?'

'Just a drop of milk. I thought I'd wait for you.'

Smiley weighed the cub in his hands and checked the fur. 'Roughly six to seven weeks old, I'd say. No good as pets you realise?'

'I'd like to get them back in the woods if I can. But what's the point if some moron's going to kill them?'

'Hey. One thing at a time. Lets take care of the cubs and my mates will take care of the scum-bags.'

Smiley put the cub on the worktable and opened his bag of tricks. 'There are some excellent centres taking proper care of these animals, you know? There's one in Tunbridge Wells. Wildlife Centre Project, it's called.'

'I know. I looked them up. If I find I can't cope, I'll give them a call. I'd like to have a go and see if I can get them back in our woods.'

'Okay. Is that cloth over there clean?'
'Yes.'
'Right. Rip it into several strips. That's the way. Now soak one strip under that tap. Pass that here. We have to make sure they are empty before we go filling them up. Watch this. Lift up the front legs. Now gently wipe this rear end to stimulate them and out it all comes. Boy, that stinks. This ones empty now. You do the same with the other two. Use a clean towel each time. Not exactly Chanel number nine. You've got it. Now at this age they can have a mix of special milk formulae. They can possibly be allergic to ordinary cows milk.'

Smiley mixed some up. 'I've a special feeder here. Wash it out each time. Okay. Hold the cub like this and let it lick around the teat so it gets the idea. This little chap knows what's going on. Hold the tip of the teat to the roof of its mouth. Then, just stroke the throat a little bit to encourage him and away he goes. Now. Very important, as soon as he stops suckling, stop feeding. Otherwise you might be getting it down his lungs and kill him. Here. All yours.'

Ferret took over.

'You're a natural mother, Ferret.'

'Thanks.'

'When we've fed and emptied them again, I'll give them some shots.' Whilst Ferret fed the cub, Smiley checked the cage. 'This is plenty big enough for now, but we need bedding we can clean out and throw away.'

'Some old newspapers over there.'

'Perfect.' Smiley got the other two cubs out and placed them on the table. Being daytime, they were still sleepy. He shredded up the newspaper and layered the bottom of the cage. 'Another daily job for you.'

'Fine.'

'Tomorrow we can make a bigger enclosure where they can run about when they're ready.'

'In that corner should do.'

'Just the job. The good news is, pretty soon they'll be just on solids. Dog food, scrambled egg. I'll give you a list.'

'I really appreciate this, Smiley.'

'No worries. Now all we have to do is catch those responsible and show them the error of their ways.'

Ferret winced from the smell as he emptied one of the other cubs. 'Now that I'm looking forward to.'

Chapter 22

'Sleep okay?' said Ferret.

Smiley stretched and yawned. 'There's more lumps in that mattress than there is in this porridge.'

'Thanks. Keep insulting my cooking you won't get any of my free range eggs and bacon.'

The men sat at the huge rustic oak plank table. There were those in the neighbourhood who were convinced the table came first and the house was built around it.

'I was up early to see to the badgers,' said Ferret. 'I gave them scrambled egg. They loved it.'

'Good. Did you remember to empty them?'

'Before and after. I heard dad moving about earlier. I'll take him some grub up later.'

'Ferret. It's your decision, but I really think you should think about sending the badgers to a sanctuary where they can get the care they need.'

'I can manage. It isn't like this is a dairy farm. No milking at four in the morning. Like I said, if I find I can't manage, I'll send them to the centre.'

'Fair enough. It could be a few months before you can let them free. One thing you mustn't do is let them get too fond of humans. Just do what you have to do and then let them be.'

Ferret scraped the last of his lumpy porridge up. 'It's only like the pigs. I don't get chummy with something I'll be killing and eating.' He pushed the bowl away. 'See. That's what gets me about all this. It isn't even as if the badgers are killed for food. Just tortured and slaughtered for so called sport. I got no problem with an animal that's had a good life being humanely killed for food.'

'Me neither.'

Ferret poured out dark brown tea and dished up bacon and eggs. 'So. What's the plan?'

'Hmm. This looks good. See, the problem is, not knowing when or even if they'll come back. Most of us have jobs to do. But we think they'd most likely return at the weekends.'

Ferret nodded. 'It was Saturday night I saw them here.'

'We didn't really think they'd show up this weekend, not after you seeing them off with your gun. What we propose is, we take turns staying the weekend, three or four of us at a time. With you as well, we'd soon deal with them. We can try that for say four weeks and hope to catch them.'

'I didn't realise so many bikers cared.'

'We're just people who like bikes and animals. That's pretty much my whole life.'

'I never had a bike. The old Land Rover does for me. I'll get Dad his breakfast.'

'Okay. I'll look at the cubs and take their temperatures and see they're alright.'

'You can give me a hand putting an enclosure together later, if you like.'

'No sweat.'

Ferret started on his father's breakfast and Smiley put his boots on and made his way to the shed. The badgers were sound asleep wrapped up in each other, as cute as any kittens. 'Sorry to wake you lot. Come on. Out you come.'

* * *

Smiley knocked in another nail. 'How's your dad?'

'Not too bad. He has good days and bad. More bad, lately. This doesn't look to shabby.'

'It should keep them in. We can put their cage in for them to sleep in and leave the door open for them to get in and out. They look pretty healthy. At least they got to a decent size before they were orphaned.'

Smiley stood back after the pen was finished and let Ferret do the feeding and cleaning of the cubs. The less people handling the better, he explained. With that done, Ferret took Smiley to look over his piggery.

'Good old Gloucester Old Spots,' said Ferret. 'A lovely temperament.'

'They would be happy in a five star accommodation like this.'

They watched the happy pigs and piglets forage like they would in the wild and then they went to the woods to look at the setts.

'They kept their distance from the house,' said Ferret. 'This one's closest to the road. I reckon they parked in the lane, climbed the fence and let the dogs find the badger.'

Smiley could see the way the men had dug into the sett to get the badger once the dogs had found it.

Ferret said, 'When they saw me, they ran off in that direction.'

'Hmm!'

'What?'

'Nothing. Just an idea.'

Smiley gave Ferret a hand around the farm for a few hours and then they had a chicken dinner. Late that afternoon, Smiley said he had to get going.'

'It's meant a lot you coming over,' said Ferret. 'Thank the others for their support, will you?'

'I will. Expect them late Saturday.'

'I'll make sure to have plenty of beer and grub in. Watch how you go.'

'You too. But no heroics, okay? Wait until my mate's get here.' Smiley started his bike and rode off.

Chapter 23

'I hate maths,' said Fran.

Su agreed. 'Me, too. I mean. What the hell have we got calculators for? It just doesn't add up. I'll be glad when all this crap's over.'

They were both stretched out on Fran's bed, in-between the heaps of schoolbooks. 'I'm gonna have a look at Tiger,' said Su.

'I'll come with you. I could do with a break.'

It was getting dark outside, so Fran flicked on the outside light, which instantly had a moth fluttering around it. Getting the keys off the hook on the back door, they crossed the yard to the large garage workshop. Su turned the lights on. Somewhere in a dark shadowy corner, a mouse scurried for home. They went to the back of the garage and with a sigh, Su pulled off the tarpaulin that covered her Tiger. It gleamed from the continuous polishing. Most weekends she visited Fran and they would chat as Su messed with the bike. She would kick it off and let it tick over for a few minutes.

'It bloody sucks that I can't just ride off on it.'

'Gotta have rules and stuff, I suppose,' said Fran.

'I should just take her for a ride and to hell with the stupid rules.'

Fran shook her head. 'My dad would do his nut if you do that. You know he said he'd sell it if you pulled a stunt like that again.'

Su sighed and stroked the tank fondly. 'Yeah, I know. 'It's right game to get my full licence. All I can ride is a little putput moped until I'm seventeen. Might as well just catch the bus.'

'You'll soon be on Tiger. It just looks a long time away. Anyway. You'll have to get a job to even pay for a moped. All that tax, insurance and stuff. By the time you've coughed up for all that, you'll be too broke to go out on it.'

'Oh, cheer me bloody up, why don't you?' Su lovingly covered the bike back up. 'So I'll get a job. No big deal.'

'What sort of job?'

'Dunno. Old Ponsonby said she'd look into a few things for me. Something to do with animals.'

'I suppose it all depends on the exam results. If I do really well, I'll think about A levels and Uni.'

Su shook her head. 'All that book learning. Sitting in classrooms listening to old farts droning on. Stuff that.'

They went outside and Su turned out the light and Fran locked the door.

'Night, Tiger,' said Su.

* * *

'Am I glad that's over,' said Fran.

'It wasn't as bad as I thought it might be,' said Su. 'Just sums.'

'Typical. You hadn't even picked up a maths book until last week. Isn't there anything you aren't good at?'

Su wondered what Fran was on about. 'Meet you at the Nagging Bladder?'

'After a week like this, I need to let my hair down. I'll see you at seven.'

As Fran walked off, Mrs Ponsonby appeared. 'Just the girl I was looking for.'

'I was just about to go home, Mrs Ponsonby.'

'This won't take long. I may have something of interest for you. Come along.'

Su followed Mrs Ponsonby along the corridor, the plump woman's heels making a click-clack sound on the hard polished floor. Su found herself heading in the opposite direction to the other students making their way to the exit. They entered Mrs Ponsonby's small but well organised office.

'Take a seat, Miss Kane.'

Su sat and waited, eager to be on her way but concealing her impatience. Ponsonby sat in her swivel chair and shuffled some papers on her desk.

'Now, then. Last time we spoke, you expressed an interest in working with animals. Does that still appeal to you?'

'Yes. I think it does.'

'Well I got to thinking you would perhaps like to test the water, so to speak. Something that wouldn't tie you down if it didn't work out.'

'Makes sense.'

'Good. Glad we're on the same page. I was reading a magazine the other day, and I read about an animal sanctuary. They look after all sorts of animals, domestic, wild, you name it they look after it. So I gave ...what's her name? Here it is. Mrs Fletcher.

There's a picture of her here with one of the horses they look after. Anyway, I told her about you and how hard you were working on your studies and that you were keen to work with animals. Mrs Fletcher said they do from time to time have one or two school leavers helping out, especially this time of the year. Usually for a few months. Now, the thing is, it's a token wage because it's a charity, but free board and meals.'

'Free board and meals?'

'Ah! I should have said. It's a living in position. You'll have your own room, everything provided.'

'I'd stay there?'

'Yes. Is that a problem?'

'I dunno.'

'Obviously you need time to think about it. Not too long, though. They do have to fill the position by the end of this month. Well. What do you think?'

'Is it far?'

'About ninety odd miles from here. A little village called Little Neston.'

'It's a lot to take in,' said Su.

'Look at it as a long working holiday. All that countryside, away from the West Midlands. And the best part of it is, you'll have saved up a little money and had some wonderful new experiences.'

'It does sound interesting.'

'It could be very good for you. Go and have a nice weekend and think it over. Talk to your parents about it. Then on Monday, let me know and I'll make the arrangements with Mrs Fletcher.'

'Okay. I'll do that. Thanks, Mrs Ponsonby.'

Chapter 24

It was a few minutes before seven as Fran and Su approached the Nagging Bladder. 'How come I never get offered things like that?'

'You wouldn't go anyway. You said you were going to do A levels.'

Fran said, 'I didn't say I would go. I just said, why am I never offered things like that.'

'But if you wouldn't go, what difference does it make?'

'A bloody big difference. Are you going?'

'I dunno, yet. I said I'd think it over and let her know on Monday.'

'What's your mum say about it?'

Su said, 'I haven't told her. I think she'd be cool about it. She'd probably be glad to have me out of the way so she and Mick can have the place to themselves. Still at it like rabbits.'

'I wish I could get away from this dump for six months and get paid for it,' said Fran pushing open the pub doors. There were only a handful in the room. Bluesdog, Carol, and Todd had set up early and were at a table with a drink. Fran and Su said hi to Phil Crowe who gave them a cola on the house, then they joined the rest of the band.

'Hey, Dudes,' said Bluesdog.

'Hi. Any news about the badgers?' asked Fran. After hearing the gory details from Smiley the week before, she had images of tortured badgers on and off ever since.

'The cubs are doing well, according to Smiley,' said Carol. 'He's gone over there tonight with Oddball and Scrubber. They've got some big ideas about something. No idea what.'

Su said, 'At least they're there with Ferret if those bastards turn up again. I'd like to go over myself one of the weekends, but I'm not sure I'll be around.'

'How come?' said Todd.

'It came out of the blue today. The careers advisor knew I was wanting to work with animals. She got me the chance to work in an animal sanctuary. Not a lot of money, but a room and meals.'

'Might be a good thing for you,' said Carol. 'How long for?'

'About six months. I have to say yes or no on Monday.'

Bluesdog said, 'We'll miss you if you go, Dude. Come on. The place is filling up. Lets belt out some tunes while we still got you.'

* * *

Ferret was impressed. 'And it all works off a couple of twelve volt batteries?'

'Solar charged,' said Oddball. 'Fit and forget.'

'Putting it all together will keep us out of mischief,' said Smiley, watching the badgers running around their pen. They were eating mostly solid food, now.

'Or get us into it,' said Ferret. 'A job for the morning, anyway.'

They left the cubs to sniff around and turned off the light as they closed the barn door. It was a mild night, so they sat with a few beers on the front porch. Somewhere in the distance an owl hooted. The bikes were nearby, the moonlight glinting off the reflective surfaces.

'I wouldn't mind a bike,' said Ferret.'Nothing flash. Just a runabout.'

'Ha!' said Scrubber. 'You mean like Smiley's bike.'

'It looks cool enough to me,' said Ferret.

'If you wanna ride a tranquillised slug,' said Scrubber.

'Nothing wrong with my bike,' said Smiley.

'Yeah, said Oddball. 'As long as you just wanna polish it. Sounds nice, though.'

Ferret said, 'I probably won't bother. Just day dreaming. I'll stick to the Land Rover.'

'Very wise,' said Smiley.

Several beers and much fat chewing later, the friends called it a night.

Chapter 25

'Well, I think it's a good idea,' said Mick. 'A chance to meet new friends.'

'Slave labour if you ask me,' said Barbara.

'It's a charity, Mum. They need the money to run the place.'

'Sounds like you've made your mind up.'

Su said, 'It's only for six months. I'll be back before you know it.'

'You got my vote,' said Mick. 'Good work experience. It'll be hard work, though.'

Su shrugged. 'I don't mind hard work.'

'Hmm!' snorted Barbara. 'Never seen much evidence of you doing hard work around here.'

Mick disagreed. 'She's really put the hard yards in with her exams this last few weeks. I wouldn't be surprised to see her get top marks.'

'True. I can't believe the effort you've put in. Mick's right. It will do you the world of good. Mind you, I'd like to talk to this woman who runs the place just to see what you're letting yourself into.'

'I'll get the number from Mrs Ponsonby on Monday,' said Su.

Barbara said, 'How soon before you have to go?'

'I'm not sure. I'll find out everything on Monday and let you know.'

* * *

'Are you quite sure, Miss Kane?'

'Yes, Mrs Ponsonby. But my Mum said she wanted to talk to her herself.'

'Let's call Mrs Fletcher. Hang on a moment.' Ponsonby called the sanctuary and it was picked up right away. 'Ah, Mrs Fletcher. Mrs Ponsonby, here. Fine thanks. I have that girl we were talking about....that's the one. Su Kane is her name. She's really looking forward to it. Her mother has expressed a wish to speak to you before they make the final decision...No. She isn't here. This will be this evening when the girl gets home. Between seven and seven thirty? I'll tell her that. Now, Mrs Fletcher. I almost forgot. Exactly when are you wanting Miss Kane to arrive? I see. Well, that gives us a couple of weeks to get organised. Just a moment please. Su. Two weeks time suit you?'

Su thought about that. It was her sixteenth birthday on the next Monday and she was booked in to do her compulsory basic training all that week. As long as she passed, she could go to the sanctuary after that. 'Yes. That's okay.'

'Mrs Fletcher. Miss Kane says that works out for her. No. Once Miss Kane has made her mind up, she generally sticks with something. That's fine. Right, Mrs Fletcher. Thank you very much. Bye.'

'It's still on, then?'

'As long as your mother is happy with you going. Here's the number. Ask your mother to call Mrs Fletcher any time between seven and seven thirty. Let me know the outcome in the morning. If it all goes well, you start in two weeks time.'

'Thanks, Mrs Ponsonby.'

Chapter 26

'She seems a nice lady,' said Barbara as she hung up.

'I thought so,' said Su, stroking Starlight as she purred contentedly on her lap. 'So you don't mind me going?'

'No. Not now I've talked to Mrs Fletcher. Apparently they do this every year. You won't be alone, either.'

'Oh?'

'There's another girl arriving after you. Abigail something. So you'll have company.'

'Oh, right. What did she say about the money?'

'Just a few pounds a week as a token wage. Everything else will be provided. Yes. It'll be a good experience for you.'

'And you'll have this place to yourselves.'

'You make it sound like I want to get rid of you. I'm going to miss you. And if I thought for one minute you wouldn't be looked after, you wouldn't be going.'

'And she wants me there a week next Monday?'

'Yes. There's a train that gets to the village at eleven on Monday morning. She or her husband will meet you there.'

'Okay. Only I wanted to go somewhere this weekend.'

'Is that right? Like where for instance?'

'Just with some friends. I've been invited to a bit of a thing.'

'Not those biker friends of yours? I don't like the look of those people one bit. All hair and tattoos. And those bikes are dangerous.'

'Not if you ride them properly.' Somehow, the topic of Su getting a motorcycle licence hadn't been discussed. 'They're good people, Mum.'

'Hmm! *You* would say that. All weekend?'

'Fran will be there, too.'

'And Aunt Joan is happy about that?'

'She knows we can take care of ourselves. I'm going, Mum.'

'Well. I suppose if you're going to be all those miles away for six months, a weekend away won't make much difference. But no funny business, okay?'

'Mum...'

'You know what I'm talking about, young lady. I'm trusting you. Don't you let me down.'

'Me and Fran will be fine.'

* * *

After school on Friday, Su was round Fran's. Uncle Bill was looking pleased with himself.

'I got that scooter off Old Charlie. It only cost me a few beers. Come and take a look.'

Su and Fran followed Bill into the garage, and there it stood, in all its sublime scruffiness. Even when Old Charlie had been riding it, the idea of actually cleaning it had never occurred to him.

'Now. I know it looks a bit rough at the moment, but the engine's sweet and the tyres are fair. The paintwork does need a little bit of work I must admit.'

'No shit,' said Fran. 'It's a wreck.'

Su said, 'Not when I've worked my magic on it; isn't that right, Uncle Bill?'

'That's the spirit. It'll have to wait until you come back, but that's okay. The training centre have their own bikes for your C B T. Your job next week is to go and pass that. If you don't, you can pay to retake it. Fair enough?'

'Don't worry. I'll pass.'

'I know you will.'

'Of *course* she will,' said Fran.

* * *

The Friday night session at the Nagging Bladder was a solo set by Carol. Bluesdog, Smiley, Su and Fran were in Bluesdog's old van for the trip to the farm to be with Ferret. As usual, Bluesdog wasn't over the moon about two teenage girls going on a potentially dangerous weekend. He decided the breath he saved not arguing with them could be put to better use when he got older. It was dark when he pulled up outside the farmhouse.

'Hey, Bluesdog. I've not seen you for years.'

'Hey, Ferret. Good to see you, Dude. I'd like you to meet a couple of friends of mine. Su Kane and Fran Hartshorne. We got a bit of a band together.'

'No shit. Well, come on in.'

The kitchen was warm with cooking and baking. 'I got some grub if you're hungry. Plenty of beer.'

'Not still making that home-brew crap, Dude?'

'You don't have to drink it, mate.'

'It'll make a change from the Nagging Bladder's beer.'

Ferret opened a door to a small cold-room off the kitchen, filled with wall to wall bottles of home-made wine and beer and three pressurised spheres, each holding forty pints of beer or cider.

'That'll do for me,' said Bluesdog. 'What are the rest of you drinking?'

Ferret found pint glasses for everyone and poured three for the men. He looked at the girls and glanced at Bluesdog who just shrugged and kept out of it. He filled up two more pint pots for the girls. 'It's an acquired taste,' he warned them. 'I have some pretty lethal cider if you're feeling especially adventurous.'

Su and Fran winced as they both sipped the distinctive tasting beverage. 'Mind if I try the cider?' Su asked.

'Don't say I didn't warn you.' From another barrel with the letter C followed by a question mark written with black felt tip pen, he poured two half pints. 'This'll put hair on your chests.'

'Jeez,' said Fran. 'This would unblock drains.'

'Everyone's a critic. After half a pint your taste buds become terminal and you sort of don't notice the taste. Cheers.'

'Ferret,' said Su. 'Before we fall over in a drunken stupor, can we see the badgers?'

'Yeah. This way.' He took them to the barn and turned the lights on.

'They are adorable,' said Fran. 'How can anybody want to hurt them?'

'If I get my hands on them...' said Su.

'You two take a back seat if things get nasty, you hear me?' said Smiley. 'We three can sort things out.'

'We might not even have to,' said Ferret.

'Can I pick one up?' asked Su.

'Best not,' said Smiley. 'It isn't a good idea to get them too used to people. A Ferret's different.'

'Ha, bloody ha. Time to let these little critters have some playtime. Come on and leave them be.'

It was fresh drinks all round and on the porch watching the stars. Su told Ferret about her plans for the coming months at the sanctuary.

'Sounds like something worthwhile. Hey, Bluesdog. You got your harmonica?'

'I never leave home without it, Dude.'

Ferret got up, went in the house and returned with a guitar. It was a magical evening of slow drinking and slow, slow soul and blues. Ferret strummed, Bluesdog blew, Su and Fran sang in sweet harmony, and Smiley was just happy to be there. Then after an hour, an upstairs window opened.

'Are you scalded cats ever going to bed? I'm trying to die up here.'

'Okay, Dad,' said Ferret.

Chapter 27

'I'm never going to drink cider ever, ever again in my bloody life. Fran? Fran? Are you still alive?'

'Hell, no. At least I hope not. If this is being alive, bloody shoot me now.'

They had shared a bed; more comatose than sleeping. Both were naked but neither had any recollection of getting that way. Su felt like Todd was playing a particularly vicious drum solo in some dark cavern of her mind.

'What happened to my teeth?'

'Dunno,' said Fran. 'Somebody pickled mine in battery acid.'

'Vindictive bastards. Have you tried opening your eyes yet?'

'I'm not doing that this side of Christmas.'

Su said, 'I will if you will.'

'Do we really have to?'

'On the count of three. One, two, ouch!'

'Bloody hell. Where the hell am I?'

'If I knew that, I wouldn't be sharing a bed naked with my cousin.'

By mutual support, they dragged each other to the bathroom, showered, resurrected their teeth, then dressed.

'Anybody else up yet?' Fran asked.

They passed a bedroom door and deep snoring from two distinctively different nasal cavities that made the walls vibrate.

'Smiley and Bluesdog at a guess,' said Su. 'Is it me or are those stairs moving?'

Fran placed a tentative foot on the first step down. 'It looks like jelly, but it feels okay.'

They stared down the stairs and it looked a hundred feet at least to the bottom. They held onto each other and the handrail either side and taking their lives into their hands, they made it one step at a time to base camp.

'Morning, ladies.'

'Ferret,' said Su.

Ferret was doing strange things with bacon and leeks in an ocean of oil. 'Hungry?'

Su held a hand to her mouth. 'Let me even see that, I won't be responsible.'

'Same here,' said Fran.

'Not hungry, then.'

Su found her leather jacket draped over a chair. 'Only one thing that'll make life worth living right now, and I have that right here.'

The girls went outside, Fran breathing in the country air with a faint smell of pig dung, Su lighting up and drawing in the will to live. The door opened and Ferret stepped out.

'Is that it. Smokes for breakfast?'

'You got a better idea?'

'As a matter of fact, I have. Come with me.'

'Are you kidding me?'

'I've never been more serious in my life. Come on.'

Su took a last drag and followed Ferret inside. He went up the stairs and she started wondering what it was all about. Ferret knocked on a door.

'Dad?'

'Piss off.'

'Can I come in?'

'Piss off.'

'I'm coming in, Dad. Cover yourself up. I got a young lady with me.'

'Go away.'

Ferret opened the door and went inside. Su followed him. In the bed was a man. Or perhaps the shell of a man that once was. He was propped up on his pillows; an oxygen mask over his face. His eyes were baggy, dark rimmed and sunken. His skin was an unhealthy yellow, and his breathing was his way of defying the gods.

'Who the hell is that?'

'I'm Su Kane,' said Su Kane.

'Oh. You must have been the one making that infernal racket last night. Much appreciated.'

'Sorry.'

'Dad. Can I get you anything?'

'Yes. A new pair of lungs and an ounce of common sense to go with them.'

'Dad. Su smokes cigarettes.'

Ferret's dad wheezed into his mask and his eyes shared a moment of understanding with his son.

'Su Kane.'
'Yes.'
'Strange. You *look* intelligent.'
Su Kane bristled. 'I've just taken seven O levels.'
'That's exams. Nothing to do with intelligence.'
'But..'
'How old are you?'
'Nearly sixteen.'
'Sixteen,' he wheezed. 'Do you know how old I am?'
'No.'
'Take a guess. Have a real good look at me and then take a guess.'
'I...I dunno. Seventy? Seventy five?'
'That's just how old I feel, not how old I am. I'm fifty three.'
'I'm sorry, only you look older.'
The man coughed hard and Ferret became concerned, but his father brushed him away. 'Any idea why?'
'I suppose because you're not well.'
He tried to laugh, but that only made things worse. He fought to get his breath back. 'Hear that, Grant? I'm not well. Hmm. You got that right, young lady. How old did you say you are?'
'Nearly sixteen.'
'Right. Nearly sixteen. O levels, hey?'
'Seven.'
'Seven. Any idea what made me the way I am today?'
'No.'
'Smoking. Bloody cigarettes. Know how long I've smoked?'
'No.'
'Since I was fifteen. Do you know what I want right now this minute?'
'No.'
'I want a cigarette so bad I could leap out of this bed and rip your pretty face off for one.'
Su instinctively stepped back, strangely scared of a sick old man.
'Do you know what else I want?'
Su shook her head. She was crying, now. 'No.'

'I just...' He wheezed and gasped and his eyes rolled. He took the oxygen in as deep as he could. 'I just want to bloody die. Grant?'

'Dad?'

'Piss off.'

Su ran out of the room and down the stairs and out of the door.

'Su?' Fran said.

All Su could do was to wave her cousin away. 'Don't.'

She took out the cigarettes she craved for more than life itself and put one between her lips. Ferret was right behind her.

'You are seriously going to light that thing?'

She flicked the lighter and with a trembling hand brought the flame up to the end of the cigarette. She couldn't do it. She shut off the lighter and took the cigarette from between her lips and she crushed it in her hand. Then she took out the packet and did the same with that, throwing it onto the ground. She stood up and stared at Ferret.

'You bastard.' Su and Ferret stared at each other, and then Su took off, disappearing into the woods.

'Is she okay?' asked Fran.

'I think she just gave up smoking.'

Chapter 28

'Just for the record, Su might be a bit awkward today,' said Ferret.

'Is that right, Dude? Nothing new there then.'

'She quit smoking today.'

Bluesdog and Smiley looked at each other.

'Crap,' said Smiley. 'I was hoping for an uneventful weekend.'

Ferret grinned. 'She's going away, isn't she? You could come back when she's gone.'

'Women are one thing,' said Bluesdog. 'A nicotine deprived Su Kane could be nasty. If I could see straight, I'd be on the road right now, Dude. Just how much did we put away last night?'

Smiley said, 'More than enough. I suggest we chill for the rest of the day and avoid Su like the bubonic plague.'

Bluesdog slapped an unhealthy amount of free range bacon between half a loaf and went outside. Fran was sitting on the steps of the porch. 'Morning.'

'You reckon?'

'Not a bad thing, stopping smoking.'

'Hello? Have you met my cousin?'

'Strange little teen chick, about this short?'

'Not nice to be around when she's pissed off.'

'I noticed. She'll get over it.'

'More than likely. Given enough time she might revert back to human. For now, I might just give her some space.'

'Point taken, Dude.'

* * *

Fran did what she could during the rest of the day. Su cried, swore, ranted, begged for smokes nobody gave her, thumped Ferret in the chest, called everyone a bunch of hypocrites, searched the house for smokes, cried, swore some more, told Ferret what a shit he was, twice, took several walks in the woods, then finally calmed down and apologised to everybody.

'Feel better now?' asked Smiley.

'I couldn't feel more stink if I tried.' There was a drawn-out pause. 'I've been a bit tetchy.'

'No shit,' said Fran.

'I'll try to pull my head in,' offered Su. 'Sorry, guys.'

They tried to take Su's mind off things by letting her feed the cubs and then had a low key blues session not loud enough to interfere with Ferret's dad's full frontal attack on death. Finally, after a serious feed, they decided to get their revenge on the booze. It was close to midnight, when it happened.

Chapter 29

In the woods, lights went on. Big bright ones. Sirens wailed. Loud 'come and get me' sirens echoing like banshees in the depth of the trees. Men shouted, animals squealed. The window above them opened and an angry frustrated man yelled, 'If you bastards don't let me die in peace, I'll come down there and kick shit out of the lot of you.'

'Okay, Dad. We'll sort it out.'

They ran into the woods and pandemonium didn't quite cut it. Four men and a very displeased badger shared the same net. Oddball and Scrubber had rigged it to fall on anyone stupid enough to try badger baiting on this sett. It was hugely satisfying to hear the men scream as the badger showed her displeasure at having her home invaded. Wicked claws slashed and sharp teeth decided fresh human meat was the way to go.

Smiley yelled, 'Fran. Go back to the house and call the cops.'

Fran legged it back through the dark woods towards the house and the phone. Su, Smiley and Bluesdog savoured the moment as the badger took umbrage at having her nightly quest for food for her cubs disrupted. Trapped inside the net, their dogs having the good sense to disappear, the men had no defence against the vicious claws and angry disposition of the mother badger.

'Get it off me,' screamed one man.

Bluesdog squatted casually on the ground, quite impressed with the amount of blood the men were shedding. The badger sank her teeth into an exposed calf muscle and spat out a chunk of warm meat. 'But I thought you liked blood sports, Dude.'

One man wriggled free and took off towards the fence.

'He's mine,' snarled the nicotine deprived Su Kane.

She ran after the man and as he was straddling the wire fence to escape, she pulled hard on the top wire, like a cheese cutter against his genitals. As he screamed in agony, she got hold of him in a headlock and pulled him to the ground.

'I am not in a very good mood right now,' she growled. 'And you are not on my Christmas card list.'

'Don't hurt me.'

'As if I would. Well, maybe a little.'

His screams and cries for help rang through the night air only to be unheeded. Back at the nets, the other three men were still trying desperately to avoid the wicked teeth and claws of the badger.

'Sounds like Su's got him,' said Ferret.

'Poor bastard,' said Smiley. 'Maybe we should go pull her off him?'

'No rush,' said Ferret. 'Do you think these guys get the message yet?'

Fran ran up the path towards them. 'The police will be about five minutes.'

'Yeah,' said Bluesdog. 'That could be a very long five minutes for these jokers, Dude.'

'Where's Su?' Fran demanded. Then she heard the cry for mercy. 'Never mind. I'll find her.'

Fran ran towards the screaming. A man was face down in the dirt and Su was sitting on top of him, smacking him over the head with a dead branch she'd found.

'Su, stop it. The cops are coming.'

'They ain't here yet,' Su growled, hammering the branch on the top of his head again.

'Please stop hitting me.'

'I ain't even started yet.'

Su was about to hit the man again when Fran grabbed her arm. 'Okay, 'cus. I think he gets the point.'

Su threw the branch away. Then she grabbed the man's ears and yanked his head back. 'I'm going to get off you now,' she said in a voice that was low and assured. 'But if you dare to move, I will rip out your eyeballs and make you eat them. Are you going to move?'

'Hrmeph.'

'I didn't quite catch that.'

The man spat out mud. 'I'm not going to move.'

Su got off him and Fran sat on top of him to make sure he kept his promise. 'I'm so glad you said that. You see, she's just quit smoking and she's not thinking straight. You just be a good boy and if you're very lucky, the cops will soon be here to rescue you from her.'

From somewhere down the lane, two police cars appeared, all sirens and flashing lights, hoping to make a contribution. They pulled up on the drive and the sound of many car doors opening and slamming back shut, echoed through the night air.

'Over here,' cried one cop. 'Oh, shit. Call an ambulance. Hurry.'

'Sarge. There's something else over here.'

'Shit!. Okay. You two girls back away from him. You. Can you stand?'

The man with blood running down his forehead scrambled to his feet and ran behind the police sergeant, his face pale and his eyes wide with terror. 'Don't let her hurt me again. Please. Don't let her hurt me.'

'You two keep away from him, hear me?'

'Sarge,' called another officer, deeper into the woods. 'You need to see this.'

'Now what?' The sergeant saw something new for the first time in years. Three grown men trapped in a net, at the mercy of one pissed off badger. There was quite a lot of blood everywhere. 'Bloody hell.'

'Don't worry, officer,' said Smiley. 'I'm a veterinary nurse. I can look after her.'

'But what about these jokers?'

'I hear an ambulance, officer Dude,' said Bluesdog, helpfully. 'Maybe they can help them.'

Smiley wrapped the net around the badger, giving the three men time to scramble out of harms way to the welcoming arms of the law.

'I'll have you for this,' said the oldest of the men.

'And I'll have you for trespassing,' said Ferret. 'Not to mention disturbing a badgers sett.'

'Bollocks. We came over just to answer a call of nature. You'll never prove anything.'

'You came to take a leak with a spade and dogs?' said Smiley.

'Yeah, so what?'

'See that?' said Smiley. 'That camera, tripped off by the motion detectors. It was all recorded.'

Two paramedics rushed into the scene and saw the blood soaked men. The sergeant had heard enough for one night. He called two of his officers over. 'You two go with these fine gentlemen and make sure they don't decide to leg it.' Two more policemen were half dragging another man along.

'That bitch assaulted me,' he yelled, keeping the police between him and a small, wild haired teenage hell cat who would give him nightmares for the rest of his life.

'No shit,' said the sergeant. 'And yet she looks so sweet and dainty. Go with him to the hospital. I'm staying here to take statements. I've got an idea it could be a very long night.'

Chapter 30

'You take care, that's all I'm saying.'

'Mum. I'll be fine. I'll just be on a moped. I have to do the two theory tests before I can even sit on that.' She had almost overslept after getting home late from Ferret's.

'If anything happens to you, I'll be livid with your Uncle Bill.'

'I have to go, Mum, or I'll be late.'

Barbara kissed her daughter and sighed as she went off to catch the bus. She would take some persuading that anything less than four wheels was a good idea. It was the same routine for the next four mornings, but on Friday evening, a beaming Su Kane held her certificate to show she had passed her Compulsory Basic Training. She could now ride her tatty little Vespa. But that Saturday morning, Bill had other ideas.

'No. Absolutely not. Don't you pout like that at me, Su Kane. It isn't MoT'd, insured, taxed and not even properly roadworthy. No, end of discussion.'

Su sighed. 'Okay. It'll keep until I get back.'

'That's right. There was no point getting it legal if it was only going to sit in the garage for six months. She'll be waiting for when you get back.'

Su hugged her favourite uncle. 'Thanks, Uncle Bill.'

'You got through the training. That's the main thing. You'll be on your Tiger before you know it.'

Chapter 31

Su spent the weekend with Fran, just happily being teenagers. It was nine thirty on Sunday night when she got back home.

Barbara said, 'I've packed your bags and case. You have an early night and I'll take you to the station in the morning.' She passed Su an envelope. 'This is from Mick and me. Just to keep you going until you get paid. If you get stuck for money, phone me and I'll do what I can.'

Su hugged her mother. 'Thanks, Mum. Thanks, Mick. I'm going to miss you.'

Tired but happy, Su went to bed, Starlight curling up with her. She thought about the weekend and the result. She grinned as she recalled bashing the man with the lump of wood. It was something she would never forget. There was a stronger bond between herself, Fran and the bikers. Suddenly, she had an extended family, like minded people with common aims. To have fun, live life to the full, and deal with anyone who was cruel to animals.

'All this started with you, Starlight,' she said, stroking the sleeping cat. 'You were the first, but I think there's a lot more stuff out there to sort out. But that's cool. We got an army, now.' The cat opened her eyes, looked at Su and licked her face. 'We got the Starlight Army looking out for the animals.'

But Starlight wasn't listening. She was fast asleep.

* * *

'Now I want a phone call at least once a week, okay?'

'I'll call, Mum.'

'Just work hard and stay out of trouble.'

'Mum...'

'I mean it. I'll be worrying enough about you as it is.'

'I'll be good.'

The train started to move and Su waved to her mother as it left the station. It took two stops and ninety minutes to pull up at the Neston station. Su picked up her bags and case and got off the train. The large station building looked neglected and uninviting. Several people were waiting on the platform, and one of them, a woman, approached Su.

'Su Kane?'

'Yes.'

'Welcome to Neston. I'm Gwen Fletcher.'

They shook hands 'Nice to meet you, Mrs Fletcher.'

'Call me Gwen. We're a very informal lot around here.'

Gwen was on the short side, about the same height as Su, but carrying more weight. Su guessed her age to be late forties. Her hair was fair and cut in a no nonsense style and given little attention too, as if belonging to a woman with better things to do. Her clothes told much the same story, the top half covered up in a vest, the neck of which showed above a check shirt, which was partially covered up by a cardigan with most of the buttons missing and finally a waxed Belstaff jacket Su had seen on several of her biker friends. The lower half of Gwen's attire was jeans tucked into green gumboots. Everything about Gwen, including her ruddy complexion, shouted here was a woman who lived more outdoors then in. Su liked her instantly.

They both picked up bags and went along a slab path at the side of the building. 'Not a very nice thing for first time visitors to see,' said Gwen. 'There's talk about it being demolished. Sooner the better, in my opinion.'

There was a Land Rover in the car park, its army green paintwork liberally coated with mud. Gwen opened the back door and heaved Su's bags inside, pushing them along for the rest of the luggage to be added to it, then Gwen got in the drivers seat and Su sat next to her.

'It isn't far. Just a few miles.'

They drove south, onto the High Street, passing the church of Saint Mary and Saint Helen's.

'This is Neston,' said Gwen. 'Our place is the other side of Little Neston. Mind you, there's not much separating the two, these days.' They drove onto Burton Road. 'This is Little Neston. All much of a muchness, these days. It's grown a lot since I was your age.'

Out of the village, they went along Neston Road, out into farmland. After another few miles, they turned south west along another lane, and into Fletcher Park and Animal Sanctuary. On one side were horses and on the other, alpaca's. Turning right, they came to the house with several outbuildings scattered seemingly randomly around it. As they pulled up, a man came out of the front door of the house and Gwen and Su got out of the vehicle.

'Hello,' said the man. Like Gwen, the man was all about the outdoor life. 'I'm Tom.'

Su shook hands with Tom. His hands were rough and strong; the hands of a man used to working hard with them. He was a little taller than Gwen, but lean and wiry looking. He was about fifty, Su figured. Like his wife, Tom was dressed for any weather that came his way.

'I'm Su. This is a nice place.'

'Nine acres, there about,' said Tom. 'It was a rough boggy mess when we bought the place. It's been a labour of love getting to this standard, I can tell you. Still. That's why we got the place cheap all those years ago.'

Gwen said. 'We have two chalet's for our helpers. A girl named Abigail arrives tomorrow, so you get first pick. Give us a hand with the bag's, Tom.'

The chalets were fairly recent additions to the Sanctuary, painted an inviting yellow. Gwen opened the door to both. 'Not much in it,' said Gwen. 'This one had a coat of paint last year, so it's a bit fresher, I suppose.'

The chalet was basically one room with a bed and two old armchairs at one end and a basic kitchen at the other.

'There's a toilet and shower through there,' said Tom. 'All nice and clean.'

'It looks fine,' said Su.

'No washing machine,' said Gwen. 'You can use our laundry when you need it.'

'It all looks nice to me,' said Su.

'Good. Now. You sort your things out and come and join Tom and I for lunch in about half an hour.'

'Thank you.'

Chapter 32

'Settled in?' asked Tom, slicing a crusty loaf of bread up.

'Pretty much.'

'Take a seat. Gwen's just on the phone. She'll be in in a minute.'

The farmhouse kitchen was spacious with a red tile floor and beams of ancient blackened wood on the walls and ceiling. The units looked old and well used.

'When do you want me to start work?' Su asked.

'Tomorrow will do fine,' said Tom. 'After we've eaten, we'll show you around and explain things.'

Gwen entered as Tom was dishing up. 'That was my daughter, Elaine on the phone. Not that we get much chance to talk with the grandchildren. Nathan's such a chatterbox. And all he ever talks about is football. This looks nice, Tom.'

'One tries to please,' said Tom.

'He's a much better cook than me. I'd be lost without him.'

As they ate, they got to know each other. 'Done anything with animals, Su?'

'I have a cat called Starlight. Always up to mischief. Actually, I fed some orphaned badgers this weekend.'

'Really?' said Tom. 'Why were they orphaned? Did their mother abandon them? I do know they do that sometimes.'

'Baiters killed their mother. A friend rescued the cubs.'

Gwen shook her head. 'There are some wicked types about.'

'That lot isn't any more. We set a trap for them and caught them. The police have them now.'

'That's great,' said Tom. 'I hope they get locked away for awhile.'

Su told them about the dog fighting gang and how the bikers taught them a lesson and rescued two injured dogs.

'Amazing,' said Gwen. 'I look at you, just a slip of a girl and I'd never have dreamt you'd be doing things like that.'

'It's why I'm here, because I love animals.'

'There's always something to do around this place,' said Tom. 'We basically survive by getting in donations, but we do have an organic produce shop that keeps our head above water, just about. We're also fairly self sufficient in food. Everything on this table comes from our land.'

'It's really good,' said Su.

'One of the things we do as well,' said Gwen, 'is have regular coach parties to visit us. We don't charge as such, but most make a donation. So one way or another, we manage. Right. I'll show you around. Coming, Tom?'

'I'm making a fresh batch of chutney, so I'll pass.'

Gwen and Su went outside. 'One thing for sure, is you won't have time to be bored. Lots to do, but lots of variety. Come and meet Maggie, Dobbs and Polly.'

In a large paddock were two adult shire horses and their foal.

'They're gorgeous,' said Su.

'Gentle giants. The mare is Maggie. Stands sixteen hands. That's Dobbs, her partner, just over seventeen hands and of course, Polly. They're purebreeds. We can trace their line back to the beginning of the century. They eat a lot, but they pay their way. We have a cart used for weddings and they look a picture all spruced up.'

The mare walked over to the fence. 'Hello, Maggie. I suppose you want a little treat, do you?' From her coat pocket, Gwen pulled out a carrot. 'There you go, Su. Make a friend for life.'

'What do I do?'

'Just put it on the palm of your hand and let her take it. That's the way. Keep your hand flat.'

Su did that, a little nervous of the animal that towered above her. Maggie took the carrot and chewed it up. Not to be left out, Dobbs and Polly came over and they too got a treat. 'We've a wedding coming up this weekend. You'll be helping to get them ready for it.'

'I don't know anything about horses.'

'We'll be working together. Don't worry, by the time your six months is up, you'll know one end of a horse from the other. Come on.' They crossed over to the other enclosure. 'Alpacas,' said Gwen. 'Mad as hatters, most of them.'

'Were they mistreated?'

'No, not at all. The elderly couple who had them couldn't look after them and offered them to us as part of our attraction. We only had four, two pair. Now thanks to Mother Nature, we have eleven. On we go.'

'Vietnamese pot belly pigs. A trendy pet suddenly became too much trouble for some of the ladedah brigade. See, the beauty of working here with us is that you'll learn about many different animals. Over here we have our various chickens. We keep two types of Frizzle. That's the Lavender Frizzle, called that for obvious reasons. Lovely colour. But these are my favourites. The Lemon Cuckoo Frizzle. I just think they're hysterical looking.'

A little further on, were several pygmy goats. 'They all have their own needs and wants,' said Gwen. 'Now we are coming to our care and rehabilitation centre.' They went into a large barn. 'You aren't the only one who's looked after badgers. These little darlings were orphaned, too.' There were four cubs, larger than the ones Su had seen at Ferret's farm.

'Baiters?'

'Not this time. Mum got hit by a truck one night. The driver was most distraught over it. It was just an accident. He stopped his truck and had a look around and he found these nearby, outside the sett, waiting for Mum. They were weaned, so we are just feeding them up to release into the wild. Over here we have Oliver the barn owl. He was found caught up in a soccer net. He'd chased a rat or something, got wrapped up and couldn't get free. When we got him, he was badly injured and his right wing never healed completely. And so he's a permanent resident. He can't fly too great, but he gets around in here and keeps the mice and rat population down. Here we have a hedgehog some boys thought made a cool football. He seems to be on the mend. Don't get too close. They all have fleas. We just never know what somebody will bring in next.'

'You certainly have your hands full.'

'I love every minute of it. One of the things Tom and I are keen on is education. We often go into schools to teach the children about respecting nature and the wildlife.'

'I think I'm going to enjoy being here.'

'I know you will. Lets go and see how Tom's getting on.'

At the back of the house was a purpose built kitchen, just for Tom to make stuff from their home grown produce to sell to visitors to the sanctuary. There was a huge pot on the gas stove full of tomatoes, onions and a dozen other things. Tom was stirring it all up with a huge plastic spoon. He pulled out the spoon and presented the business end to Su.

'See what you think of this.'

Su wiped her forefinger across the spoon and sampled the chutney. 'Now that is bloody good.'

Gwen said, 'Five hundred jars which will make us three hundred pounds profit for the sanctuary.'

'What can I say?' said Tom. 'I'm a culinary genius.'

Chapter 33

It was seven thirty the following morning when there was a loud and persistent knocking on the door of the chalet. Su had amazed herself by responding to her alarm clock radio and was already up and dressed. The cravings for cigarettes were still strong, but she just closed her eyes and focused on Ferret's dad. It was an unshakable image and one that like the dying man's dire warnings, served to make her determined to stay off them.

'Coming.'

'Morning, Su,' said Tom. 'Sleep well?'

'Good, thanks.'

'Ready for a days work?'

'Yes.'

'You might want to put these on.'

Tom handed over dungarees and gumboots. 'I guessed your sizes. If I'm too far off the mark we have others you can try.'

She tried them on. 'Dungarees a bit tight and the boots are a bit big.'

'Enough to bother you?'

'No. Not really.'

'Good. When you knock off for lunch, we have others to try on if you want. Right. Lets see how you handle a shovel.'

The Shire horses shared a stables at the side of their paddock. And by the side of that was a compost heap, three times the height of Su.

'It needs turning over,' said Tom. 'But first we have to make it even bigger.'

'That's a lot of shi...shovelling. Is it even possible making it bigger?'

'Come on.' Tom opened the stables and made a fuss of Polly. 'Time for some fresh air, Polly. And you two sleepy heads, come on. Out you get.'

Maggie and Dobbs dwarfed both Tom and Su as they walked out into the morning sunshine.

'When you do it, just be firm with them and they won't argue. Just say it with a bit of authority. Now big horses make big messes. Your job first thing is to let them out and clean it all up. Okay. Grab that shovel and bucket and that old broom there.'

Su did that and had a good idea what to do next, so she swept the horse droppings up and soon filled the bucket.'

'Good,' said Tom. 'That gets thrown on the heap. See all that old straw? That's about had it. It can be worked into the heap. Very important to have plenty of straw in a compost heap. There's a barrow over there if you need it.'

Su filled the barrow and wheeled it outside.

'Okay. There's a fork by where you got the broom from. You'll need that.'

Su went back in the barn and returned with the fork.

'Deep down inside the heap is the good stuff. We get a good price for that. Just shovel the stuff on top, out of the way.' He watched her dig away for a few minutes. 'Okay. Come and look at this. Worth good money.' He picked up a handful up. 'See how rich and crumbly it is? That's what we're after. Just inside the stables by the door is a big pile of sacks. Grab as many as you can carry.'

Su got the sacks.

'All you have to do is fill as many sacks as you can and when you've got it all, turn the rest over with the shovel or fork, but mix in as much of the straw as possible.' Tom watched her for a while. 'That's the way. I'll leave you to it. Have fun.'

Tom, grinning, returned to the house, went into the kitchen and put the kettle on just as Gwen walked in.

'What's tickling you?' Gwen asked.

'Su's turning over the compost heap.'

'You swine. You've been putting off doing that job for ages. Now you've got Su doing it.'

Tom chuckled. 'You know how much I hate doing that. A bit of exercise will do her the world of good.'

There was a knock on the door and a young woman walked in. A strong Liverpudlian accent said, 'Hi. I'm Abigail but everybody calls me Abbey.'

Chapter 34

Abigail Jones was...unique. She didn't try to be, she just was. She was nineteen going on thirty-five, had already been married and divorced, hitch-hiked around half the globe twice. Had served two months in a juvenile detention centre when she was fifteen for knocking a man unconscious. She'd done it with a single punch and hadn't denied it. When the time had finally come for her trial, the magistrate discovered that Abbey had run away from home after years of abuse and was living on the streets of Liverpool.

When a middle aged man had offered her money for sex, she'd refused and he'd pinned her up against a wall to molest her. A passing police patrol car officer saw Abbey land the punch, breaking the man's nose, sending him crashing to the ground. Instead of the man being arrested, Abbey, an obvious street kid, was charged with assault. When the trial came around, the man she had hit was serving time for the rape of another street kid. The case against Abbey was dismissed.

Four years and many miles and adventures later, the irrepressible Abigail Jones ended up at the animal sanctuary. For her it was a roof over her head for six months.

Abbey also looked unique. She was the thickness of a pencil off six feet tall. Five years of eating anything that came her way and washing it down with any alcohol that came to hand, gave her a body most men would have been proud of. Her hair was cropped close to her head, she had a scar above her left eye from a regrettable incident in Morocco, and tattoos acquired during alcoholic binges were even in places previously considered anatomically impossible to perform the noble body art. Abbey Jones was delightful.

Tom took Abbey to her chalet. To Abbey, it was a slice of paradise. 'It'll do fer me, pal,' said Abbey. From what passed for a car, she got her tote bag and dropped it on the bed. Her whole world was in that thick canvas, well travelled bag.

'Well,' said Tom. 'Come and meet Su Kane.' With only passing references to the animals as they walked along the path, they came to the stables, more specifically, the compost heap outside it. Somewhere under several layers of...under several layers, was Su Kane.

'Su. Come and meet Abbey.'

Su was in the middle of emptying a gumboot of something unpleasant. The dirty job, coupled with her persistent desire for tobacco had put her in a rather unsociable mood. Yet, she was mature enough to realise this wasn't the fault of Abbey. Jamming the gumboot back on, she hobbled over to the young woman who towered over her.

'You stink,' said Abbey by way of a greeting.

'Nice to meet you, too,' said Su.

'See?' said Tom. 'I just knew you two would hit it off.'

Strangely, they did.

Chapter 35

'How did you get in a state like that in less than an hour?' Gwen asked.

'Don't ask,' said Su.

She had gone back with Tom and Abbey to the house, Gwen insisting Su not only remove her gumboots and dungarees, but everything except her underwear. Gwen found her clean clothes to make do with.

'Tom should never have given you that job. Not on your first day, anyway.'

Su shrugged. 'It's what I'm here for isn't it?' taking a bite out of her chicken sandwich.

'When I ask *him* to do it, he usually runs a mile.'

Abbey said, 'I worked on a camel farm in Australia for a few months. Now what they crap out brings tears to your eyes.'

'Hello. I am trying to eat here, you know?' said Su, the sandwich midway to her mouth.

'I'm just saying,' said Abbey. 'Much worse jobs than horse...'

'Abbey!'

'Poo, I was going to say. Never mind.'

'Been around a bit, Abbey?' said Gwen.

'Yeah, like, it's Tuesday, so it must be Bangladesh, right?'

'You're an interesting lady, Abbey,' said Tom. 'Your experience with animals will be very useful around here.'

'It wasn't all good. See this?' She rolled her sleeve up. Much of her left arm was heavily scarred. 'Croc. Again in Australia. There was a creek where the camels drank. I was just having a bit of a cool down at the waters edge, I see something I think is a log. A log with teeth, all right. Bastard jumped up and latched on.'

'No shit,' said Su. 'How did you shake it off?'

'Well, luckily it was a baby. No more than seven feet long. The little sod wouldn't let go, so I dragged it on land, twirled around and smashed the joker against a tree.'

'And that got rid of it?' said Gwen.

'No. Not the first time. Three times I was spinning round like a bloody ballerina but the third time it got the message and dropped off me. Back in the creek it went leaving me irrigating the bloody desert with my blood.'

'And the hospital stitched you up?' said Su.

'What bloody hospital? Five hundred miles the nearest one was. Even the farmhouse was ninety miles away.'

'So what did you do?' asked Tom. 'You had a vehicle, right?'

'My vehicle had four legs and very questionable breath. I rode a camel. Only all the camels had run off when they had seen me fighting the croc. Fortunately, my saddle bag had dropped off in the commotion. I had a sewing kit....'

'Abbey. Tell me you didn't,' said Gwen.

'It took me an hour to close it all up. I'd just finished, when Pete turned up.'

'So you had some help, then?' said Su.

'Pete was my camel. He had teeth like a boyfriend I once had so I named the camel after him. I managed to get on his back and smack his backside. Pete the camel, I mean. Next thing I knew, I was back at the farmhouse.'

'I bet they were relieved to see you,' said Gwen.

'Not really. I got the sack. All the herd were scattered all over the place and they weren't happy about that. Shit happens. Talking of shit, Su. Why don't you and me conquer horse dung mountain?'

Chapter 36

'This is the life,' said Abbey.

Eight hours of toil that would have put a whole gang of navvies to shame, had conquered horse dung mountain and a dozen other jobs. It took both of them twenty minutes to feel human and clean again. A substantial feed had been provided by the Fletcher's and Abbey and Su were staring at the stars as they sat on the porch of Abbey's chalet. From her cornucopia of a kitbag, Abbey had took out a full bottle of bourbon. They passed it back and forth as they chewed the fat.

'You've really been around,' said Su.

Abbey took a long pull on the bottle and passed it back. 'It ain't all it's cracked up to be. Six months here will be the longest I've stayed put in three years. Maybe I'll settle down one day.'

Abbey had her arms exposed as she sat and admired the night sky. Su tried not to look at the croc mangled arm but the tattoos were too enticing not to look at them.

'What's that one there,' she asked, handing the bottle back

'This one? That's supposed to be a mongoose fighting a cobra. I was stoned out of my brain in Delhi; no idea why I was even in Delhi. Anyway, I'm staggering along this backstreet slum and I see some bloke tattooing. Like it's in some kind of tumble down shack, all exposed for the whole bloody world to see, and this joker is tattooing this blokes back. The bloke calls me over. Like an idiot I do. I tell you, stoned as I was, the stuff on this blokes back was a work of art. And it was blue, and black and green. And I just sat and watched and it was amazing.'

'So you had that done?'

'I must have dosed off. Next thing I know, the artist was tapping me on my naked back, demanding money. The tattoo looked great, so I paid up.'

'Everyone's happy, then?'

'Not quite. It got infected and I spent the next three days in a state of delirium, wandering the streets of Delhi. Like I said. It isn't all good.'

'I suppose not. I might still get me a tattoo when I'm eighteen.'

'Why not?' said Abbey, draining the bottle. 'At least it will outlive you. Years after you get buried, the tattoo will linger on. Unless you get cremated, of course. I'm off to bed. Night, Su.'

'Night, Abbey.'

Chapter 37

Abbey seemed unscathed from a night of heavy alcohol consumption, but Su Kane just wanted to leave her head on the pillow and send her body outside to do something useful. No such luck.

'We've a wedding on Saturday,' said Tom. 'We need all this tack cleaned and polished. Don't bother about the cart until the day before. Have fun.'

It was about to rain, so Abbey and Su got all the gear undercover in the stables and dragged up bails of straw to sit on. Abbey was applying dubbin to the collars, on with one soft cloth, off with another, Su was dealing with all the leather reins with an aim to polish the brass-work next.

'I might phone my Mum, tonight,' said Su.

'At least you got one to phone. If she's halfway human, call her.'

'My mum's okay. I just really want to know if she's had my O level results yet.'

'If you done O levels, you done more than me.'

'Nobody on this planet's done more than you. I'd like to travel some day.'

'They say it broadens your mind. I say you really end up with more third world diseases than you can shake a stick at. I remember this one time. I was in... where the hell was I? Algiers? Libya? It might have been Turkey. Anyway, I'd eaten some weird local dish. It might have been dog. Can't remember. By the time I got to my room, I didn't need drugs or booze to feel strange. I reckon by the time it had passed, I'd lost four kilo's of crap, sweat and self esteem. I think I went to Malta after that.'

Su loved Abbey's stories. How many were true, seemed irrelevant. The simple, factual way she recounted the stories, not bothering to exaggerate or embellish, only made them more tangible and believable. Perhaps it was Abbey's Irish Blarney Stone roots, but there was magic in the honest retelling of the adventures. Su told Abbey about saving the cat, thumping the dog fighters, and whacking badger baiters with lumps of wood. They just seemed small potatoes compared to anything Abbey had done. Su was just reflecting on this, when the door of the barn swung open. Gwen walked in with a dapper looking man.

'Abbey. Su. This is Kevin Couling, Lord of Little Neston Cum Hargrave. He's also a celebrant and he's doing the wedding on Saturday. Kevin, this is Su Kane and Abbey Jones.'

'Hello,' said Kevin. 'Nice to meet the two of you. Good heavens. That's a jolly good shine you've put on that tack.'

Su had never met a Lord before. She didn't know if she should stand up and curtsy or just say hi. She just said hi.

'Thanks, Kev,' said Abbey. 'Nothing like a spot of elbow grease to get a proper shine on things, hey?'

'Absolutely. And I'm sure with the shires dressed up to the nines we'll have an absolutely splendid occasion.'

'Absolutely,' agreed Abbey.

'Right,' said Gwen. 'Carry on girls. Kevin. We have to discuss the arrangements for the fair.'

'Absolutely,' said Kevin. 'Great work, girls. Top class job and all that.'

Gwen and the Lord of Little Neston cum Hargrave left the barn and Abbey and Su stared at each other.

'Absolutely top class job, Su.'

'Absolutely, Abigail.'

Chapter 38

'Are you sure you want me to open it? I can always post it to you so you can open it yourself.'

'No, Mum,' said Su. 'Let's get it over with.'

As she sat with the telephone in a slightly shaking hand, Su could imagine her mother at home, opening the letter.

'Okay. It says. Dear Su Kane. We are pleased...ladeladelah...the following results...ladeladelah...'

'Mum!'

'Right. Calm down. Maths. A 'B'. B's very good isn't it?'

'Yes. Not bad. Go on.'

'Chemistry, another 'B'.'

'Did you say B or C?'

'B. B for baboon. English an 'A plus'. Oh, well done. Geography C minus. Oh, well. Can't win them all, hey?'

'It's still a pass.'

'That's okay, then. History another B. Oh, sorry. B minus. Still, a thing of the past, history. What's next? Physics. B plus. Art. A minus. And finally, social sciences. That's cooking, isn't it? You got a C for that. You must have burnt the toast or something. Happy with that lot?'

'I'm just amazed I didn't fail anything.'

'See? If you'd spent more time at school, you'd have done even better. Why don't you call Fran and see how she's done?'

'I will later.'

'How are you getting on?'

'Yeah, okay. Abbey, she's another helper, we get on great. Oh. And I met a Lord something of somewhere this morning. He's marrying a couple on Saturday.'

'Bloody typical of the aristocracy. Us peasants can only marry one at a time.'

'No, Mum. He's a celebrant. He can perform the service.'

'Oh! Got it. Right. How are you for money?'

'I haven't had a chance to spend the last lot you gave me, yet. I've been too busy working.'

'Well, I'm glad you're giving it a go. But don't let them take advantage of you. Mick. Stop it. I'm on the phone. You take care, Su. You know I love you.'

'Love you too, Mum. Oh. Don't forget to feed Starlight.'

'I will. Bye for now.'
'Bye, Mum.'

* * *

'No shit?' said Abbey. 'Seven O levels. You must be some kinda genius.'

'I doubt it.'

'We need to celebrate. Go out and get bevvied. I've run out of booze, so I need to go and get some. I noticed a pub less than a mile away. I reckon you could pass for eighteen at a push. Put a bit of slap on our faces and we'll get well bevvied, yeah?'

'Not too hammered. I've only just got normal vision back from last night.'

'You'll live. Come on.'

Half an hour later, dressed in the best gear they had, they walked up the lane to the start of Little Neston and the pub. The Harp Inn was situated on Quayside, a two story building with white painted rendered walls. Inside, a few customers looked sideways at the girls, but Su and Abbey ignored them. The barman cast a professional eye over the pair.

'Evening, Ladies. What can I get you?'

'A couple of pints of bitter would be a good start, thanks,' said Abbey.

'Coming right up.' As he poured the beer, he glanced over at Su again. 'You are old enough, aren't you Miss?'

'She's my mam,' said Abbey, fixing the man with a "wanna argue with me about it" stare.

'Hmm. Wearing very well, if I may say so. I don't suppose you have any identification on you?'

Abbey said, 'Mam. Did you bring your over sixties bus pass, like I asked you?'

'Slipped my mind.'

'That's what old age does, I suppose,' said Abbey. 'Are you gonna let a couple of women keel over with dehydration, barman?'

He looked at the huge woman who he was sure could beat the living daylights out of him had she a mind to; the muscular scarred arms with the tattoos and the face with the scar. Self preservation and the desire for a trouble free night got the better of him.

'There you go, ladies. Enjoy.'

Abbey paid and gave the man a wink and a look that said, "wise move" and then they found a quiet corner.

'Well, Mam. Here's to you and your O levels. Cheers.'

'Cheers, Abbey.'

Another seven pints of beer each was enough for one night, although both girls running out of money was the main reason. Abbey belched, blew the barman a kiss and staggered out with Su.

Chapter 39

'Lots of soapy water then hose it off,' said Tom. 'Then once it's dry, polish all the painted surfaces. Make sure all the seats are spotless, because we don't want a wedding dress ruined on the brides big day. At least the forecast says dry for the next couple of days. I'll see you later.'

It was a pleasant job in the morning sunshine, and Su was happy to be outside in fresh air. She only had a moderate hangover, but bullet proof Abbey looked as fresh as a daisy, as if she'd gone to bed with cocoa and a good book.

'Not a bad night last night,' said Su, unrolling the hose.

Abbey was squeezing washing up liquid into a bucket. 'Yeah. A bit tame, though. I went to a party in Hong Kong, once. I'd worked my way over on a cargo ship from Mexico. Anyway, I'd had a bit of an altercation with the captain, who told me when he regained consciousness that I wasn't welcome back on board for the return trip. Not that I gave a stuff about that. So, there I was, minding my own business having a quiet drink and this little bloke comes up to me. I think he fancied me. Offered to buy me a drink. Just be friendly, I said okay.'

After Su had blasted off the loose dirt, Abbey worked a soft, soap covered brush into all the nooks and crannies and then Su hit it again with the hose.

'Four days and nights of none stop partying. I tell you, for small people, they can put it away when they want to. Happy days.'

'Sounds like fun. I think we should let it all dry off so we can polish it.'

Abbey said, 'Yeah. Time for lunch, I reckon.'

Gwen had a substantial feed waiting for them. 'How's it going?'

'It'll look a picture,' said Abbey.

'Good. Actually, Tom and I thought you might like to drive the cart tomorrow and transport the wedding party to the ceremony at the golf course.'

'That sounds like fun, hey, Su?'

'Yeah, but I never had anything to do with horses before.'

'They're very gentle,' said Gwen. 'They practically know every street in Little Neston and they've been to the golf course a few times.'

'Can't be any harder than bronco busting in a rodeo,' said Abbey. 'I haven't much in the way of fancy clothes to wear, though?'

'Just clean jeans and shirt will be fine,' Gwen assured them. 'Keep out of the way when the photographs are being taken and they'll be happy.'

It was renewed gusto that the girls prepared the cart. 'How about that?' said Abbey.

'It'll be fun,' said Su. 'Were you really a bronco buster?'

'I only did it the once. Seven seconds I stayed on. Landed a bit awkward and bust my arm. Could have been worse. It could have been my drinking arm. I reckon this rig's as good as it's going to get.'

* * *

'You beat me in everything but history,' said Fran, lying on the settee with the phone.

'It's just a bit of luck how the questions came up,' said Su. 'I'm off to a wedding tomorrow. Me and Abbey are driving the wedding cart.'

'Typical. You have all the fun.'

'Aren't you going to the Nagging Bladder tonight?'

'Yeah, but it isn't the same without you there. It seems ages since I saw you.'

'I'll soon be home. Look. I gotta go. I gotta sort out my best gear for tomorrow.'

'Okay. I miss you.'

'I miss you too. I'll call you next week. Bye, Fran.'

'Bye, Su.'

Chapter 40

'Easy. Easy,' said Tom as he backed the horses to the front of the cart. 'Okay. If you grab that, Abbey. There. All secure.'

'They look beautiful,' said Gwen. 'You've plenty of time, so just let them go at their own pace. You have that route I gave you, Su?'

'Right here, Gwen,' said Su, tapping the pocket of her clean and ironed white shirt.

'Just help everyone on and off,' said Tom. 'I'm just going to take a couple of photos, so smile. You too, girls. Done. Off you go and good luck.'

Abbey flicked the reins and the horses pulled the heavy cart like it was made of tissue paper. Gwen and Tom watched them go off onto the lane.

'Annie Oakley and Calamity Jane ride again,' said Tom.

Su navigated and Abbey steered the cart. Maggie and Dobbs looked superb, their coats shining; their purple and gold plumage bobbing on their heads and their brass bells jingling with each step. It took twenty minutes to reach the address. The wedding party was standing on the pavement, waiting for the transportation. The bride was a middle aged lady, about to take the plunge for the second time. No flowing white dress for her, but a very nice two piece outfit in a powder blue. The bridesmaids were her two daughters and the pageboys and girls were her grandchildren.

Su jumped down and went to the back of the cart where the steps were. She let the lady hold onto her arm as she climbed the steps, and her daughters helped their children on board.

'Sit tight please, everybody,' said Su. She jumped back up and Abbey flicked the reins and away they went.

The weather was being kind that day, and it was a long and steady plod along Burton Road, and from Tom's instructions, it would take nearly one and a half hours to get from the grooms home to the Heswall Golf Club, where the ceremony and reception were to be held. All others would be going by car. It wasn't the horses first time along that route, so they pulled the cart at a singularly steady pace. Abbey held the reins, but it was hardly necessary. Su periodically asked the wedding party if everyone was happy and they all seemed to be enjoying the special occasion. Abbey gave the horses guidance to take the left turn onto Church Lane, to avoid Neston High Street. Then onto the short Mill Street, to join Leighton Road.

'We're about halfway,' said Su.

'Good. We're making good time. Which road is next?'

'Right onto Boathouse Lane.'

A few more lefts and rights and they were finally on Cottage Lane where the entrance to the golf club was.

'This looks posh,' said Abbey. The clubhouse and reception centre was just a hundred yards from the entrance to the club and the manager was waiting to great them, along with the groom and the rest of the guests. Both Su and Abbey got down, glad to stretch their legs, and helped the bride and her family down the steps at the back of the cart. The wedding photographer took several photos of the bride and her entourage with the horses before they went in to join the groom and the others. Su and Abbey kept out of the way as instructed, Abbey holding onto the reins to keep the horses calm. They just stood calmly like the seasoned professionals they were.

'That was a lovely experience,' said the bride. 'Thank you so much.'

'Our pleasure,' said Su. 'Have a lovely day.'

Lord Couling quickly said hello to the girls as the wedding party went inside. 'You girls have done a magnificent job with the rig,' said Lord Couling. 'Don't Maggie and Dobbs look proud of themselves?'

'Nothing to it, Kev,' said Abbey.

'Right. Have a safe journey back. Duty calls.' Kevin went inside

Su and Abbey climbed on the cart again, this time. A beaming groom hurried outside just before his wedding, gave them twenty pounds each, thanked them and hurried off to leave the single life behind.

'Not bad for a couple of hours work,' said Abbey, kissing the note and putting it into her pocket.

Su did the same. 'I've really enjoyed today.'

'Made a change from shovelling muck. Time to go home, you two.'

The horses shook their plumes and jangled their bells and set off for home and a well deserved feed.

Chapter 41

A happy routine developed and Su and Abbey became close friends. The Lord of Little Neston always made a point of saying hello to them when he called in. He didn't seem to really mind the way Abbey called him Kev. He was organising the annual fête. Kevin was a strong advocate of animal welfare, both wild and domestic. He had supported Tom and Gwen for many years, and did what he could to promote them and their cause. The weekend of the event was fast looming up.

'The vintage car club are putting on a bigger display than before,' he told Tom and Gwen. 'Clowns, stilt walkers, tombola, an acrobatic display, tug of war, mud wrestling, a raffle to win a television, a territorial army display with an assault course, the archery club, a secret celebrity from Liverpool Football Club, not sure which one at the moment, and of course you with the horses giving children rides. I think that's about the lot.'

'You've done really well, Kevin,' said Gwen 'It's helped us a lot over the years.'

'It's been a big help,' agreed Tom. 'I think Abbey and Su might be keen to be involved. They might want to drive the cart.'

'They seemed most confident with that wedding the other day,' said Kevin. 'Well, I'd better be going. Lots still to do.'

'We'll have the cart there about eight in the morning,' said Tom.

'Splendid. I'll see you on the day, then.'

* * *

Both Su and Abbey were only too pleased to get involved. On the morning of the event, they were up earlier than usual, and a little after seven thirty, Maggie and Dobbs were pulling the cart along, with Polly tied up to the back of the cart so as not to be left out. A few minutes after eight, they entered the show-ground. The grounds didn't open to the public until nine, so that things could be organised. Fifty vintage cars, vans and motorcycles were being lined up, a steam traction engine was already belching out steam and smoke, a dozen stalls were getting ready for a busy day, and the Lord of Little Neston was in the thick of it, organizing things with the marshals.

'Hello, Su. Hello, Abbey. All nicely turned out as usual.'

'Thanks, Kev,' said Abbey.

'If you just move over to that side? A little quieter for the horses, perhaps.'

'Okay, Kev.'

A flick of the reins and the huge horses pulled the cart to the end of the field.

'We can just chill out for a bit, I reckon,' said Abbey.

'Suits me.'

They sat back and watched the field fill with activity, and at eight thirty, Tom and Gwen pulled up in the Land Rover, with a trailer on the back with a photographic display of the sanctuary. In cages were the hedgehogs, badgers and Olly the owl. They set up at the end of a row of other stalls and arranged fold-up chairs and table and put the cages on the table with pamphlets and a collection tin for donations.

Cars were being parked up in the visitors car park and marshals were ready to take money for entering. Tom got a hand painted sign nailed to a wooden stake and took that with a mallet up to the cart. He hammered it into the ground. Cart trips every half hour the sign read.

'Keep to that and you won't go far wrong. The perimeter of the field has been kept clear just for you. Don't forget to collect the money. Good luck.'

He returned to his table with Gwen and by nine, the cart was covered with children and their parents. Maggie and Dobbs set off for their first plodding trip around the field.

It was six in the evening and time to wrap up the event. An excited crowd had gathered around the podium and the celebrity guest was introduced by Kevin.

'Ladies and gentleman. I hope you have all had a great day. To everyone who have worked so hard to make a success of this event, a big personal thank you from me. From Tom and Gwen Fletcher, we have learned about their work at their sanctuary and important lessons in respecting our fellow creatures. But now I would like to introduce out special celebrity guest who has given his time freely to be here today. A warm welcome please to none other than, Wayne Wilkinson, striker for Liverpool Football Club.'

There was a rousing cheer from the crowd as Wilkinson stepped forward. 'Thank you. Thank you. What a great day. But now, I'd just like to give you the tally of money raised for the sanctuary. We have a total of, wait for it, nine thousand, four hundred and eight pounds. Fantastic effort. But it gets better than that. I held a meeting of the players yesterday and we agreed that whatever was raised here today, we would match pound for pound. Now I'm a footballer, not a mathematician, but I make that a grand total of, eighteen thousand, eight hundred and sixteen pounds.'

'Brilliant,' said Kevin. 'Absolutely brilliant.'

Back at the sanctuary in the Fletcher's kitchen, Gwen opened a bottle of their home-made wine and poured four glasses. 'Well done, girls. That's the most money ever raised by the fair. We can do so much with that money. Cheers.

'Nice one,' said Abbey. 'Cheers.'

'I'm so pleased for you,' said Su. 'Cheers.'

That night they all went to bed exhausted, but happy.

Chapter 42

A week later was another special day. It had started off as work as usual for Abbey and Su. Su was ankle deep in pig slurry, feeding the little black Vietnamese pot bellied pigs, when she heard a familiar voice.

'Doesn't she look glamorous?'

'Fran! Jeez. Mum, Mick.'

'Just passing, so we thought we'd drop in,' said Barbara.

Su left the pigs to eat and went to her mother.

'Don't you dare hug me. Not until you've showered and put something clean on.'

'But I've work to do.'

'No you haven't. Tom and Gwen said you can have the rest of the day off. Well, it isn't every day your cousin is sixteen.'

'You're catching me up, Fran. Happy birthday.'

'Thanks. Anyway, I'll never be as old as you.'

'Kids today,' said Su. 'No respect for their elders. Give me twenty minutes to clean up.'

Mick drove them to the Hamilton Inn, named after Lady Hamilton, Lord Nelson's mistress.

'This is fantastic,' said Su. Because her mother was there, she stuck to coke. 'I've missed you all so much. I still can't believe you're here.'

'I had a chat to Gwen Fletcher before I found you,' said Barbara. 'When she told me how well you've been doing, I was so proud.'

'Looks like you've found your vocation,' said Mick.

'It's hard work, but I love it.'

Su told them of the things she and Abbey had been up to. Even as she told them, she could hardly believe herself how much she had achieved.

'*And* you beat me in the O levels,' said Fran. 'I've decided to stay on and do my 'A' levels and maybe uni.'

'No more school for me,' said Su. 'I like the real world too much, now.'

Barbara looked at her daughter and marvelled at how she had matured in such a short space of time. 'My baby's a woman, now. All grown up.'

'Had to happen sometime, Mum.'

Mum and daughter had a special moment of understanding.

'Hey, Fran. I managed to get you a little present. It's in the chalet. I was going to post it but I haven't had the chance.'

'Well, now you don't have to post it.' said Fran, 'There's also special present waiting for you back home.'

'What? Tell me or I'll burst.'

'No way,' said Fran. 'My lips are sealed.'

'You pig.'

'At least I don't smell like one. I'm only joking.'

They had a fine meal and then Mick drove them back to the sanctuary. Tom and Gwen were waiting with Abbey by their front door.

'This has to be the amazing Abbey we've heard so much about,' said Barbara.

'Whatever she said, I ain't that bad.'

'We've only heard good things. She says you are a very special friend.'

The big woman wrapped her scarred and tattoo covered arm around the much smaller Su. 'Gotta look after our buddies..'

'I feel better knowing she has you looking out for her. We'd better get going.'

'Fran. Come to the chalet and get your prezzy.'

Fran followed her inside the chalet and Su passed her a parcel. 'Happy birthday, Fran.'

'Can I open it?'

'Yeah. Go for it.'

It was two large, matching black picture frames. One had an enlarged photograph of Su and Abbey with the Shire horses, the other was empty.

'Turn it over,' said Su.

'Fran turned it over. On the back. Su had written, *for Fran's university degree*.

'That's smashing. Thanks.'

'Glad you like them. Now. Are you going to tell me what my big surprise is?'

'Hell, no,' Fran said with a chuckle. 'See you in three months.'

'You can be so annoying but I love you to bits. Come here, 'cus.'

'Always the drama queen,' said Fran as they hugged. 'Take care, 'cus.'

Chapter 43

'She's nice, your mum,' said Abbey.

'Yeah, she's cool. Fran liked her present, I'm glad to say.'

'My last birthday at home before I took off for good was a thrashing with one of those garden canes. She used to keep it by her chair and if she thought I'd been naughty, or even if I hadn't been....'

Su hadn't seen Abbey show her emotions much. She had never mentioned her family, just her many adventures after leaving them. Her big shoulders started to shake and she could hardly breathe as raw, deeply suppressed memories of a childhood no little girl should ever have gone through were unleashed. It was an eruption of emotion and whatever was buried inside her, just had to come out. The lips began to quiver and the tears flooded out. Su went to her, holding her, feeling her friends trembling body, and felt the tears on her neck and held her hand.

'Let it all out,' said Su, softly. 'You're not as strong as you pretend to be.'

Abbey cried her heart out for a full ten minutes, soaking Su's shirt. She pulled away and Su could see the hurt in her eyes. Su placed a hand on each shoulder.

'Abbey. Lately, I've met some amazing people. Big hairy bikers that cry if their pet dog dies, or go all silly holding an orphaned badger. But you've also done so much; taken on the whole bloody world and won, because you had to. My biker friends have become family to me and my cousin. Now you are a part of my family.'

Abbey couldn't speak and got up to go to her own chalet. She wiped away her tears on the sleeve of her shirt. She opened the door and paused, looking back at Su.

'I've waited my whole life to hear those words. Thank you.' She went out, gently closing the door behind her.

Chapter 44

The next few weeks went surprisingly quickly. More wild creatures found their way to the sanctuary. A duck that had survived being shot with a crossbow, staying alive like a good mother to look after her ducklings. Another injured owl with a broken wing, who kept Olly company for awhile before being released fully fit into the wild. A swan that had collided with power lines, surviving just long enough to lay a clutch of eggs, and they had watched each one hatch in an incubator Tom had made. There were no dry eyes that night. The constant stream of creatures needing loving care and a home, just went on and on. They all had many nights of staying up to take care of something, even after a hard days labour. None of them ever complained. But inevitably, their time was up. It was the night before Abbey and Su were due to leave. They had packed their bags and they were sitting on the deck of Su's chalet, counting the stars.

'Where will you go?' Su asked.

'No idea,' said Abbey. 'I might go to the docks. Get a job on a ship. Go where that's going.'

'Abbey. Come with me.'

'What?'

'I mean it. There's a spare room at my home. Mum won't mind. You can stay and look for a job. You'll get a great reference from here.'

'I don't remember the last time I lived in an actual house with an actual family. No. I'd be in the way. Besides. I'd soon get itchy feet and move on.'

'Okay. If you got itchy feet, fine. I'd understand. But I reckon you really want to settle down. At least for a while. Come on, Abbey. Give it a go, yeah?'

'I'll think about it, okay. Just don't nag.'

The next morning, Su was awakened by a noise outside. She pulled her jeans and shirt on and went barefoot outside. Abbey was piling her tote bag in the back of her car.

'Abbey?'

'Are you going to hang about here all day, or are we hitting the road?'

'Two minutes.'

Su finished dressing and took her bags and case outside and rammed them in the car. 'Just one more minute.'

She went back inside, and found a pen and paper. Then from her wallet, she took out half the money she had saved up from her wages. It came to sixty pounds. Not a lot, but she knew a couple who could make every penny count. On the paper she wrote, *thanks for everything, love Su. X.* Then she folded the money in the paper and left it on the bed. Outside, she went to the car, and there on the steps of the house stood Tom and Gwen. Su ran over to them, said nothing, kissed and hugged both of them, ran back to the car and they drove away.

Chapter 45

'Of course she can stay awhile,' said Barbara. 'You are most welcome, Abbey. You being such a good friend to my daughter was very reassuring to me.'

'I'll chip in for food and stuff,' said Abbey.

'Not until you get settled in a job. You two deserve a break, anyway.'

Su was holding Starlight but the cat was never too keen on being held, so she was soon let go. 'Mum. My birthday surprise Fran was on about. Where is it?'

Barbara shook her head. 'To be honest, I have no idea. It was as much of a surprise to me as it was to you. Best phone Fran.'

'I will. Come on, Abbey. I'll show you your room.'

The third bedroom was the smallest, but it had everything a guest needed. 'Very nice,' said Abbey.

'You put your gear away, I'll go phone Fran.'

Fran still insisted on teasing Su. 'You'll have to come here and find out.'

'You minx. I'll be round in a bit.'

Barbara said, 'Didn't she say what it was?'

'No. She's just trying to wind me up. I'll go round there.'

'I suppose you'll be off out tonight?"

'Yeah. I haven't seen my pals for ages. I'll take Abbey.'

'Take me where?'

'To meet my pals at the Nagging Bladder. It'll be a good night tonight. I'm going to see Fran. Fancy a walk?'

They walked through the park as a short cut. 'Remember me saying about jumping in the lake to save my cat Starlight? That was right there. I was only eleven.'

'You were brave.'

Fran was surprised to see Abbey with Su. Her father was at work and her mother was out shopping, so they had the place to themselves.

'It was a last minute thing,' said Su. 'Are you going to the pub tonight?'

'Where else would I be on a Friday night. Come on. I know you're bursting to see your present.'

They went out the back way to the garage and Fran opened up. At the back were two lumpy shapes covered in tarpaulins. Su recognised the larger shape as being Tiger, but Fran tapped the other one. 'All yours.'

Su dragged the tarp off. 'Bloody hell.'

It was a gleaming scooter, an Italian Vespa. 'Bloody hell. That is not my scooter.' It wasn't new, but it was better than new. The seat had been recovered, the tyres were new, and the paint-job was extraordinary. On either side of the large body panels were tigers, rearing up in a wonderland of rivers, clouds and castles. Every inch of the scooter had some original Bluesdog art.

'Everyone chipped in. Bluesdog did the artwork. Dad had it MoT'd and insured last week for you.'

'It's fantastic. Even better, I can ride it now.'

'You got some good mates, Su,' said Abbey.

'You'll love them. Take a look at this,' Su said, taking the cover off the triumph.

'Nice.'

'I put it together myself. But I won't be able to ride it until I'm seventeen.'

'That's only a few months away,' said Fran. 'Come on. Lets get some fish and chips.'

As they sat at the kitchen table eating the fish and chips from just down the road, they talked about what they had done and what they intended to do.

'I'm going to see if I can get a few weeks work during the school holidays,' said Fran. 'After the A levels, I'll take some sort of university degree. Then I might go into teaching.'

'Bloody hell,' said Abbey. 'You'll be like some sort of professor the way you're going.'

'I doubt it,' said Fran. 'But I thought maybe a special needs teacher. We'll see. What about you, Su?'

'Definitely something to do with animals. The last six months just confirmed what I already knew. I'll take a week off and then see what's on offer.'

'I might check out farm work,' said Abbey. 'I noticed a few farms before we came into town. There's sure to be something.'

Su said, 'Abbey has done some amazing things. Been all round the world.'

'Not as glam as it sounds. Most of it was fun, though.'

Bill Hartshorne arrived home before his wife. 'Su. Good to have you back. Have you been in the garage?'

'I've seen the scooter. It's fantastic. Thanks so much. Uncle Bill, this is Abbey. We worked together at the sanctuary. She's staying at our house.'

'Very nice to meet you, Abbey. Barbara did mention you. Staying for dinner?'

'We've just eaten, thanks,' said Su. 'Fran's been telling us about wanting to be a teacher.'

Bill ruffled Fran's hair. 'We're very proud of her. You did well with your exams, too.'

'Yeah, but no more school. I'll find a job somewhere.'

Shortly afterwards, Joan Hartshorne arrived. More chat, then it was time to go to the Nagging Bladder. Bluesdog's trike was outside. At the bar, Philip Crowe poured a pint for Abbey and coke's for Su and Fran.

'On the house. Welcome back, Su.'

'Thanks, Phil. Hey, Bluesdog.'

'Hey, Dude.'

Su gave him a kiss. 'Awesome paint job on the scooter, Bluesdog. Thanks.'

'Just my contribution. I figured as you have a Tiger one hundred, it should have tigers in the paint job. It'll do until you can ride the Triumph.'

'Abbey. This is Bluesdog. Setting up on the stage is Carol and her brother Todd.'

'Nice to meet you, Bluesdog. I haven't seen a live band in ages,' said Abbey.

'Heard anything from Ferret?' asked Su.

'Yeah. His dad died a couple of weeks ago. Most of us went to the funeral. I spoke to him the other night and he sounded pretty depressed. I'm going over in the morning.'

'Poor Ferret,' said Su. 'Mind if I go with you?'

'I can't come,' said Fran. 'I've a job interview at supermarket. Just shelf stacking during the holidays.'

'Abbey,' said Su. 'Would you like to meet Ferret?'

'How could I not want to meet a bloke with a name like Ferret? Sure.'

"I'll pick you up about nine,' said Bluesdog.

'Thanks.'

From the stage, Carol said, 'Hey. Are you guys here to play, or what?'

'Coming, Carol.'

'You're in the band?' said Abbey.

'We all are.'

Carol, Todd, Bluesdog, Fran and Su took their places on the tiny stage. The bikers were starting to pile into the bar, and Su waved hello as she sang. After the set, she introduced her friends to Abbey. Abbey quickly realised what Su had meant about them being like her family. By the end of the night, she had made twenty new friends.

Chapter 46

As he'd promised, Bluesdog pulled up on his trike. Su had her own crash helmet, but he'd remembered to bring a spare for Abbey. Just under an hour later, they were at Ferret's farm.

'Hey, Dude. Come here.' Bluesdog got Ferret in a bear-hug. 'We have a new friend to meet you. Ferret, this is Abbey.'

Bluesdog missed it, but Su noticed a change in Abbey's expression. Ferret hadn't smiled much for weeks, but he cracked one when he saw Abbey.

'Nice to meet you. Hi, Su. Come in. I'll get the kettle on.'

They sat at the kitchen table and Ferret opened a tin of his home-made biscuits as he poured the tea.

'Sorry to hear about your dad, Ferret,' said Su.

'It's what he wanted. I'm surprised he lasted as long as he did. I hope you haven't started smoking again.'

'You smoke?' said Abbey.

'Not any more. Seeing Ferret's dad the way he was plus a few harsh words from him were enough of a wake-up call.'

'I've known her six months,' said Abbey. 'Never saw her smoke once.'

'Pleased to hear it,' said Ferret.

'No more badger baiters?' Bluesdog asked as he ate his fourth biscuit.

'I think they got the message,' said Ferret. 'They got six months inside each and a hefty fine.'

Bluesdog said, 'They'll be out by now then. If they come around again we'll set Su onto them.'

'What did you do with the orphans?' Su asked.

'When they were big enough I let them go in the woods. I've seen fresh setts so I think they're okay.'

'How many acres do you farm?' Abbey asked.

'I've thirty acres plus the twenty acre woods,' said Ferret. 'Even that's a struggle sometimes.'

'Abbey,' said Su. 'Fancy a walk in the woods. See if we can find the new setts.'

'Okay.'

* * *

'He seems a nice bloke, does Ferret,' said Abbey as they walked the woods. 'You do know badgers are nocturnal?'

'Is that right?'

'Is Ferret married or anything?'

Su smiled secretly. It was the question she was hoping to hear. 'I don't even think he has a girlfriend. He's a bit shy, I think.'

'Makes two of us.'

'Yeah, right. Just here is where the baiters were trapped in our net. The mother badger was really getting stuck in. Over there I grabbed one trying to leg it. I was dying for a smoke so not in a good mood. I was smacking him over the head with a log until Fran stopped me.'

'Spoilsport.'

* * *

'She seems nice,' said Ferret.

'Who does, Dude?'

'Abbey. Is she seeing anybody?'

'Dude. I only met the girl last night. Su was working with her on some animal sanctuary, up north.'

Ferret gathered the mugs and washed them out. 'I kinda like the look of her. She's one hell of a woman.'

'Dude. She'd break a skinny runt like you.'

'Yeah. But what a way to go.'

Chapter 47

Ferret had made a job lot of mutton stew that had been simmering in his slow-cooker all morning, to feed himself and Bluesdog. He'd intended to freeze the rest, but with four to feed, that plan was changed. With his home baked bread, it was a substantial feed.

'That hit the spot,' said Abbey.

'It'll mop up the beer later on,' said Ferret.

It had been an amusing meal, with Su swapping glances with Bluesdog as they watched Ferret and Abbey furtively glancing at each other. The attraction had been instant and mutual. Su decided they just needed some alone time.

Su said. 'We had some pigs in the sanctuary. Vietnamese pot bellied ones. Cute. What breed are yours?'

'Gloucester Old Spots.'

'A good pig,' said Abbey. 'Good bacon.'

'That's the extra fat on their backs. And they have young like they were shelling peas,' said Ferret. 'I'm in the Old Spot pig breeders club. We keep the breed pure.'

'Ferret,' said Su. 'Why don't you show Abbey your old spots?' She ignored the tap on her shin she got from Abbey, under the table. The innuendo was completely lost on Ferret.

'Good idea. Help yourself to beer. We won't be long.'

'Take as long as you need,' said Su, trying not to giggle.

When they were out the door, Su said, 'Isn't it so romantic? Falling in love over Gloucester Old Spots?'

This surprised Bluesdog. 'Falling in love? I never saw that coming, Dude.'

Su shook her head and sighed. 'Men. Hopeless, the lot of you.'

It was an hour later when Ferret and Abbey returned, when they found Su and Bluesdog on their third beer, sitting on the front deck..

'I hope you've left some for us,' said Abbey.

'You should really take a look at his stuff. It's impressive,' said Su. 'I recommend the cider.' Abbey and Ferret went into the beer storeroom. 'If the pigs don't clinch it, his booze will,' whispered Su.

Bluesdog whispered back, 'Yeah, but cider? That stuffs lethal.'

'Trust me. I know what I'm doing.'

During the evening, beer and cider flowed freely, Bluesdog played his harmonica, Abbey and Ferret got closer with each drink, and Su had trouble not peeing her pants she was chuckling so much.

'I think I'll get off to bed,' said Su with a belch. She had to kick Bluesdog a couple of times to make him move.

'Oh, yeah. Me too, Dudes. Been a long day.'

They left Ferret and Abbey staring drunkenly at the moon, watching for shooting stars to wish upon. They didn't need any shooting stars that night.

Chapter 48

Nobody got out of bed before eleven the next morning and it was only urgent bathroom visits that made it that early. Su was waiting outside the bathroom door, trying to take her mind off her need to pee. Only just in time did the door open and Abbey, wearing just her shirt and pants, stepped out. Su didn't have time for small talk, and she ran inside and Abbey could hear the sigh of relief from the other side of the door.

'Cider?' said Abbey.

'I thought you liked cider.'

'Not when it can propel rockets to the moon. I'll forgive you one day. Have you any idea how shocked I was waking up in the same bed as Ferret?'

Su laughed. 'No! Hold the front page. You slept with Ferret?'

'Hey. You knew that would happen.'

'Me? An innocent sixteen year old virgin? What would I know about things like that?'

'It doesn't matter. We were both too wasted to do anything. Maybe we talked for a while.'

'Right. And the headboard banging against the wall half the night was your idea of polite conversation I suppose?'

'No way.'

'I wouldn't be surprised if the wall needs re-plastering. Did you use the last of the toilet paper? It's okay. I've found some.'

'I've some news for you. I know we were just a little bit tipsy...'

'As drunk as a skunk you mean.'

'Ferret's offered me a job. I'm sure he...well, I think he said...Yeah. He definitely offered me a job here.'

'It's a long way to commute from my place.'

'Living in.'

'Today's full of surprises. You said yes?'

'Of course I said yes. A roof over my head, a job on the farm.'

'And somebody to keep your feet warm at night?'

'Call it a bonus. Su. Bluesdog's still alive and kicking and looking anxious, so don't take all day in there.'

The door opened and Su emerged. 'Morning.'

Bluesdog said, 'I will be after a liver transplant. Jeez. Somebody farted?'

'It isn't that bad and I've opened a window,' said Su.

* * *

Buttered toast and tea was all anyone could face. That and paracetamol.

'Ferret,' said Bluesdog. 'You have to crunch toast so loud?'

Su said, 'Abbey mentioned something about working here, Ferret.'

'I need to expand the business so I don't go under. I can't do it on my own.' He looked at Abbey. 'You did say yes, didn't you?'

'If you offered, then I said yes.'

Su said, 'Say, Bluesdog. Know any good plasterers?' She got another playful tap on her shin under the table for that. She made a mental note to bring cricket batting pads next time she visited.

Abbey said, 'I'll have to go back for my stuff, though.'

Bluesdog said, 'I need to be going soon, anyway. I've a paint job to finish today. I just need to be able to see out of my eyes.'

Half an hour later, when normal service had returned to Bluesdog's vision, he and Su said bye and Abbey gave Ferret a reassuring kiss, then they took off with a roar. At Su's home, Abbey ran in, grabbed her tote bag hastily rammed with clothes, gave Su and Bluesdog a hug, jumped in her car and drove off.

'I'd call that a result,' said Su.

Chapter 49

'Here's trouble,' said Uncle Garf, putting a small doleful looking puppy with a cast on its front leg into a cage. 'Is it Su Kane or Sunarmi.'

Su took off her helmet and gave her hair a shake. She was going everywhere on her scooter these days. 'I only dropped in to say hi, Uncle Garf. Hi, Smiley.'

'Long time no see. How've you been?'

'Great. Hi, Bumblebee.'

'Hrm,' grunted the old vet. 'Such silly names you bikers give yourselves.'

'Yes, *Uncle Garf*,' said Bumblebee. 'I haven't seen you about much lately, Su, but then again, I've been abroad.'

'I've been working at an animal sanctuary for six months. Not long been back. Are you working here full time now? Oddball told me you are away a lot.'

'On and off. I've just come back from Africa. I've been working on a wildlife reserve for a few months.'

'Like lions and things?'

'Lions, rhino, elephant, chimps. I liked working with the chimps because they reminded me of Smiley.'

Smiley bobbed his tongue out at his friend. 'She loves me, really. How was life in the sanctuary, Su?'

'Not as exotic as Africa. It was hard work, but loads of fun. And I learnt a lot about all sorts of animals, I got to ride the shire horses and cart for a wedding. Tom and Gwen are amazing. But the best thing of all was meeting my friend Abbey Jones. And guess what? She came back with me and now she's shacked up with Ferret.'

'Jeez,' said Bumblebee. 'You got Ferret fixed up?'

'She was won over by his old spots or something, apparently. Anyway, I'm looking for a job with animals.'

'We're okay for staff at the moment,' said Uncle Garf. 'Paid ones at least. Our budget won't stretch for anything but volunteers. Sorry.'

'That's okay. I just thought you might hear of something. I can get a good reference from Tom and Gwen for my time there. I didn't do too bad in my O levels, either.'

Smiley said, 'Well done. It'll be just a matter of time before you land something then. We'll listen out for things for you.'

'Thanks. Are things really tight around here then?'

'Let's put it this way,' said Bumblebee. 'Most of our stuff Noah wore out and chucked out of his ark.'

'Including Uncle Garf,' added Smiley.

'Hrmm. I am right here, you know. But sadly Smiley's right. Even about me. We could use a serious amount of cash right now.'

'I've got about one pound fifty you can have.'

Uncle Garf chuckled. 'That really is most kind, Su, but that would be just a drop in the bucket.'

'Good luck with that then. Anyway, if you do hear of a job....'

'You'll be the first to know,' said Smiley.

Chapter 50

It was Friday night at the Nagging Bladder. The band had finished their set and Su and Fran went to the bar to get a drink. It was a little more crowded than usual, and Su tried to wriggle her way through.

She was almost to the bar when a voice said, 'So you are this Su Kane I've been hearing about?' He was a large hairy biker she hadn't met before.

'Why? Who's been talking about me?'

'Quite a few people, as it happens. Mostly in a good way. Can I get you two a drink?'

'Thanks. Just cokes. This is Fran, my cousin.'

'Nice to meet you, Fran. You sing well. You both do.'

'We try,' said Fran.

'Oddball and Scrubber told me about you two getting stuck into those dog fighters and badger baiters. Well done.'

'We enjoyed sorting them out,' said Su. She suddenly realised, what she and Fran had been involved in ran much deeper than she had imagined. People had been watching how they had performed.

'We try to do our part for animals as well. I'm Cerbarus. Surf and Scrubber are with me, in the Revolting Animals. Heard of us?'

'I've heard the name,' said Su. 'Not sure what it means.'

'What the name means is, the animals are revolting against people for what they do to them. That and the fact we get a little grubby when we're out camping. Like you, we like three things, Bikes, having a good time and doing what we can for abused animals, wild or otherwise. It's good to find more kindred spirits.'

'Thanks,' said Su.

Cerbarus said, 'Are you involved in anything at the moment?'

'Not really. I was working at an animal sanctuary for six months but I need to find a job now. Are you up to anything?'

Cebarus, Surf and Scrubber looked at each other. They knew it paid to be discreet.

'We've been keeping an eye on you,' said Cerbarus. 'Checking you out as a possible member of the Revolting Animals. With some education you might even be useful.'

Fran said, 'You've been following us?'

Cerbarus sipped his beer and grinned at the girl. 'If what we did wasn't so bloody important, you two might not have been given the time of day. We need fresh blood and new ideas. We have a legacy to ensure what we've built up continues and young people like you can take over where we leave off. We needed to make sure you are up to the job. You're a long shot, but we might give you two a chance. I want you to sit in on this meeting.'

'Maybe I don't want to sit in,' said Su.

Cerbarus glared at the girl. His energy was spread way too thin as it was. This teen with the rainbow hair was either in or out. 'I'll ask you one last time. Do you want to make a difference or not?'

Fran nudged her cousin in the ribs. 'This isn't kids stuff, Su. This is bigger than you and me.'

Su looked the big hairy man in the eyes. 'Me and Fran will be more than useful. But you had better have something worth listening to.'

Cerbarus grinned and made a decision. 'Phil. Mind if we use the back room, mate?'

Phil Crowe passed the key to the small back room. 'Help yourself. Just lock up and hand the key in later.'

'Thanks,' he said, looking at the girls. 'Lets have a chat.' He opened up the back room and they followed him inside then locked the door behind them. They put two small tables together and sat around it. 'I'm telling you this because you are getting a bit of a reputation and I like what I hear. I'm trusting you two to keep it confidential.'

'You can trust us,' said Su.

'Ditto,' said Fran.

'Okay. The Revolting Animals are targeting some large corporations. We are putting together plans for a raid on a cosmetics company.'

'Like make-up and stuff?'

'Yes. Ever known an animal wear make-up or perfume?'

'No, but my cat could use some perfume now and then.' She saw Cerbarus raise an eyebrow and scowl at her flippant remark. 'Sorry.'

'There's nothing funny about testing on animals, Su. How about rabbits strapped down with their eyes opened with clamps and having perfume and hairspray dripped in their eyes hour after hour, day after day? Or beagles forced to smoke nicotine continuously. Not one beagle ever caught lung cancer. Any of that excusable to you?'

It sounded horrific. 'It's barbaric. Revolting,' said Su.

'Tip of the ice berg.'

'Why doesn't the government do something and stop it?' said Fran.

'It's the government that insist testing on animals is done before products can be approved for sale,' said Scrubber. 'But good companies find ways not to test on animals, using alternatives.'

'Shit,' said Su. 'I had no idea.'

'It's kept well under the radar,' said Surf. 'The cosmetic company is hardly going to show a full page add in a magazine with a cute bunny being tested, with a caption saying, Buy this product because it will make you beautiful and we blinded thousands of rabbits to prove it. It's called the Draize test. Check it out sometime. That might affect their profits a bit if more people did check it out.'

'Your hair dye's. What make?' asked Cerbarus.

Su told him and Cerbarus smiled. 'You might want to stop buying from that company. Not made here, but imported from America.'

'They use the Draize test?'

'One company on a long list,' said Scrubber.

'How are you going to stop them?' said Fran.

Cerbarus shook his head and sighed. 'They're billion dollar multinationals. At best, all we can do is annoy them.'

'I'd like to help,' said Su.

'Maybe next time,' said Cerbarus.

'I'll hold you to that. And here was me thinking how to raise a few pounds for the local PDSA and here's you, taking on the big boys.'

'Hey,' said Scrubber. 'Don't put down what you do. It all helps.'

'Hey, Cerbs,' said Surf. 'Maybe we can muck in and help Su raise some money?'

'Just what I was thinking. A bike run?'

'We've done it a couple of times,' said Surf. 'Why not?'

'What happens on a bike run?' asked Fran.

Cerbarus explained. 'Dozens of bikes riding through the town. The riders give a couple of quid to join in, showing off their bikes all shiny and nice, with a pillion on the back of each one with collecting buckets. Well advertised, they can raise a lot of money.'

'Count me in,' said Su.

Fran said, 'I'll be involved, somehow. Anyway. I had an idea of my own, earlier. We can do a gig with the band to raise money, too.'

'Ooh!' said Cerbarus. 'I like it. Why not have the run and end up at the gig? We would get even more cash in.'

'Now I'm definitely up for that,' said Fran.

Cerbarus offered his hand and a bond was made for life with a handshake.

Chapter 51

'I don't believe my eyes,' said Barbara. 'The money you've splashed out on that and you're trashing it?'

'Call it a wake up call,' said Su, dropping her once beloved hair products into the rubbish bin. 'This company will not get any of my money from now on.'

'I think you're going over the top a bit. What's brought this on all of a sudden?'

'Like the rabbits. I've had my eyes opened.'

'Su? Have you been taking drugs or something? All these hairy Hells Angels you hang out with.'

Su bristled. What her mother had said was like a jolt with a cattle prod. 'Do not call my friends Hells Angels. They're bikers trying to make a difference in this world. Right now we are organising a bike run and a music gig to raise money for the PDSA. Does that sound like bad people to you, Mum?'

'All highly commendable, I'm sure. And throwing pounds worth of cosmetics helps how?'

Su tapped her chest. 'It helps me, that's how. I didn't realise I had been supporting animal torturers by buying their crap. But not any more, I'm not.'

'You're exaggerating. It can't be that bad.'

'Can't it? You have no idea how bad it is out there. Mum. Will you listen to me, please?'

'That depends what you have to say.'

'Come on. I'll put the kettle on and make us a cup of tea. There are things I want to share with you.'

Barbara sat down. This was no longer like a mother and daughter talk. Her girl was growing up, becoming a woman. She respected that.

'I'm listening.'

Su put the mugs of tea on the kitchen table and sat opposite her mother. 'Mum. Just don't freak out, yeah?'

Barbara sipped her tea, unsure she wanted to hear this. 'Go on.'

'Okay. You know I've always loved animals and hated anyone who hurts them.'

'I know.'

'Ages ago, I went out on my Triumph...'

'You what? You know you're not allowed on that thing on the road.'

'It was just the once. Anyway, I stopped for a break before turning back. I heard something. When I had a look, it was a dog fighting gang.'

'Oh, now that's one thing that turns my stomach.'

'Mum. I saw it happening. There was this one dog...all its insides hanging out, blood everywhere, still trying to defend itself.'

'God. Somebody should do something about those people.'

'We did. Me, Fran and our hairy biker friends. We went out the next weekend and, well, kicked the crap out of them.'

Barbara was horrified. 'Su Kane. Are you mad? You could have been hurt.'

'The gang was taught a lesson, we rescued two injured dogs and had them looked after and saved some others from having to fight.'

Barbara looked at her daughter like she was a complete stranger. 'How come this is the first I heard of all this?'

'Because I didn't want to worry you.'

'Well I'm damn well worried now. I'm almost too afraid to ask. Anything else I should know about?

'Well, we belted the crap out of some badger baiters. We caught them, beat them up a bit and then called the cops.'

'Bloody hell. Who the hell are you and what have you done with my daughter?'

Su smiled and took her mothers hand. 'I'm not a kid any more, Mum.'

Barbara squeezed her daughters hand. 'No. I can see that. But let me tell you something. One day, and not too soon I hope, you'll be a mother and you'll discover it doesn't matter how old they are, sixteen or sixty, they'll still be your children. That's just a fact of life. Now. Is there anything else you're planning to do?'

'Yes, as it happens. We are organising a bike run and a gig with the band to raise money for the PDSA.'

Barbara breathed out a sigh of relief. 'After what you've just told me, that just sounds like a nice day out.'

'It will be, Mum. Just me and those hairy bikers collecting money for a good cause.'

'I can live with that. Now I want to learn something. Why is this cosmetic company so evil.'

'Are you sure you want to know?'

'Yes. I want to know.'

Chapter 52

It was the usual venue for a meeting, the small back room of the Nagging Bladder. Fran, Bluesdog, Oddball, Smiley, Bumblebee, Surf, Scrubber and Carol and several others were squeezed in, also.

'I've had a talk to a mate on the Express and Star,' said Cerabus. 'They're happy to do a feature about us raising money for the PDSA.'

Carol said, 'My dad suggested we have the gig on the Wakefield car park in Willenhall. He knows a bloke on the council and he's going to ask for a permit for us to put a show on.'

'That sounds perfect,' said Su. 'Shall we start the run from Wolverhampton or Walsall?'

'I know plenty of bikers in Wolverhampton,' said Bluesdog. 'I can put the word out. If we start with a circuit of the Chapel Ash roundabout, up along Willenhall Road, through Willenhall and finish on the Wakefield, I think that might work.'

Scrubber said, 'It's all about the timing. We don't want to piss everyone off by blocking the roads, but we don't want everywhere deserted either, otherwise we won't be collecting much on route.'

Cerabus said, 'I still think Saturday, but late afternoon so we still have some shoppers about, but late enough to be able to use the Wakefield. Four in the afternoon, seems about right.'

Su said, 'A lot depends on your dad and the council, Carol. We need that to plan around.'

'I'll have him onto it first thing Monday.'

'Okay,' said Cerbarus. 'Assuming we can use the Wakefield, how do we maximise on that? If we charge riders two quid instead of the usual one, but that includes the show, and we charge anyone else one quid for the show, that would work. If we get say, a hundred bikers, which would be average, there's two hundred, plus what they collect on route, conservatively another five hundred, maybe another hundred at the show. I reckon eight hundred is doable'

Oddball said, 'I've a generator for powering the band.'

Bluesdog laughed. 'I'm purely wind powered.'

Smiley said, 'Must be those pickled onions you ate.'

Oddball said, 'I'll sort out the electrics and sound system.'

'Right,' said Cerabus. 'If we work on two weeks tomorrow, that should give us enough time to get things organised. We need to work in with the police so they can control the traffic and stuff. Council permission for the use of the Wakefield car park is the first thing to sort out. That about concludes this meeting. Any other comments? No? Okay. I need a beer and to watch my favourite band in action.'

Chapter 53

It was the day of the run after a very busy two weeks for everyone. Su, Carol, Todd, Oddball and Bumblebee were busy setting the stage in one corner of the Wakefield car park. Fran was on the back of Bluesdog's trike with a PDSA sash and a collection bucket. One hundred and twenty five bikers had answered the call and happily paid two pounds, a few even paying more. PDSA banners and sashes were everywhere.

For added appeal, several Wolverhampton University female students wearing only bikini's, high heels, crash helmets and PDSA sashes, added a touch of glamour and soon found willing red blooded bikers to have them as their pillion riders. The Express and Star photographers were also keen to snap them. It was amazing how scantily clad young ladies armed only with plastic buckets, acted like magnets to men eager to through money their way.

Cerbarus led the way on his ninety three Yamaha eleven hundred X V Virago, with his girlfriend Mandy on the back, yelling and shaking her bucket for cash. They made one full circuit of Chapel Ash roundabout in the centre of the city. Then they were heading east through the city centre, and with the bikini girls, not many objected to the added congestion. By the time they had passed through the city centre, already a substantial sum of money had been collected. Fran's bucket had a respectable amount in it, even without a bikini.

On they went at a steady ten miles per hour, and many people went out of their way to throw money in the buckets. Eventually, they came to the old market town of Willenhall, established well before the doomsday book. Passing the southern end of the Market Place, the old clock told Cerbarus he had timed their arrival perfectly. The clock still kept good time long after being built in 1892.

Probably very few had bothered to read the inscription on it dedicated to Joseph Tonks, surgeon, which stated, *whose generous and unsparing devotion in the cause of alleviating human suffering was deemed worthy of public record.* The esteemed surgeon would undoubtedly have been looking down approvingly at Cerbarus and all the other bikers, determined to fight for the cause of alleviating animal suffering. All Cerbarus was thinking about was a well earned beer, so close he could taste it. Two bikers acting as marshals, waved them into the Wakefield car park and one hundred and twenty five bikes, scooters, mopeds, and trikes soon filled most of it up. Cerbarus happily thumped the air and yelled 'BEER!' then added. 'And hurry. It's an emergency.'

Chapter 54

In a small marquee in the far corner the collection buckets were handed in and the sorting and counting of the money was entrusted to Bumblebee. As she set about that, the crowd of locals worked their way to the stage area, many stopping to admire the artwork on the many bikes. Su, Carol, Todd and Oddball were still setting up the equipment. Oddball had erected a cover for the band and the electrical equipment in case the weather turned wet, which didn't seem likely right then. Bluesdog and Fran got themselves drinks and went onto the stage.

'Have a good time?' Su asked her cousin.

'The best,' said Fran. 'I reckon I had at least seventy pounds in my bucket. Mind you, I might have got more if I'd worn just a bikini and high heels like those girls over there.'

'I bet they can't sing like you, though.'

'None of the blokes would care about singing if the girls all strutted their stuff on stage. Are we nearly set to go?'

Bluesdog said, 'I see more still arriving, so hold off a while longer. Bloody hell. I don't believe it.'

A man in leather jacket and jeans was stepping onto the stage. 'Just passing.' he said, in an unmistakable Birmingham accent. 'I thought I'd say hi.'

'Hi, Dude,' said Bluesdog hugging the man. Come and meet the band. Hey everybody. Recognise this Dude?'

Fran and Su had no idea. Carol said, 'You look familiar to me.'

'Kids today,' said Bluesdog. 'Allow me to introduce the one and only, Blaze Bayley.'

A whole sack of pennies dropped all at once. 'Wolfsbane,' said Carol.

'Got it,' said Su. 'I bought all of your CD's.'

'Right. You're the one.'

'A great rock singer and writer,' said Carol. 'And you know Bluesdog?'

'And Cerabus, and Oddball. I read about the run and the gig in the Express and Star and I thought, why not? So here I am.'

'Fantastic,' said Carol.

'I gather you're more of a blues band, then with Bluesdog in it, it would have to be.'

'What have you been up to, Dude?'

'You know me, Bluesdog. Always working. Having a break from the last tour so I'm writing more songs.'

'Fancy jamming with us?' said Carol, hopefully.

'What? With a blues band, completely unrehearsed? Hell, I like living dangerously. Yeah, go on, then. You think you can keep up with us kids, old timer?'

Bluesdog grinned. 'Bring it on, Dude. I'll show you how it's really done.'

Chapter 55

At least three hundred locals had paid two pounds to see the show. While they settled, the band and Blaze practised a couple of songs until they were reasonably happy they could pull it off. It wasn't Wolfsbane, but they did have Blaze Bayley in their corner. It was time to kick things off. It was the blues set first, saving their unexpected guest until last. An appreciative audience applauded enthusiastically. They took a ten minute break and got their minds from blues to heavy metal. Blaze had been having a beer with his friend Cerbarus, enjoying the band.

'Going to introduce me, mate?'

'I'm onto it.' Cerbarus said. The band, a little apprehensive at having such a seasoned professional with them, were ready to go. Cerbarus took the microphone. 'Well, I reckon the band did an awesome job. Fantastic. I'm glad I came now. But it gets better. We have with us, one of this country's best heavy rock singer and writer. Give it up for legendary, Wolfsbane lead singer, the one, the only, Blaze Bayley.'

To a roar of approval, Blaze picked up the microphone and Todd led them in on the drums, Carol went into rock chick overdrive and Blaze let it rip as only he could. Bluesdog made some useful noises, and Su and Fran were right there in backing group mode. Nobody had ever seen or heard anything like it on that Wakefield car park in Willenhall. The noise they made would have had the whole town rocking. And all the time, the bikini girls were squeezing the pockets dry filling up the cash buckets once again. At the end of two numbers, it was time to call it a day and Cerbarus went on stage to thank Blaze for a great job.

'Don't go just yet Blaze. You'll want to hear this. I have just been handed the final sum of all the money collected. I honestly could not believe this when I saw it. For the PDSA, we have collected...' he paused, 'Five thousand, nine hundred and ninety five pounds. Fantastic.'

'No it isn't.' Blaze stepped forwards, took out his wallet and produced five pounds. 'Six thousand pounds. Now, *that's* fantastic.'

There was roar from the crowd and as the band got off stage, people were clamouring for autographs from the whole band.

'Can I have your autograph, Miss Kane?'

'Of course. Jeez. Mum. Mick. I had no idea you were here.'

'We were at the back of the crowd,' said Mick. 'Brilliant gig.'

'I'm so proud of you. You, Fran and all your biker friends. I can well understand why you love all of them.'

'You're this young lady's mother?' said Blaze.

'I am,' said Barbara, glowing with pride.

'I'll tell you this. If Wolfsbane ever need a couple of girls in the band, these two are on top of my list. It's been fantastic fun, people, but I really do have to fly.'

Chapter 56

'What's all this?' Su asked.

Pictures from the Express and Star were all over the table. 'Something to show my grandchildren one day. And this one of Cerbarus handing over the cheque to Uncle Garf. I'm sure Uncle Garf has tears in his eyes.'

'I think he's a bit of a softy at heart. Right. I'm off for an interview at an employment agency.'

'Well, you look very nice. Good luck.'

Su Kane hadn't been for any kind of interview for employment before and even for somebody with all her confidence, it was still an daunting prospect. Dale and Prior Employment Agency the sign on the door said. Su took a deep breath and entered. There was a receptionist typing on a computer who looked up and smiled at her when she walked in.

'Can I help you?'

'Hi, yes. I'm here to see Mrs Prior.'

'Right. Nine thirty, you're a little early. Would you mind filling in this personal information sheet, please. Mrs Prior will be a few moments.'

Su took the clipboard and printed form to a chair and filled it in. it was just basic information. She had just finished when a woman in her thirties appeared. 'Su Kane?'

'Yes.'

'Nice to meet you. Please come through to my office.' Su followed Mrs Prior into a well ordered office. 'Take a seat. May have the form? Thank you. So. Not long left school, hey?'

'A few months ago. I need to find a job now.'

'So what have you been doing for the last few months?'

'For six months, I was working for Mr and Mrs Fletcher on an animal sanctuary. I have a written reference from them here.'

Prior scanned it with her professional eye. 'Hmm. They speak very highly of you. And you enjoyed the work?'

'Loved it, brilliant. That's why I want to work with animals.'

Prior smiled. 'That's obviously your passion. One thing I pick up on right away is sincerity when people talk about their chosen line of work. I know when somebody is faking it to impress me. Yours is fourteen carrot genuine.'

'It's what I really want to do. Here's my O level report.'

'Right. Not bad at all. Very good in the ones that matter. I mean geography? Only any good if you wanted to be a long distance lorry driver. No. Very useful, these.'

Mrs Prior leaned back in her chair, removed her glassed and studied Su. 'Su Kane. That name sounds familiar. I think I read it somewhere. Su. An unusual spelling, I thought. That's why I remembered it. I thought it was a typo, but it appeared twice, so it wasn't. Got it. I read about in the Express and Star. You were in that band on the Wakefield. I saw you singing.'

'Just a bit of fun. We raised a lot of money for the PDSA.'

'I know. Three pounds fifty was from me. It was all of my change after going shopping. You're a versatile young lady, Su Kane.'

'Thank you.'

'Do you have transport?'

'A scooter. I've a bigger bike, but I won't be able to ride that for ages.'

'Best not have a job too far away then. Unless it was live in. Would you mind living in?'

'I'd prefer to be at home, but if it was a good job, I might do it.'

'I see. I think I see the sort of direction you'd like to be heading. To be honest, you have quite unique requirements that are going to be a challenge to tick all the boxes with. Nothing really suitable at the moment, Su, but things come in all the time here. I'll certainly be keeping an eye open for you. So. Thank you for coming to see me today. I'll let you know as soon as anything becomes available.'

'Thank you, Mrs Prior.'

Chapter 57

'I wouldn't hold your breath,' said Mick. 'In my experience, those agencies can only find people work when there's enough work about for people to find their own jobs.'

'Well what would you do, then?'

'I did say I'd see if I can get you something in my company. I'll try for you if you like?'

'Mick. No way can I work cooped up in an office day in day out. I need to be out and about.'

Mick said, 'Ah! You say that now. Your work at the sanctuary was during the summer. You'd soon have a different view of things if there was two foot of snow and you couldn't feel your fingers from the cold.'

'Look. Mick. I appreciate the offer, I really do. But give me a couple of weeks and if I haven't found what I really want, I'll take you up on it.'

'Fair enough.'

In the heart of the industrial Midlands of England, it was a big ask finding her ideal job working with animals. The words of Mrs Prior were going around in her head. 'Would you mind living in?'

The downside to that was missing all her friends, Fran, singing in the band. She had already missed all those things so much. She didn't mind compromises, but it was something to think about, what she really wanted and how badly did she want it. The money didn't have to be great, just enough to live on.

Trying to think of some proactive things to be doing, she decided to call the employment agencies in the phone book. She got the yellow pages open and opened it to the appropriate page, which was when Starlight decided to jump on the table and sit on the phone book.

'Thanks a bunch. This is your way of being helpful, is it?' She picked the cat up and sat it on her lap. 'You know, there must be just the right thing out there for me somewhere. I feel it in my bones, Starlight. It's what I'm supposed to do.'

With the cat curled up on her lap, she went through the motions calling the agencies. They all wanted to meet with her but did they have anything to do with working with animals? No. None did. One suggested trying some of the nearby farms. Milking cows twice a day was not what she was all about.

They had no computer at home, her mother seeing no real need for one. Mick worked with them every day in his office, so he didn't need one at home. Arguments for getting one were generally defeated by her mother saying, 'No problem. If you want one, save up and buy one and pay to go online.'

She called Fran. 'Yeah, Su. Are you in all day? Can I use your computer? I'm looking for work. Right, thanks. On my way.'

In Fran's bedroom, her cousin had her own computer. Su said, 'You are so damn lucky. I just can't get my Mum to come out of the dark ages. You'll have to help me, though.'

They sat together at the desk. Fran was secretly pleased that she was ahead of her cousin on something at least. She turned the computer up. Of course Su had used computers at school so she had a basic understanding, but accepted she was a novice.

'We'll do a few general searches. We have to be a bit specific, though. You want to work in the West Midlands, so lets put that in the search bar. Now, jobs with animals and working with animals. Enter.'

Several web pages came up. 'Right. Some of these are volunteer jobs for charities, like the RSPCA. You need a wage, so we can forget those. Trainee dairy farmer?'

'That's just a job and with only one type of animal. What else is there?'

'Assistant keepers wanted at Dudley Zoo. Two positions available. That could be interesting.'

'A bit of a commute. Lets take a look anyway.'

'Hmm,' said Fran. 'They need the animal management degree.'

'Right. To get a degree I'd have to stay on and do A levels, like you. That's two years down the drain.'

'Thanks,' said Fran.

'It would be for me, not you. Then if I do okay at that, I take another two years becoming qualified at uni, then if I'm lucky I might get a job I can exist on.'

'Not for you then, I take it?'

'I'd be really old, like twenty two or something by the time I was getting anywhere.'

'Well, the only other way in is as a volunteer. No money, though.'

'Exactly. I wouldn't even be able to afford to get there. It isn't an option.'

Fran scrolled the screen. 'The rest is mostly volunteer stuff, too.'

'Typical. As much work as I could get, as long as it's for free. Hey. That's interesting.'

'Stop U K corporations torturing animals. That's what Cerabus was on about. Lets take a look.'

Su said, 'Hell. There's those rabbits he was on about. I mean look at that poor creature. Strapped down, its eyes clamped open and cosmetics being dripped into its bloody eyes. That's research?'

'That Draize test. Sick, that's what it is. How did they get the pictures?'

'Here,' said Su, pointing at the screen. 'They broke in and took photographic evidence. I got rid of all my stuff. Anything from that outfit, anyway.'

Fran looked anxiously at her own cosmetics on her dressing table. 'You don't want me to bin all my stuff, do you?'

'I'm saying nothing, Fran. This is the way they test the stuff you buy from them. You do what you want. If you can use that stuff and sleep at night, that's fine by me.'

Fran looked at the image of the rabbit and then at her beloved make-up and perfume. 'Okay,' she said with a sigh. 'I'll do it.'

Fran picked up the waste paper basket and picked up each item one at a time, and with an exaggerated sigh, dropped them in it. She picked up the last one, her favourite perfume. 'Perhaps I'll just keep this one.'

'Rabbit,' said Su, tapping the monitor screen.

'Okay. I can do this.' She dropped in the waste bin. 'There, happy?'

'Nothing to do with me, Fran. You made the right choice all by yourself.'

'Yeah. No pressure at all from you.'

'What did I say? I just told you the truth.'

'But I can't go around without make-up. It isn't ...natural. They can't all be testing on animals. Some must find a way round it.

Shove over. Let's see what alternatives there are. Here we go. Here we go. Well, that's the one I just binned. And that one there. They both say they don't test on animals unless the law demands it. See? It's the bloody government.'

Su said, 'Yeah? So why do these others not test on animals at all?'

'They're American. I suppose they just export it to us. We can still buy stuff, we just have to know which outfits to buy from.' Fran wrote a few names down. 'Come on.'

'Where?'

'Shopping. I need some new stuff. It's either that or walk about with a bag on my head.'

Chapter 58

'Maybe you're being too picky,' said Barbara. 'Besides. In the meantime there are real jobs out there, paying real money.'

'I keep offering,' said Mick.

Su said, 'And I've decided to take you up on it Mick, if you don't mind.'

'Seriously?'

'Yes,' said Su. 'Like you said. It's okay money and it'll do until I get what I really want.'

'Okay. I'll see what I can do. You have to promise me you'll knuckle down and look busy. If not, it will reflect on me for recommending you.'

'I know how to work hard.'

'I know. I'm just saying. Anyway, I think you're making the right decision. Welcome to the real world.'

* * *

Head of Interglobal Insurance, Walsall division, Christine Spooner, looked at Su Kane and then at Mick. 'I tell you straight, Su. The job is as tedious as it gets.'

Su held her smile even though her heart sank. One part of her mind screamed, get up, run out the door and don't stop. A slightly more persistent part said, ignore her. You'll be in a cosy office, meet new people *and* get a wage packet with real money in at the end of the week. It was a hard fought battle but she heard herself saying, 'Not a problem, Mrs Spooner.'

'Right. How about we give each other a months trial and no hard feelings at the end of it?'

If nothing else, thought Su, It would be a months money. She was totally broke after being dragged around the shopping centre by Fran to buy new cosmetics.

'That suits me. Thank you.'

'Christine,' said Mike. 'Mind if I spend the rest of the day with Su? I know the job inside out, so I could show her the ropes.'

'Very well. As long as your own job doesn't suffer.'

'It won't if I have to, I'll work over to catch up.'

'Right. I'll leave you two to it.' She gave Mick an "on your own head be it," look to make sure he knew she was holding him responsible.

Su followed Mick along the corridor passing rows of offices. 'She seemed a bit stuffy to me, Mick.'

'Shush! Keep your voice down. Mrs Spooner has a lot of responsibility running this place. Sixty three, actually, sixty four staff with you, a five hundred million pound turnover. Not everyone gets a job here as easy as you just have.'

'Even one as tedious as it gets?'

'I've always believed a job is what you make of it. You're in here,' he said, opening a door.

'A broom-cupboard?'

'Your home during the day if you play your cards right. Rumour has it, there's a desk under here.'

'More likely the body of the last girl who worked in here. She died of chronic boredom and nobody has found her body under this lot yet.'

'It has been a position a little hard to fill, to be honest.'

'No shit?'

'It just needs organising and streamlining. Lets clear the desk for a start. Here. Start piling these over in that corner.'

Five boxes later, they discovered a computer. 'Ooh, goody. Something to play with.'

'Su....!'

'I'll be good.'

'Do you even know how? Hang on. Here it is. A chair.'

'Nothing lost on you, Mick. Sorry.'

'I'd say pile everything onto these shelves, but they look a bit suspect. I'll have a word with Harry, our janitor handyman. In the meantime, at least you have a desk, a computer and somewhere to park your backside.'

'First rate,' said Su, trying the swivel chair. It squealed ominously when she swivelled on it. 'Let's hope Harry has an oil can. So. Mick. What exactly is it I'm supposed to do?'

'You are now the Extinct File Coordinator. You coordinate the extinct files onto a data base accessible to the rest of the company.'

Su heard the words and her eyes glazed over. 'Right. So all this crap is old shit nobody will ever look at again?'

'Boy, you're hard work. But, for ninety percent of it, you're correct. The trouble is, nobody could tell which is the useful ten percent and which is the rubbish. So we, and by we I mean you, put all of it on the database...'

'The what?'

'The computer system; and whenever anyone in the company wants to look up an extinct file, there it is.'

'Why?'

'Why what?'

'Why would they want to look up old insurance files?'

'A whole raft of reasons. For instance. My department covers household building and contents. Suppose I get an enquiry from a potential customer. But my radar goes off. Something not right about this. So I put in a few names into my computer and bingo. Mr Joe Somebody, has had two houses go up in flames, his car has been stolen nine times, and three of his televisions have blown up. Now what goes through my mind?'

'Poor Mr Somebody, what an unfortunate man you are?'

'How about, Mr Somebody, you are nothing but a lying shyster, please feel free to take your business elsewhere. I have then probably saved this company thousands of pounds.'

'Right. So I am the first line of defence from the Joe Somebody's getting one back for the little man from the multinational, billion dollar insurance businesses that have fleeced off everyone else over the years.'

'Exactly. What? No. Su. Go with the flow. You get all this paper shit and enter it onto the data base. That's it, end of. Now will you bloody well cooperate with me?'

'Fine. I'll do it. There's just one thing. How do I turn this computer on?'

Mick closed his eyes and sighed.

Chapter 59

'I need a drink,' said Mick.

'Su. What have you done?'

'I thought I applied myself very well under the circumstances.'

'Mick?'

'Two hours of explaining the system, ninety seven entries we made together, spreadsheets, data bases, statistics. Your blo...lovely daughter has thirty seconds flying solo and wipes the lot out.'

'You should have saved it,' said Barbara.

'You should have saved it,' agreed Su. 'Anyway. Nothing was lost. We just had to do it over again. Actually, I blame you, Mum.'

'Me? I wasn't even there.'

'If you'd have bought a computer to practice on I would know what I was doing. I mean, Fran has her very own computer. She knows all about megabites and gigabites and termites. I hardly knew how to turn the thing on.'

'Well, now we don't have to buy one. You have one to play with all day long. So stop making excuses and learn as much as you can.'

Su sighed. 'I give up. What's for dinner for a working girl?'

* * *

'You should have saved it,' said Fran.

'No shit? Here I am, a slave to the system...'

'A slave? After one cushy day?'

'Excuse me. I'll have you know I worked these two fingers to the bone today. Beats me how I'm still standing.'

'You're not. You're flopped out on my bed.'

'Metaphorically speaking. Besides. Mick's a crap teacher. The way he goes droning on and on, I'm surprised I'm not in intensive care in a Mick induced coma.'

'Ungrateful cow. He's got you a job and he's teaching you the ropes. Pull your bloody head in.'

'Why is everybody picking on me today?'

'Telling you how it is, more like. Just do the job for a few months and save some cash up. After that, you can look out for the job of your dreams. Like chief shit shifter for Noah.'

'Fran Hartshorne, I resent that. I came round here for some TLC and all you do is exacerbate the situation.'

'Exwhatabate?'

'Screw things up even worse than they already are. Why is life so bloody complicated, Fran?'

'In my experience, because we make it that way. And the higher up the food-chain people are, the more they try to complicate things.'

'Shit, Fran. Have you been reading Freud again?'

'I'm just expressing my personal observations. Dad's just come home.'

'Good. I want to ask him something.'

They went down stairs and found Bill Hartshorne in the kitchen with Joan. 'Hello, Su. How's the new job going?'

Su shrugged. 'Yeah. It's a job.'

'That good, hey?'

'Uncle Bill...'

'See, Joan? That's Su's big eyed "I want a favour" voice.'

'Only a little one. Can we take Tiger out for a spin, please? That place we went before so I can ride her.'

Bill looked at Joan. 'Well,....'

Joan said, 'I don't like motorcycles. Noisy dangerous, horrible things.'

'The old warehouse we go to isn't that far,' countered Bill. 'We'll be fine. She needs the practice and the bike could do with a run.'

Joan glared at her husband. 'What you mean is you want an excuse to ride it yourself. Go on. You don't need my permission.'

Su said, 'Thanks Aunt Joan.'

Bill said, 'Sunday morning. The roads will be quieter.'

'Thanks Uncle Bill. You're a legend.'

'I'm glad somebody around here thinks so. Be here on Sunday at ten in the morning.'

Chapter 60

Bill Hartshorne let Su kick-start the Tiger and it fired up second go.

'She sounds sweet, Uncle Bill.'

'A pity it will be another few months before you can take her out. It was a lot different in my day. Things needed to change, but I think the powers that be went a bit over the top. Okay. Me on the front, you on the back.'

Fran watched them ride off, her mother not wanting to know about it.

'I hope you don't go getting one of those dangerous things, Frances.'

It was only Frances when a particular point was being made.

'I was kinda thinking of a Mini. At least I can drive that before Su can ride her bike.'

'A Mini. I like that. Safe and economical.'

Fran didn't tell her she was thinking about the nippy Cooper S model. A bridge to cross later.

* * *

Su was ecstatic to be on her Tiger again, even as a pillion. She knew Uncle Bill was really happy to be on a bike again. After half an hour of open road they came to the old abandoned warehouse car park and Bill dismounted and Su got on the front seat.

'Okay. You haven't ridden for a while, so I suggest a few slow laps, just getting used to things again. Off you go.'

Su pulled the clutch in and toed it into first. She could only get her Tiger into second for the first couple of laps, trying to keep her speed down. Bill watched his niece as she familiarised herself with the machine again. After three more circuits, she pulled up alongside of him.

'Right,' said Bill 'I'm going to make a figure of eight obstacle course like we did last time.' He found rubble and bricks and placed them in a wide figure of eight. 'Off you go.'

It was a relatively simple course and Su didn't go above second gear and went around with ease.

'Now we make it harder.' He made a much tighter course and this time she had to work harder to maintain control and at one corner she wobbled so much he thought she was about to come off, but she regained control without putting her foot to the ground and finished three more laps.

'Okay. You almost lost it that time. What can I say? Become one with the machine. It has to become an extension of yourself. You don't have to do this.'

'I can do it.'

'Good girl.' He made the course even tighter, the corners sharper.

'Uncle Bill...'

'We can go home now if you like?'

'You dare.'

She flipped her visor down, focused on the task ahead and set off. Bill made a silent prayer to the god HonSuz-TriBsa, the watcher over all two wheeled petrol heads and crossed his fingers behind his back. In hindsight, he had set those corners impossibly tight. This was going to end in tears. As he bit his free thumb, sweat beading on his forehead, she made it around the first time.

'Well done,' he shouted encouraging her. "*Just don't drop the damned thing or I'll never hear the last of it,*" he was thinking.

A couple more wobbles as she maintained the walking speed, steady into the straights and another circuit completed. Her third and final lap. He wanted to let her gain confidence, not pull it from under her. She clipped a brick marker with her front wheel on the tightest curve and her right leg shot out and Bill's heart was in his mouth, but she became one with the bike and by will power alone coaxed it upright and she pulled up, rider, bike and their uncle-niece relationship still in one piece.

Su flipped up her visor. 'Well?' she said, defiantly.

'Pretty average, I thought. I suppose you'll get the hang of it one day.'

'Bill...?'

'You were bloody terrific. If ever there was a bike chick, you're it.'

'You'll let me ride us home, then?'

'On yer bike.'

'I am.'

'Yeah. Just a foot too near the controls. Move along the bus, Su.'

Chapter 61

Su tackled the office itself. Harry Potts had cured the squeaking chair and not only fixed the original shelves, but found some more shelving to add to it. He even helped organise and fill those shelves until the desk and floor were clear.

'Should have been done ages ago,' said Harry. 'All done now, though.' Harry was in his late forties, wore a cloth cap with greying hair sprouting out from under it and a brown work coat. There was a smell of oil, bleach and tobacco about the man.

'Thanks, Harry. At least I can move in here now.'

'Anything else needing doing while I'm here?'

'If you could give me a hand turning the desk around, please. Where it is, the light from the window makes it hard to read the screen sometimes.'

'Okay. I'll just unplug everything first so we don't snag the cables. Right. You grab that end. Nice and easy and there. That should do. I have a Venetian blind somewhere that should fit that window. That should help. I'll find you a bank of sockets so you'll be able to move the computer anywhere on the desk you want it. I'll be back in a bit.'

As Harry disappeared, Su looked around the tiny office. With the boxes off the floor, the room seemed less oppressive. The wall next to her desk would have a few posters of her own, she thought, just to make the office seem a little more her own space. Harry returned with the extension lead with the bank of sockets and the blind.

'Here you go. If you plug everything back in, I'll get the blind up.' A few minutes later, the blind was in place and the computer up and running. 'Hasn't *that* made a difference?'

'Home from home,' said Su.

Harry said, 'I've a feeling you won't be here long enough to call it home.'

'Why? What have you heard?'

'Hey? Nothing. I just meant the bright young girls who've done this job were bored out of their minds in no time. They either talked their way into other departments, or got a job elsewhere. I give you...three months tops.'

'And that'll be pushing it.'

'See? I told you. Just don't up and walk out. Give them proper notice and you'll get a bit of a reference. And if you can, make sure you already have a new job to go to.'

'That's good advice. Thanks Harry.'

'What would you really be doing if you could?'

'Working with animals. I did six months on an animal sanctuary working for peanuts, but it was great fun. Most jobs I've looked at since have mostly been volunteer work and I need to earn some money.'

Harry smiled. 'The right job will come along one day. Like my little job. It suits me down to the ground. No pressure, as long as I keep busy. Always something different to do. Okay. I'd better get going or Mrs Spooner will be on my case. Nice chatting with you, Su.'

'Yeah. Same here, Harry.'

With the room to herself, she picked up a box crammed with folders and took one out. 'Three months of this? Maybe.' She sat down and started working.

Chapter 62

As time marched on, Su's ambitions to work in the animal world was being placed more and more on the back burner. She had to admit, there were aspects about her job at Interglobal Insurance (Walsall Division) she either liked, or actually didn't loath. Which was why when Harry brought her an iced bun with a little candle in it, it hit her just how long she had been employed by the multinational company.

'You beat all the sweepstakes,' said Harry, flicking his lighter over the candle. 'We all stopped betting in the end.'

'With handsome men like you about to provide eye candy Harry, why would I want to be anywhere else?'

'True,' said Harry, slipping off his cap to wipe the top of his bald dome with his handkerchief. 'I can see I'd be an added attraction.'

Su sighed. 'I'm in a bloody rut, aren't I Harry?'

'Beats going round in circles, I suppose. Why *have* you stayed here?'

'Well, for a start, Mrs Spooner gave a me a rise after I made the system more efficient, cutting the processing time down by half.'

'Not a bad achievement for a girl who hardly knew how to switch the computer on when she arrived. There must be more to it than that.'

'I clock on, do my thing, nobody bothers me, I go home. I sing in a band on Friday night's, have a load of mates. I can buy the things I want, mostly. It'll do for now.'

'All good points.' He went to the door but didn't open it. 'In a few years time, don't be one of the sheep that suddenly wonders where their lives have gone and done nothing that they really wanted. Just reflect on that a moment. And if you think I'm eye candy, there's an optician right across the street from here. See you later.'

There were things Harry wasn't aware of. She had adjusted the position of her computer so anyone entering wouldn't see what she was looking at on the monitor. A part of the furniture she might be during the day, but unfettered internet access during quiet times gave her opportunity to study. She also had time to plan. She blew out the candle and took a bite out of the bun and returned to her studies. This time it was chickens. Battery farmed chickens.

She had heard Cerbarus talking about it and what he had to say appalled her. After an argument with her mother, and offering an increase in her board money to cover the cost, it was agreed that only free range eggs were ever going into their home from then on. But that didn't stop the suffering. She had seen the videos, the shocking pictures; the successive governments without the backbone to outlaw the barbaric practice. It was time to have the courage of her convictions.

This was a job for herself alone. It would take surveillance, planning, and when the time was right, positive action. There were two so called farms in the region, just outside the town, one to the south, one to the north. Both owned by the same outfit. Eggstatic Fresh Eggs, Ltd.

'Yeah, right. Not bloody eggstatic for the poor hens, though.'

Su had debated with herself for hours about the consequences of releasing the hens. Realistically, with about twenty thousand hens in tiny cages, if she could let a hundred free, it wouldn't even be an annoyance to the so called farmer. Not only that, breaking in would be noisy and risky. There was another way; one that would hit the farmer hard in the pocket. To kill the chickens. Pretty horrible, but the chickens would no longer be suffering, and an expensive point to the farmer would be made. Over the last week, a plan was forming in her mind. A night visit to check things out was called for.

Chapter 63

One of the Eggstatic farms was not far from Essington, about ten miles from her home. It was one thirty on Saturday morning as she wheeled her scooter away from the house. Su had decided to go equipped to carry out her plan, just in case she had the opportunity to actually do it. It involved taking the thirty metre long garden hose from their back garden, and the special crude but effective fitting she had made. The hose was around her head, over one shoulder and under another. She had the route in her head and keeping to the speed limits in case police patrol cars were about, she reached the farm in fifteen minutes.

She turned off her lights about half a mile from the barn, riding slowly along the dark, country lane. The sky was overcast, not even the full moon caring to make an appearance. For what she intended to do, she needed to have her scooter parked up on the grass verge, as close as possible to the barn. With that done, she took the hose and placed it on the saddle.

It was likely, she'd assumed, that some security system had been installed, probably security lights with a motion sensor. Standing on tiptoe, she could just see over the hedge. She was looking at the gable end of the steel clad barn. The door to the barn was on the side facing the gate. It was likely, she figured, that any sensors would be facing the gate where intruders would most likely approach. And had she intended to open the barn door, that might have been her chosen way in..

Su had no intention of opening the barn door. Her plan wasn't to free the birds, but to humanely kill them all. It was a close call, but the hose would just about reach. She could feed the hose through the base of hedge but getting herself through was another matter entirely. Bending low, she examined the bottom of the thick hedge, but it looked impossible to squeeze through anywhere. Su had walked along it for close to a hundred and fifty metres before she she came to a small gap. On her hands and knees, she examined it. It still looked too tightly packed to get through. With her gloved hands, she tested the ground at the roots. It was soft and she found she could remove the top layer down to about the length of her hand.

Spending a few minutes digging, Su cleared the soil before hitting the root system. That was as far as she was going to get.

Lying almost flat, she was sure she could wriggle through. Going back to the scooter, she took a look around her; the lane was reassuringly dark and deserted.

Attaching the crude handmade adapter to the end of the scooter's exhaust pipe, she inserted the hose into it. It was a tight fit which was what she wanted. She fed the other end of the hose through the bottom of the hedge and with that done, she hurried to the enlarged gap and wriggled through, almost getting herself trapped halfway in. A sharp branch snagged her jeans ripping the material. She almost yelped out as the branch stuck in her backside. Ignoring the pain, she pushed on, finally out and into the field.

Looking up at the gable end of the barn, she couldn't see any more security lights. Racing to the hosepipe, Su carefully pulled the slack through, hoping not to disconnect the hose from the exhaust. It was difficult examining the barn for a place to push the end of the hose into. Above her head, roughly central, was a vent. It was just out of her reach but she realised from the awful smell, it was expelling stale air not drawing fresh air inside. Even if she could reach to insert the hose, the vent wouldn't do because it would be drawing out the exhaust gasses and stopping them killing the birds.

Down on all fours, she felt along the bottom of the barn where it was raised off the ground to prevent corrosion to the steel cladding. It took a few minutes but she found what she was looking for, a gap in the wooden framework just large enough to force the end of the hose inside. There was only enough for about a metre to be pushed inside. That would have to do. She made a mental note to herself to get longer hose for the next barn.

Running back to the gap in the hedge, she quickly wriggled through and then raced to the scooter. She checked the fitting hadn't become dislodged and kicked off the scooter. She didn't use the throttle, not wanting to make any more noise than necessary. What noise there was still woke the birds up. Her heart hammered at the noise twenty thousand hens could make in the night air. Gradually, as the barn filled with the toxic gas, the noise decreased until only a few hens were creating a racket. Her plan seemed to be working. Just another few minutes to make sure they were all dead. That's when the security lights came on.

She heard men's voices, two of them, she thought. 'Shit!'

Leaving the engine ticking over, she pulled the fitting off the end of the exhaust pipe and started pulling the hose back through the hedge. She had retrieved several metres before somebody on the other end grabbed it. The other man was opening the barn door and from the profanities, Su could tell he wasn't too pleased right then. She heard the gate being opened and in the light from the security lamps, she could see him clearly.

'Wait till I get my hands on you,' he yelled as he ran towards her.

Su jumped on the scooter and keeping her lights off, rode away into the shadows of the night.

Chapter 64

An exhausted Cerabus had his own problems and he was in too much of fragile state of mind, what he heard on the radio, did nothing to improve his demeanour. He had not slept properly for three days and nights, taking care of a sick kitten and the time he had invested in her was taking its toll on him. But Cerabus being the man he was, wasn't about to put his own health before a sick animal, totally dependent on him for her survival.

As the cattery manager for the local RSPCA, the kitten had been brought into him. Once again, he felt sick to his stomach at man's inhumanity to defenceless animals. This one made him so angry, anyone who knew him, gave him a wide berth. He recalled the RSPCA inspector handing her over to him.

'You have your work cut out helping this one, Cerb's. Might be better off putting her down.'

'What happened here?'

'We had a call. Some gypo's had buried her in sand leaving her head out, and were throwing bricks at her.'

Cerbarus's comments were unrepeatable.

'About four weeks old you reckon?' the inspector asked.

'Yeah. Was this kids?'

'Adults, if you can call them that.'

'Shit. Well, if I have anything to do with it, we'll save her. She's hung on this long, she deserves the best help we can give her. Leave her with me.'

Cerbarus had taken her to the animal hospital where the manager took a look at her as Cerbarus told him the story.

'Total bastards,' the manager had said. 'You get her cleaned off so we can assess the damage.'

With hands uncommonly gentle for such a big man, Cerbarus cleaned her off and took the almost dead kitten back to the senior vet.

'This is as bad as it gets on a kitten that's survived,' said the vet. 'Her eyes have been badly damaged. She may be blind. She can hardly breathe from her injuries. The left front leg's twisted out of shape.'

'Is that burns on her back? She had petrol and oil on her.'

The vet nodded, sadly. 'She's been burnt. I'd say this abuse has been going on for some time. She has bruises and cuts on her body. Some are infected.'

Cerbarus so wanted to be in a locked room with those responsible. Ten minutes would have been enough. 'Can we save her?'

'Cerbarus...'

'If we don't try, those bastards have won.'

'We can only do so much, but we'll give it ago.'

'Thanks.'

The vet had performed miracles on the kitten. Cerbarus was determined he would become her guardian angel for as long as she needed him. Three weeks of sleepless nights after doing a days work to take care of her, were starting to pay off and amazingly, she showed signs of recovery. But she was still frail and the vet diagnosed cat flu, due to the injuries sustained. The vet discussed the case with the manager and between them they decided the kitten was to be put down.

The exhausted Cerbarus was incensed. 'No way,' he said, but not quite so politely. 'She's got this far.'

'Cerbarus,' said the vet. 'We have to be realistic.'

'Please. Give her some jabs and twenty four more hours.'

The vet sighed and gave in. 'Okay. I can't see her surviving the night, but I'll do it.'

The tiny fighter survived another twenty four hours, with Cerbarus with her all that time. Three more days and nights and she was still hanging on and improving.

'She's beaten the odds, Cerbarus. Thanks to you. We might be able to do something for her eyes in another week or so.'

As the kitten improved over the next few days, Cerbarus managed to catch up on his sleep but still felt drained. He had already sounded out his aunt to take the kitten into her care. And now on top of everything, the trouble at the battery farm he could do without. The interview with the owner was as twisted as it got.

'Disgusting, that's what it is. Nothing less than torture and terrorism,' he had told the reporter.

The reporter asked, 'Can any of the hens be spared?'

'Maybe a few. I mean what an idiotic thing to do? This is big barn. How was the gas from the scooter going to kill them all? A handful dead, but a hell of a lot got toxic carbon monoxide poisoning so they can't function. We've began putting them out of their misery. Heartbreaking it is. Years of building a respectable business, paying taxes and providing employment. Then what happens, we are attacked by some criminal element. Mark my words. I expect the police to make an example of this hooligan.'

'You say you actually saw the person involved?'

'I wouldn't recognise the sod. Had a full face helmet on. Police say they couldn't get prints off the hose left behind. Being dragged through the wet grass wiped that away and I saw the bugger wore gloves. All I know is, he or she rode off on a scooter. No lights on it, but I think I saw some animal painted on it. These terrorists want shooting.'

There was no doubt in Cerbarus's mind who was getting them all branded as terrorists and he intended to have words with that young lady.

Chapter 65

It was late morning when Su finally got out of bed. Still half asleep, she was greeted by her mother and Mick looking decidedly unhappy.

'Well,' said Mick. 'Finally crawled out of your pit, have you?'

'Just having a bit of a lie in.'

'Is that right?' said Barbara. 'I can see being up half the night wreaking havoc could be exhausting.'

Su tried her best "innocent" shrug and "no idea what you're talking about" expression.

Mick said, 'I went to wash the car down this morning. Guess what? The hose has disappeared. Naturally, I thought somebody had just stolen it. Then I was having a cuppa and I heard the news on the radio.'

Su poured herself a cup of tea and sat at the table, unable to look either of them in the eye.

Barbara said, 'It doesn't take Sherlock Holmes to figure out a missing hose and somebody on a scooter killing chickens. I'm expecting the police to be banging on the door any minute now.'

'You could tell them I was here all night,' Su suggested.

'You want us to lie to the police for you now, do you?' said Mick. 'Bloody unbelievable.'

'Don't then. I don't feel bad about what I did.'

'No?' said Barbara. 'You haven't heard the news on the radio. One thing you don't come out like is any kind of a hero.'

'They were better off dead.'

Mick said, 'In your opinion. You actually killed just a handful. All you achieved was to make many hens so ill they had to be destroyed. As if they hadn't suffered enough, you go and make things a whole lot worse for them.'

'I'll not sleep for a month,' said Barbara. 'Every time I hear somebody at the door I'll be a nervous wreck. Do you want to end up in prison?'

'Of course not.'

The telephone rang and Mick answered it. 'Somebody for you called Cerbarus.'

Su took the call, didn't get much chance to say anything, then put the phone down. 'I have to go and see somebody.'

Barbara said, 'Don't you go near that scooter. You walk from now on.'

'I was going to walk, anyway.'

'Good,' said Mick. 'And don't you come back here without a new hose.'

Chapter 66

'I hope you bloody walked here,' snapped Cerbarus. 'Because if you are still riding that damn scooter of yours after what you did, you're even a bigger idiot than I thought you were.'

Su Kane had received that barrage from Cerbarus the second she stepped foot into the back room of the Nagging Bladder.

'I did walk here as it happens. And I don't have to stay and take that crap from you.'

She was about to walk out when Cerbarus hit the table hard. 'When you go hurting the cause like that, putting *our* reputations on the line, you bloody well hear what I have to say. Now. Close the damned door and sit.'

Su tried to match his angry stare, but she was nowhere close. She closed the door and sat opposite him at the far end of the big table and they glared at each other.

Pointing angrily at her, Cerbarus said, 'That was you, wasn't it. And don't you dare insult me by denying it.'

'So?'

'So? So? Just be very glad you're a girl. If you'd been a bloke you'd be a few teeth missing by now.'

'I wanted to stop them...'

Cerbarus slammed the table so hard it made her jump. 'I know what you wanted to do, bloody Sunarmi. Have you any idea what you've done?'

'I saved hens from barbaric conditions, that's what I did. Better they were dead than suffer like that.'

'Unbelievable. Didn't you hear that farmer on the radio? Talk about handing ammunition to the enemy. You've been around five minutes. The Revolting Animal's have been at this for years, gradually building up the public trust. You go swanning off on your bloody put-put and wreck our image and destroy what we've achieved. You know what? I might forget you're a girl and thump you anyway.'

'I was trying to help.'

'God help us if you were against us then, if that's you helping us. For a start, we do not kill animals if there are alternatives. You were never going to gas a barn that size the way you tried. All you ended up doing was to make birds already suffering, suffer even more. With all that lot to put down, they wouldn't be too gentle about it.'

'All I wanted...'

Su clammed up when Cerbarus pointed at her. She became scared when he stood and went over to her. Being small and sitting down made him look more like a giant and not the friendly kind. She was relieved when he sat on the table by the side of her, his arms folded, his expression deadly serious.

'If you were in my club, you'd be out on your ear. No two ways about it. I thought I knew you, Su Kane. I thought here's a kid who wants to make a difference.'

'I do.'

Cerbarus sighed and nodded. 'I know. I know.' His voice was calmer, softer even. 'Su. To be honest, I don't know what to do. I thought you had potential. And I still do, I suppose. God knows if the cops will track you down. If they do, keep the rest of us out of it. I'll deny I even know you if they ask me.'

'I understand.'

'Do you really? Shit! I got some serious damage limitation to do. We need people to believe we, and at this moment in time I'm not including you, are the good guys.'

'I'm sorry, Cerbarus.'

'That's the first sensible thing you've said since you walked in here.' He sat in silence, figuring out what to do about the situation. 'Su. Your heart's in the right place. God knows where your bloody brain is. Here's what you do. Keep your head down, don't ride your scooter until the heat's died down, and I'll be the judge of that. And if you as much as look sideways at a bloody chicken or any other creature, you won't know what hit you. Got that?'

Su nodded glumly. 'I can see I went about things all wrong. And like I said. I'm sorry. I really am. But I get so angry...'

'Su. We all do. Over the past few weeks, I've been ready to kill and I don't mean animals.' He told her about the kitten and soon hard-case Su Kane was crying. 'It wasn't the kitten I wanted to put down. But leave me alone with the bastards who hurt her, I'd happily spend time for taking them out.'

Su wiped her tears away. 'Cerbarus. Please don't tell me to stop trying to help.'

'Okay. Get out of my sight. Keep your head down and hope you get away with it. But you never go solo without talking your crazy ideas over with me in future. And if I say no, that had better be the end of it, right?'

'Thanks.' She got up to leave. 'What about me coming in here again?'

'Like I said. Lay low for a while. Your mates in here will be as disappointed in you as I am. They might not be as sweet and understanding as I've been. It'll blow over. Let them stew about it and I'll pour oil on troubled waters when the time is right. Now get the hell out of my sight until *I* want to see *you*.'

Chapter 67

Cerbarus went out into the bar and ordered a much needed pint from Phil Crowe. Smiley hadn't long walked in and he was sipping on a beer.

'You look like you've had a hard day,' said Smiley.

'You could say that.'

'Su Kane just walked by me like she had her tail between her legs. Actually, I heard something about a botched job last night. A scooter rider, by all accounts. There wouldn't be a connection I suppose?'

Cerabus just shrugged.

'Ah! And her less than happy expression was you having a quiet word?'

'Both barrels. She's a worry, that kid.'

'She needed telling. Are we still off to Ferret's next weekend?'

'In light of what's happened, it might be a good idea to let things cool off for awhile.'

'Maybe. It doesn't have to be business. Just a bit of ride out to see the love-birds.'

Cerbarus cracked a slight smile. 'Perhaps enough of Ferret's rot-gut will improve my frame of mind. Yeah. Why not?'

* * *

The following Saturday evening, Smiley and Cerabus descended on Ferret and Abbey. The glow surrounding the couple was almost blinding, Cerabus noticed. An unnatural incandescence that turned normal human beings into things you wouldn't want to touch for fear of electric shock from them. The cause for all this luminosity was standing by Ferret's side, her scarred and tattooed arm wrapped around him like a boa constrictor.

'Shit, you two got a bad dose of love,' said Cerabus parking his bike.

'Nothing contagious, I hope,' said Ferret.

'I'll let you know when I get back to Mandy. Now I know it seems peculiar, but me and Smiley here got a real craving for your cider.'

'You ain't pregnant are you?' Abbey asked.

'Not the last time I took a test.'

'Don't mind me,' said Smiley. 'I'll just turn into a pile of dry dust for the lack of something alcoholic.'

'Suckers for punishment some people,' said Abbey. 'You know where it is.'

It was a warm night and the idea of spending quality time on Ferret's back porch with copious amounts of questionable cider, was well worth the journey. They talked for awhile, then Ferret asked, 'Is this pig thing on?'

'There's been a complication,' said Cerbarus.

'Has Su been caught yet?' Abbey asked. Both she and the Ferret knew what was going down.

'I was tempted to turn the bugger in myself, but I couldn't bring myself to do it.'

'You'd have me to answer for if you did,' said Abbey, in a voice even Cerbarus wouldn't question. The two of them going toe to toe would be short odds.

Smiley said, 'She's a loose cannon, Abbey. She has all the local cops looking for her, and the rest of us will be tarred with being terrorists.'

Abbey said, 'Hey. I worked with her for six months. She's a great kid. You have a problem with Su, you have a problem with me.'

Cerubus countered, 'I've had enough problems lately. But how the hell are we to do anything if she screws everything up for the rest of us?'

'She's raw energy,' said Ferret. 'We need that. Keep putting off the raid on the pig farm and we lose our momentum. Why not use this case to bring her in line? If she's with us on this one, maybe she'll be useful.'

Cerabus said, 'She needs to understand we don't go all guns blazing into things. Do you seriously think she deserves another chance?'

'Another of these ciders and even *I* might think she does,' said Smiley, holding out his glass for a refill.

'I'll remind you you said that when you've sobered up,' said Ferret. 'We're off to bed. Goodnight.'

Chapter 68

Cerabus's and Smiley's brains slowly regained an awareness of their surroundings and their internal organs were gradually forgiving them for being abused. Abbey had little sympathy for either of them.

'I told Ferret he should try to get the army interested in his cider for use in chemical warfare,' she told them.

'No enemy deserves that,' said Smiley. 'You two look happy.'

'We are. To think I had to travel twice around the world to fall in love in this country.'

Cerbarus said, 'That makes up for Ferret not going even as far as Blackpool for a day trip.'

'Talk of the devil,' said Smiley.

'Morning. Any tea on the go?'

Abbey poured it and they all sat at the table. Ferret kicked the conversation off. 'Me and Abbey have put a lot of time and effort into this,' he said. 'I want to know what we are doing.'

Smiley said, 'Sow crates will be soon gone altogether. One of the few things our government got right.'

'So for the next few months, those poor bloody animals suffer?' said Abbey. 'Every major pork producer has already pulled out of it but there are still joker's like Ainsworthy hanging onto the vile practice.'

'I had a sneaky look in his barn,' said Cerbarus. 'Most of the stalls were empty, but about twenty were still in use. Some of the sows were in a bit of a state.'

'I don't want all our hard work to go to waste,' said Ferret. 'I say we free the pigs.'

Cerbarus said, 'Thanks to Su, anything else we do will get tarred with the same brush. I can just see the headlines. Animal terrorists strike again. First chickens, now pigs.'

Abbey glared at him. 'What are you more interested in; the public calling us names or the welfare of the animals.'

'I resent that. The animals will always be the top priority. But you know as well as I do that we need the public support. For this job, we'll be labelled as thieves as well as terrorists. How does that help us with other cases?'

Smiley sighed. 'I hate to think of the sows having to suffer even one more night in those barbaric conditions, Cerbarus. If we can free them and get them here, I'll do all I can to get them right. I'm with Ferret and Abbey on this one.'

'Okay. I get the point. We'll do it. I'll organise the truck for around two in the morning, next Saturday. We need about ten of us as a minimum to get the pigs rounded up and on the back of the truck.'

'We have four here,' said Abbey. She fixed Cerbarus with a steely stare. 'I want Su involved if she wants to be.'

'Who the hell put you in charge all of a sudden?'

'I think it would be a good idea,' said Smiley. 'I know she stuffed up, but I like her. If she's given a second chance with us, I'm sure she'll become a useful member of the team. I think we can stop her being so eager to go tilting at windmills on her own.'

'What's windmills got to do with this?' said Abbey.

'Don Quixote. So determined was the bloke he thought even windmills were evil giants, so he charged at them on his donkey with his lance.'

'And...?'

'Su is Quixote, her scooter is her donkey and her mule-headedness is her lance,' explained Smiley. 'Keep our enemies close, keep Su Kane even closer.'

Abbey snapped, 'Su isn't our enemy.'

'I didn't mean she was,' said Smiley. 'Just keep her where we can keep an eye on her, that's all I'm saying.'

'So, are we saying she's in on it then?' Cerbarus asked.

'Yes,' said Ferret. 'She's in.'

Cerbarus sighed. 'Okay. She's in.'

Chapter 69

'I tell you for nothing,' said Cerbarus. 'I was against the idea. Abbey Jones persuaded me otherwise.'

'Thanks,' said Su. She had half expected another roasting when he'd summoned her to the Nagging Bladder for a one on one.

'But I'll be watching you like a hawk. You will be part of a team who could all be in serious trouble if it all goes wrong. You do exactly as you're told and no going off tilting at windmills.'

'Windmills?'

'Don't you kids ever read anything these days? It just means you will be a part of a team and you'll be expected to behave like one.'

'That's all I want. Thanks. I won't let you down. I was looking into sow crates on line. They're banned from the first of January next year.'

'I know. Which was my argument against this job. But Abbey and Ferret have put in a lot of time and effort into sorting out a separate area well away from the Old Spots. The pigs we'll be letting free will not be in as good a condition as the Spots. We don't want any infections passing to them. Smiley will be on hand to treat the pigs once we have them on Ferret's farm. We have use of a truck one of our mates will be driving. Jimbo Smith. Great bloke.'

'Right. So we release the pigs, get them up in the truck then over to Ferret's, job done.'

Cerbarus nodded. 'That's the plan. You can ride in the truck with Jimbo. Riding anywhere on that scooter of yours is a no no. Have the cops been kicking your door down yet?'

'No. Nothing. I suppose they have better things to do.'

'Maybe. Don't get complacent. Stay off the thing for another month at least.'

Su understood. 'My stepdad's taking me to work, so no worries. I can wait a month.'

'Glad to hear it. Be outside here at just after eleven thirty, Friday night.'

* * *

Su had told her mother she was staying at Fran's that night, after the band finished. Fran had expressed her interest in going along to Ferret's but Su advised against it.

'There's still a few not happy with me after what I did, Cerbarus included. This is my way of making peace with everyone.'

'I don't like being left out of things,' said Fran.

'Hey, Fran. Let me do this then I'm sure you'll be more involved. Then you and me can go tilting at windmills together.'

'Come again?'

Su grinned. 'Kids today. You should read more. Fran. We'll be off in a few minutes. You may as well get off home.'

'Okay. You be careful, okay?'

'No worries.'

Chapter 70

'So. Yo om this notorious chicken killer I been 'earing all abart,' said Jimbo Smith in his heavy Black Country accent, slipping the truck into first and pulling away with a small convoy of motorcycles following behind.

'Jeez. Nice to meet you too, Jimbo.'

'I actually thought that was a ballsy thing to do, even if it woz misguided.'

'I've had all the lectures, thank you very much.'

'It'll blow over. Dow yo tek no notice.' Even after his introduction, Jimbo's grin was infectious.

Su smiled back at him, thinking he must be younger than he looked. It must have been that Santa style white beard that did it. 'Do you get involved with much stuff?'

'On and off. I seem to be most popular when a truck is needed. Still. Hard to ride a bike with a pig strapped on yer tank I suppose. I must admit though. I was having second thoughts about this little job. It wo' be easy mekin' a couple of dozen mental sows goo willingly into the back of this thing. Yo lot have yower werk cut out, I reckon, our kid.'

'Won't you be helping us?'

'I'll be sittin' right 'ere ready to bust the land speed bloody record, dow yo fret. I'll leave the pig chasin' to yo youngn's. I ay got the legs fer it no more.'

Su chatted to Jimbo all the way to Ferret's farm, even finding herself slipping into the Black Country way of talking. Ferret and Abbey were waiting for them on the porch and the truck and the bikes were parked up in a row.

Su jumped out and happily had the wind crushed out of her by Abbey Jones. 'God, I've missed you, Abbey.'

'Come on in the house. We've a lot to catch up on.'

Everyone entered the house and crowded around a table of snack-food. It was twenty minutes after midnight and the adrenalin was starting to flow. After a few minutes of friendly banter, it was all about the job. Ferret had made a plan of the operation with black felt tip pen on a large, flattened cardboard box, held onto the door of his beer cellar with drawing pins.

'Your attention please,' said Ferret. 'First of all, thanks everyone for getting behind this. Most of you have seen my Spots, and how happy they are. I realise a couple of you are vegetarians and one or two are vegan and I respect that. My stance is that I'm a meat eater and I raise pigs and chickens to eat and to sell. I make no apology for that. One thing I will not compromise on however, is respect for the creatures I farm. They are well looked after and humanely killed. Smiley will testify to the care I take of them.'

'They're the best kept farm animals in the district bar none,' testified Smiley.

'Thanks, mate. What I do object to, is the disrespect of the creatures that give up their lives that we might eat. Within the industry I work, I am well known as an advocate of responsible farming and a campaigner against sow pens. Thankfully in a few months time, that barbaric practice will be banned in this country. If people like ourselves hadn't protested and petitioned relentlessly, that would not have happened. Most of the pig farmers have already abandoned their old ways, but there is one just ten miles from here still holding on with at least twenty sows until he has no choice but to stop. Most of his stock has been thinned off as he goes towards free range, but for reasons I don't understand, he still has a few sows penned up. I know it's only a few months until those pigs are set free, but that's a few months of unnecessary torture as far as I'm concerned.'

'Ferret,' said Surf. 'Just how close is the house to the barn?'

'Between two hundred and fifty and three hundred yards.'

Shadow asked, 'And the barn from the entrance of the farm?'

'About fifty yards.'

'Security lights?' asked Su. She remembered how her heart had almost leapt out of her mouth the last time she had seen security lights come on.

'None since my last trip over here,' said Oddball, grinning hugely 'I just happened to be passing the other day and found some wire cutters in my pocket. No lights.'

'Dogs?' asked Cerbarus.

'An arthritic German Shepard with cataracts,' said Ferret.

'Right,' said Jimbo Smith. 'I jus' wanna say I ay gonna be puttin' one foot outside me cab. Yo lot get the poor buggers free and leave me in me waggon and I'll piss off outer there. Jus' so we om clear, okay?'

Cerbarus said, 'You just sit tight and play your Dolly Allen tapes and leave the rest to us.' He looked meaningfully at Su Kane. 'Are we ready to rock and roll?'

'Ready when you are,' said Su.

Chapter 71

Ferret and Abbey were in the back of Jimbo's truck as it trundled along the dark country lane, Su in the passenger seat, mentally preparing herself for action. This was every bit as adrenalin fuelled action as soldiers had going into battle. The only difference was, they were unarmed and it was quite possible some farmers gun could be discharged in their direction. Before they reached the gate to the farm, everyone killed their lights and then their engines, pushing the bikes the last hundred yards, facing them towards the direction they would be heading back to Ferret's farm. Jimbo passed the entrance, then reversed it close to the gate.

'Good luck yo lot,' said Jimbo, slipping a Dolly Allen cassette into his tape player, the volume down low. If ever Jimbo needed the rambling wisdom of that earthy Black Country comedienne, it was right then.

Su got out as quietly as she could, not slamming the door shut. Abbey and Ferret did the same out of the rear of the truck, dragging the wooden ramp out so it sat on the ground as a way in for the pigs. That done, they joined the others behind the hedge by the gate.

'Okay,' said Cerbarus. 'Listen up. These pigs will be in a hell of a state. Their minds a mess because of the way they've been penned up all this time. They'll have no idea we are the good guys, so watch out for them trying to bite you. We need to form a tunnel from the barn door to the back of the van. Watch out for runaways. If one gets an idea to take off and gets too far away, let it go. We need to be in and out in a couple of minutes. Ready?'

'Ready,' said the bikers.

Cerbarus opened the gate and led the way inside. The barn they were aiming for was the one nearest the drive, one of ten in a row. The door was at the end nearest to the house which was reassuringly in darkness. The door of the barn wasn't locked, so Cerbarus dragged it open. Oddball found a light switch and with the door partially closed back up, they were all inside.

'Oh, shit,' said Su. The way the sows were confined into crates so small they could barely lie down, made her blood boil to see. These were gestation crates, so there were no piglets, but the crates were so tight, the pigs couldn't even lie on their sides. 'How long are they kept like this?'

'Most of their lives,' said Cerbarus. 'Okay. Keep the door just open. I'll let them out one at a time. Funnel them up into the truck.'

He let out the first one who just looked at him. Having been confined in a steel straitjacket for so long, she had no idea what to do. He slapped her rump and she got the message, cautiously stepping out of her crate. He slapped her again and she bolted for the door. Deranged and confused, the sow squealed, and dodging the humans, ran straight up the ramp. Abbey stayed at the foot of the ramp in case the animal had a change of heart. One by one, the other pigs were let go and encouraged by the others, all raced up the ramp.

The final sow had other ideas. She missed the ramp and fled by the side of the truck, onto the road. There she stopped, her damaged mind hardly knowing what was going on. Su was the closest and she knew she had only one shot at it. She took off her jacket and slowly approached the animal. The pig was about to take off again, but Su threw her jacket over her head and wrapped it around the terrified creatures neck. Abbey saw the drama, and used her considerable strength to help Su hold the animal in one place as Jimbo Smith started his truck, moving it onto the lane and then he stopped to let the others get the last sow on board.

Keeping the jacket over the pigs head, they pushed her as close to the ramp as possible, let her go and were delighted to see her bolt up to join the others. Abbey heaved the ramp into the truck, slammed the door shut and then she and Su squeezed up onto the passenger seat together, leaving Ferret to jump on the back of one of the bikes. Jimbo Smith had pedal to the metal and after a mile, dared to turn on the lights. Fifteen minutes later, Jimbo was reversing the truck, guided by Ferret, into the new enclosure. Only when the pigs were safely confined did the bikers dare to breathe and make their exhausted way to the warmth of Ferret's kitchen. It was time for celebration and Ferret was only too happy to provide the fuel.

'Good job, everybody. Cheers.'

'Hang on a minute,' said Cerbarus. 'A fantastic effort, everyone. But I think somebody really shone tonight. Well done, Su Kane. Welcome back.'

Su said, 'Thanks. I really learned something tonight. Working together, we can achieve anything.'

Chapter 72

The jubilation and self congratulating stopped at daybreak, when they went out to examine the pigs. Nobody was smiling. The animals were traumatised from their experience; one lying dead. The others were just standing as if being outside in the fresh air and sunshine was like being on some alien world, and in many respects, it was. For sows spending months and years confined in metal straitjackets, the intelligent animals had little understanding of their new environment. Most just stood and stared vacantly hardly moving at all.

'People did that?' Su Kane asked, already knowing the answer.

'Not only did,' said Cerbarus, 'we are still doing it. In Europe it will probably be going on for many more years. Even in countries like New Zealand, they're just not in any hurry to stop doing this.'

'More intelligent than most dogs are pigs,' said Ferret. 'Yet this is how we treat them.'

'These could be the last of this in this country,' said Smiley. 'I'd better have a good look at them.'

Cerbarus said, 'Oddball. You got that camcorder ready?'

'I'm ready.'

'Right. Follow Smiley. He'll show you what to film.'

Smiley approached the pigs, who still had a vacant expression in their eyes. Most hardly moved at all, being conditioned to being confined for most of their lives. Nearly all had some kind of physical problem along with the psychological scars they suffered. Smiley slowly reached down and stroked the head of the first sow.

'Easy, old girl. We'll look after you. Oddball. See these lesions on her lower jaw? Get a clear shot of that. This is typical of her trying to be a good mother to her litter when she had them. She was trying to make a nest as she would in the dirt. Trying to do that on concrete caused this. It's infected, but treatable. They've been so pumped up with antibiotics, they haven't become sick from their sores, but that doesn't help the wounds heal up.'

Oddball was close enough to record what Smiley had said and have a good shot of the injuries. He kept Smiley's face out of the shot. They went to each sow in turn recording their sorry state.

'That should do it, Oddball. I need to be working my magic on these old girls.'

Oddball returned to Cerbarus and the others. 'That's plenty of evidence, should we need it. Made me feel sick looking at them.'

'Thank God we won't be seeing much more of it in this country. Make a few copies of that. One thing we don't want is to go to the trouble with getting them well again, only to have somebody accusing us of just stealing them. We'd still get sent to hell, but maybe not for so long.'

Smiley left the pigs to get his bag so he could start treating them. Ferret said, 'Anything they might have that could be passed on to my Spots?'

'No. They'll all need cleaning down with a hose before I can treat the injuries. If you make a start on that, I'll follow you along and work on them.'

Ferret said, 'Abbey and me will do that. I can see this being a long day.'

It took nine hours to clean off and treat all the sows. Su and Cerbarus provided tea and sandwiches for everyone. By the end of the day, the pigs were clean and starting to relax into their new environment. Under Ferret's instructions, Oddball, Shadow, Surf, Jimbo Smith and the others built a shelter for the animals, where when the time came they could have their litters in good old fashioned dirt and straw. At the end of another hard day, they could finally relax pleased that they had once again made a small contribution in the fight against animal abuse.

Chapter 73

Over the next couple of months, some things happened, other things didn't happen. The main thing that didn't happen was the police not hammering on the front door to arrest Su. It seemed strange asking Cerbarus for permission to ride her own scooter. She had helped out on two other cases and the chicken incident was pretty much forgotten about. The lone hell raiser had earned her absolution.

'It should be okay by now,' said Cerbarus, sipping his beer at the bar of the Nagging Bladder. 'On your own head be it, though.'

'Thanks. Actually, I was wondering. My seventeenth birthday's coming up and I'm booked in to take my test on a one two five. Do you know of one I could borrow for a couple of months?'

'I thought they could provide a bike for you to take your test on?'

'They can, but I want to get used to the bike so I'll be ready on the day.'

'Makes sense. Hey, Bluesdog. Haven't you got a one two five knocking about in that garage of yours? Su needs to borrow one for a couple of months.'

Bluesdog was setting up the stage with Carol for that nights session. 'I've a Honda CB one two five doing nothing. It should pass the MoT test. You'll have to pay for the insurance and tax and stuff.'

'I can do that. Thanks, Bluesdog.'

'No worries, Dude. Your seventeenth coming up, yeah?'

'Yeah.'

Cerbarus said, 'That's coming into big bike age. Something to celebrate, I reckon.'

Phil Crowe had been listening. 'You could hold it here, if you like. No charge for the room and I can supply the grub.'

'There you go,' said Cerbarus. 'Sorted.'

Fran turned up, ready to belt out the blues and the band was up to an impressive repertoire of fifteen songs.

Su told her, 'I've booked this place for my birthday. It should be a good night.'

'About time we had a party. We can also celebrate you staying out of prison.'

Carol played a short warm up riff on her guitar backed up by Todd and Bluesdog. 'Our audience awaits.'

As they played their songs, Su felt happier about herself than she had in a long time. In the morning she could ride her scooter over to Bluesdog's and check out the Honda. She had her birthday to look forward to and in no time at all she would be legally riding her Tiger. It was good to be alive right then.

* * *

Bluesdog had his garage door open as Su pulled up on the scooter. He cast an expert eye over his artwork to check that it had been looked after. He didn't find a mark anywhere on the scooter.

'Still looking good,' he said.

'It looks great.'

'Come and check out the Honda.'

Su followed him to the back of the garage. 'Nice.'

'She runs well. Needs a clean. She's a seventy-five. They were still making them in the States up until eighty-five. Bulletproof little tool. Disc brake on the front, drum on the back. Four stroke, so no messing about. Five speed box. Flat out down hill with the wind behind her, she'll do sixty five miles per hour. Tootle along all day at fifty. Oh. One thing to remember, they'll go on forever, but change the oil every seven to eight hundred miles, otherwise you'll soon wear out the cam shaft bearings.'

'She's just what I need. Being used to this will make it easier when I do my test.'

'Okay. Just look after it. I'll take her for her MoT test on Monday. If you can sort out the insurance and that, it'll be good. You realise you need to be seventeen to ride a one two five?'

'That's only a couple of weeks away. I'll be able to get some practice in for the test.'

'Fine. Go get organised and come and collect it when you're seventeen. Just bring it back in one piece, Dude.'

'I'll be careful.'

Chapter 74

It was the same dull routine at work, and she'd reached the point where she could enter the data blindfolded. It always seemed to Su that five p.m. came around barely minutes before she wanted to open the window and scream. At least she had her scooter to get home on. Mick sometimes had to work late with no notice, and Su had no intention of hanging around if she didn't have to. Her seventeenth birthday conveniently fell on the Saturday, and with that only two days away, she wanted to make sure with Phil Crowe that everything would be ready on time, so instead of going straight home, she called in at the Nagging Bladder.

'Here she is, birthday girl.'

'Hi, Phil. Just thought I'd call in and see how it's all going.'

Phil gave her the thumbs up. 'All under control. I've an extension until midnight for the night. Everyone knows that they can crash out in the back room if they want to bring sleeping bags.'

'Brilliant, Phil. Thanks.'

'Better for me. They can drink as much as they like. Mind you, I don't want to *see* you or Fran drinking alcohol in here, okay?'

'Phil,' said Su, fluttering her eyelashes at him. 'I assure you no alcohol will pass my lips before I'm eighteen.'

'I've no doubt about that whatsoever,' said Phil with a grin. 'No band on Friday night I believe?'

'We said we'd do a few numbers on Saturday instead. Okay. I'll get going. Thanks for everything, Phil.'

'My pleasure. See you Saturday.'

* * *

'Are you sure they fit properly?' Barbara asked.

'Perfect. Thanks, Mum. I'll wear them the first time I ride my Tiger after passing my test.' Su did another walk across the lounge in the new motorcycle boots her mother had bought for her birthday present. 'And the gloves are great too, Mick. Thanks.'

'Well, you look the part now,' said Mick.

Su changed back into her trainers and was ready for a night of fun at the Nagging Bladder.

'I'd better get going. Don't get worrying about me. I'll just crash out with the others.'

'You go and have fun. Say hi to Abbey for me.'

'I will.' She kissed her Mum and Mick and set off to meet Fran on route to the pub.

It was the usual walk through the park where she found Fran waiting at the south side gate. They linked arms and chatted merrily as they walked along. The street was full of bikes and trikes and Su could just imagine her Tiger taking her rightful place amongst them. When they walked through the door they were nearly bowled over by the cheer that went up. Carol was already on stage and played a Hendrix styled version of happy birthday to which everyone sang along to.

'Wow, thanks everybody. I hope you haven't scoffed all the grub. I'm starving. Hey. Abbey. Ferret.'

Abbey said, 'Come here and give your old pal a hug. You look good.'

'Thanks. So do you.'

Ferret said, 'Considering we were mucking out our new pigs, she's scrubbed up okay.'

'How are the pigs?' Fran asked.

'Coming along nicely,' said Abbey. 'Most have had their litters, in hay and dirt like nature intended. Another couple of weeks and the piglets can come out of the shelters to run around.'

'I think we'll see the biggest improvements in the sows when that happens,' said Ferret.

'When do you take your test?' Abbey asked.

'Monday. I'm all set. I've sorted out my car provisional licence, but I won't bother with passing the car test for awhile. I'll be happy with my Tiger.' From the stage, Todd gave a drum roll and Bluesdog blew some notes. 'I think we're wanted on stage, Fran.'

Fran and Su climbed up onto the stage as Carol played the Laurel and Hardy theme tune. Seconds later, they were bringing the house down, letting rip with the first song. With the promise of more later, they did just two more numbers and everyone dived into the billiard table that was covered in food. Cerbarus had booked a D J that was shaking the walls with "Born to Be Wild" and AC/DC hits.

By midnight, Phil called for last orders and thirty-eight bikers crammed into the back room where previously stashed bourbon, whiskey, vodka and brandy, and beers, that to Phil Crowe had somehow become invisible, made the small hours totally one for the history books. Legend had it, the noise from the snoring when they all finally passed out, shook loose some of the rendering from the outside of a house at the end of the street.

Phil had let them sleep it off until ten the next morning, then yelled at them to make a move to the bar where bloodshot eyes saw the coffee pots ready with a reviving black brew. After becoming reacquainted with their brains, Phil reminded them all he still had a business to run and he soon had the place to himself.

Chapter 75

On Monday morning, Su was ready to ride the Honda to the test centre and Barbara and Mick wished her good luck. Mick passed Su a small jewellery box and said, 'I got you another little present just for today.'

Su opened it. It was a little gold motorbike on a gold chain. 'Oh, Mick. I love it. Thanks.'

'Here,' said Barbara. 'Let me put it on for you.'

With the necklace on, Mick said, 'I hope it brings you luck and you pass with flying colours.'

'I'd better go and find out.'

She set off on the Honda, getting used to the feel of the bike. Apart from a slightly different centre of gravity, gears to change and being a little faster, it was just like riding her scooter. Uncle Bill had taken her to the old warehouse car park a few times to get the hang of it. She was doing well on the one two five, but with three miles to go to the test centre, it simply died on her.

'Now is not a good time,' cursed Su.

She understood a lot about the workings of bikes, but she wasn't familiar enough with the Honda to figure out the problem. She fiddled with a few things but it wasn't going to happen and if it wasn't fixed in a hurry, she would miss her test.

'Problems?'

Su hadn't seen the tall, thin young man walk up to her. 'Dunno. I can usually fix these things.'

'Mind if I take a look?'

'Know something about bikes?'

'I suppose it's why I'm called the Bike Doc.' He nodded to the van parked twenty yards behind the bike. The sign-writing on the front and the sides declared this dude was indeed the Bike Doc. He rolled the bike back towards the van and got his tool box. Then he sat astride the bike and fired it up. 'It wants to run. I'm thinking fuel.' He got back off and started tinkering with a few things. All the time Su was becoming anxious about missing her test. 'Here's the problem. You would never have picked this one up I'm guessing.'

'The idle mixture screw?'

'You know your stuff,' said the Bike Doc. 'See the end? That should taper to a point. Needs a new one.'

'I haven't time for all this,' said Su. 'If I don't get moving, I'll be late for my bike test.'

'I carry a few odds and ends. Let me take a look.' After a rummage in the back of his van, he came out grinning. 'Bingo.' He screwed the new part in fully and then back one and a quarter turns. Jumping on the bike he kicked her off and away she went. 'Just another tweak.' With a screwdriver he made the slightest of adjustments. 'All done.'

'You are a life saver,' said Su. She looked up at him, thinking she had never seen anyone quite like him. His hair was dark and long, pulled back in a pony tail and he had a horseshoe moustache. But what she liked the most about his face were his eyes, so full of life and good humour. It took her a moment to realise she was staring at him. 'What do I owe you?'

'Just go and pass your test.'

'Shit, yeah. I almost forgot.' She got on the bike, but before she started it, said, 'Do you know the Nagging Bladder?'

'I know the place. A Banks's pub. I haven't been in there for ages.'

'I'll be in there tonight. Call in and I'll buy you a pint.'

'Too good an offer to turn down. Go. Test. Pass.'

Chapter 76

'Your face says it all,' said Barbara.

'I aced it, Mum.'

Mick said, 'Well done, Su. That lucky charm was useful after all.'

'Hardly. I nearly didn't get there. If a bloke hadn't happened to be there at the time, a bike mechanic no less, I'd never have even got there.'

Mick looked at Barbara. 'Sounds bloody lucky to me.'

'I gotta call Fran.' Fran picked up right away. 'Hey. I passed.'

'Like I'd expect to hear different from you? Well done.'

'Wanna meet me at the Bladder?'

'Again? There are other places, you know.'

'I have my reasons. I'll see you in half an hour.'

And so the cousins were sipping cokes at the Nagging Bladder; just a handful of bikers at the bar and the odd non-bikers daring to sup beer in a notorious watering hole where strange large hairy types hung out.

'You had a good day, I take it?'

'For a start, I got this from Mick. He said it would bring me luck.'

'He was right. You passed your bike test. But then, Su Kane would.'

'Yeah, whatever. But I was on my way to the test centre when the bloody bike packed up. I thought, shit. Now what do I do?'

'What did you do?'

'I had a fiddle and a poke about a bit...'

'But what did you do to the bike?'

'Watch it, you. Anyway, I couldn't sort it out. Then from nowhere, I hear this voice. "Problems?" he said. So I look up and there's this bloke. Like he has to be six feet six at least.'

'Everyone looks tall to short asses.'

'Only turns out to be a brilliant mechanic. Like he fiddled and poked about...'

'But what did he do to the bike? Sorry.'

'Anyway, he got it going again. So I said...he has these amazing eyes...'

'You said he has amazing eyes?'

'No. I mean he has, but what I said was, thanks and how much did I owe him.'

'And he said nothing.'

'How did you know that?'

'Because you are Su Kane. Then what?'

'I said, did he know this place. I'm not sure about the moustache. And he said he did.'

'A sort of horseshoe moustache?'

'Are you psychic all of a sudden?'

'No. But some real tall bloke with a horseshoe moustache just walked in.'

'Oh, shit. That's him.'

'Now there's a surprise. I need a pee. I could be some time.'

* * *

'Tell me you passed?' said the Bike Doc, sipping the pint Su bought him.

'No problem. From now on I can ride my Tiger.'

'Tiger one hundred?'

'Fifty nine.'

'Pre-unit. Nice. Not overly fast, but I can see you on one of those. Look after it and it'll be worth something one day. So. This is your local?'

'I sing in a band here.'

'Yeah? What sort of music?'

'Blues with a rock edge. Soul if we are in the mood. Heavy rock if we want to mess with peoples heads. You should come along. Meet a few of my friends.'

'Bikers?'

'Most of them. You might drum up a bit of business. I know I'd put a good word in for you.'

The Doc grinned and once again Su found herself mesmerised by his eyes. Why had she never noticed this with anyone else? His smile was so genuine and warm; just glowing with the thrill of being alive. She wondered about that moustache and how it would feel to kiss him. She recalled how Fran had asked her if she were gay. No way, she had replied. But there were moments when she had seen younger girls drooling over some acne riddled adolescent with questionable breath and wondered if her own hormones had been misplaced.

She also wondered if Phil Crowe had raised the temperature in order to create customers requiring beer to cool down. That may have accounted for her own sudden rise in temperature, but not her heart beating faster than it should have been, or her difficulty in breathing. She had an overwhelming desire to grab hold of that pony tail, pull him to her and decide once and for all on the kissability of a man with a moustache.

'I have to go to the gents,' was the Bike Doc's way of breaking spells.

Su watched him go and wondered why she should meet a bloke she liked with a better backside than she had.

On his way to the gents, he bumped into Fran on her way out of the ladies.

'Hello, handsome,' Fran said, with a pout she had been practising in the mirror since she'd turned thirteen.

'Er, hi. I err, I don't suppose you know Su Kane by any chance?'

'The name sounds familiar. Why?'

'I just wondered if she was seeing anybody.'

'She is now,' said Fran with a chuckle, leaving the tall young man scratching his head.

Chapter 77

For the next four days at Interglobal Insurance, (Walsall Division), Su spent most of her time staring at the monitor. What few files that were actually added to the database, had to be re-entered again because of errors. Her mind was distracted by the face of some tall, moustachioed young man with nice eyes. She hadn't seen the Bike Doc since that Monday night, but he had promised to be at the Bladder on Friday night to watch her sing in the band. At five she turned off a relieved computer, got on her Tiger and rode home. Fourteen changes of outfit later, she was ready to go out.

The Tiger looked as if it belonged in the line up of bikes and trikes. The Bladder was full with people she knew and Fran was already inside chatting to Carol.

Carol said, 'Looks like we are in for a good night.'

'Yeah,' said Su, her eyes searching the bar. She sighed with disappointment and she looked at Fran who just gave a little "Dunno," shake of her head. Another ten minutes and the Bike Doc still hadn't turned up.

'How did you squeeze into that T shirt?' Fran said as she sipped her coke.

'I think it shrunk in the wash.'

'And when did you stop wearing a bra?'

'Who are you, my mother?'

It was time to get on stage. They started with a slow, melancholic blues number which suited Su's mood. They had just started the second number when the front door swung open and Su's heart skipped a beat as Bike Doc walked in. She suddenly forgot the words of the song and got a raised eyebrow look from Fran who then realised who had caused her cousin's mental blackout and sang a little louder to compensate. Bike Doc eased his way though the crowd to the bar and ordered a pint from Phil. He was tall enough to look over the heads of the others to watch Su who had gone into automatic mode for the words to come back to her. This of course required much deep breathing which stretched the tight T shirt to its limit. As soon as the set was over, Su was first off stage.

'I'm impressed,' said Bike Doc, trying to focus on Su's eyes.

'We're okay for a pub band.' She introduced him to several of her friends, including Smiley, Oddball, Bumblebee, Mandy and Surf. Bumblebee shared a knowing look with Mandy.

Su said, 'The band's table is over there. Come on.'

Bike Doc had already met Fran, but he was introduced to Carol, Todd and Bluesdog.

'You're the dude who fixed my Honda,' said Bluesdog.

'Just a lucky hunch. I liked your harmonica playing. I thought the whole band was pretty good.'

Carol said, 'Not bad.'

'Much work on this weekend?' Su asked.

'Not a lot,' said Bike Doc. 'Anything can happen being self employed.'

Fran whispered something in Su's ear. After a brief private conversation, Su asked him, 'Do you like cider?'

Chapter 78

Su led the way on her Tiger and Doc followed on his seven fifty Ducati Indianna Custom, the twin 'V' making its distinctive effortless throbbing beat. It was a perfect morning for a ride out to Ferret's farm.

'Come on in,' said Ferret.

Su made the introductions over mugs of tea. With his warm smile, Doc was soon at ease with the hosts.

'You just have to see this lot,' said Abigail.

They all went out to the fenced off field at the back of the farm. Su could see the transformation was remarkable. The sows were happy and roaming the field as if they had been there all their lives, the nightmare years becoming distant memories. Most of the piglets followed their mothers and Su soon lost count.

Doc said, 'Happy as pigs in muck by the look of it.'

'You'd not have said that a couple of months ago,' said Su.

Ferret shot her with a warning look. 'Su....?'

Doc sensed there was something going on. 'None of my business.'

'Come and see the Old Spots,' said Abbey.

They walked over to the Old Spots and stood and admired the contented animals as they foraged and rolled in the mud, then they had a walk into the woods where Su showed Doc the badger setts. She didn't need more warnings from Ferret about saying nothing of the clandestine activities they all got involved in. Finally, they returned to the house and the kitchen.

'I bagged a couple of rabbits earlier on,' said Ferret. 'So it'll be a rib-sticker stew later.'

'It smells great,' said Doc.

Abbey looked at Su. 'How about showing me your Tiger?' which was code for time for girl talk. Leaving the men to chat, Abbey and Su went to "look" at the Tiger.

Su didn't say anything, but waited for Abbey to start. 'Cute. And I don't mean your bike.'

'I was beginning to worry about myself. No bloke turned me on before.'

Abbey smiled. 'And this one does?'

'I'm a mess. I just can't stop thinking about him. I just don't know what to do. Abbey. I don't want to make an idiot of myself.'

Abbey knew that for all Su's confident attitude, she was still inexperienced when it came to men. 'Want some advice?'

'Please.'

'Whatever you do, don't rush. How long have you known him?'

'I met him Monday. He helped me out when my bike broke down.'

'So, basically, five minutes. Has anything happened yet?'

'Nothing. Maybe he doesn't like me that way.'

'Or he's just a bit shy. But he's doing the right thing, just taking things slowly, one day at a time. It's those jokers that pounce on women you have to watch out for.'

'I seem to remember you and Ferret didn't hang about.'

Abbey said, 'That was different. I wasn't exactly a sweet innocent virgin when we met.'

'What makes you think I'm a...Yeah. You're right.'

'Was this your idea, coming here and loosening him with Ferret's cider?'

Su shrugged. 'Fran suggested it.'

'Hey, look. Never mind what she thinks. You need to be ready and only you can know when that is. From what you say though, I get the impression it'll be you making the first move and that's as it should be. Are you prepared?'

'A little forward planning. Yes.'

'Then this is when you decide if you're a girl or a woman. All I can say is if you're not sure, don't. If he thinks anything of you, he'll wait.'

Chapter 79

'That was the best rabbit stew I ever had,' said Doc.

'Delicious,' agreed Su.

'Everything fresh off the farm,' said Ferret, proudly. 'The damn rabbits are popping up all over the place. This is the best way to keep their numbers down.'

Abbey smiled at Su, raised an eyebrow and said, 'Be better still washed down with cider,' which earned her a tap on the shin under the table from Su.

They sat on the porch and watched the odd dark cloud sail across the half moon; Bike Doc was simply being called Doc by then. Somewhere in the woods an owl hooted and Su was reminded of Tom and Gwen and the fun she and Abbey had together. Perhaps Doc would like to take a ride over there one weekend? But what was she thinking? Like Abbey had said, they had only known each other such a short time. She was a swirling mess of mixed emotions, wanting and yet at the same time so unsure. Abbey's words of wisdom echoed through her mind. "This is the time when you decide if you're a girl or a woman".

'This is...interesting,' said Doc, sipping the cider.

'You'll be used to it after your third,' said Su.

'Sounds like I'll be crashing here for the night.'

'Plenty of room,' said Abbey. She jabbed Ferret in the ribs. 'We'll see you two in the morning.'

Su refilled the glasses and returned and sat closer to Doc. 'This is nice.'

'Yeah. I'm not sure if it's the cider or just the peace of this place, but I feel decidedly mellow. Su...?'

'It depends.'

'What depends on what?'

She put down the glass, took his glass and put that down also. Then she took hold of his pony tail and pulled him to her. 'On this.' She kissed him and she knew the answer.

Chapter 80

Abbey was already making tea to go with the pile of toast. Both men were still snoring their heads off.

'So,' said Abbey. 'Any plaster left on the walls?'

Su bobbed her tongue out at her, but the grin said it all. She still changed the subject. 'I was thinking about Tom and Gwen, the other night. It would be nice to see them again.'

'An awesome couple. I can't see me being able to get away from here for months. We still have to decide what to do with the new pigs. Strictly speaking, they aren't even ours.'

'Can they be sold for meat?'

'The problem is the identification. All pigs kept should have a log kept from birth to slaughter. They're tagged, but not with our tags. Ferret does his own slaughtering, so we will have to sell them under the counter. The Old Spots can go to the butchers, but not the new pigs.'

Su said, 'At least in the new year we won't have sow crates in this country.'

A sleepy looking Doc walked in, and the first thing he did was kiss and cuddle Su. 'Morning. Morning Abbey.'

'Morning. Sleep okay?' she said with a grin.

'Eventually. I can still taste that cider.'

'Drink this tea. It might help.'

Ferret finally saw the light of day and joined them. After friendly banter and chat over a hearty breakfast, it was time for Su and Doc to say farewell and be on their way. They started their bikes and roared away.

Chapter 81

Naturally, with Su Kane's history, Cerbarus had his concerns. Not one to normally interfere where he wasn't wanted, this was more than just about the individual. He found the opportunity for a quiet word with her when they chanced to pull up together outside the Nagging Bladder.

'Hi,' said Su, taking her helmet off.

'Hi, Su,' replied Cerbarus, doing the same. 'How's the Old Tiger running these days?'

'Doc keeps it running sweet for me.'

'He seems like a good bloke.'

'He knows his stuff.'

'So. A bit of an item, you two?'

'So far so good.' She could tell from his expression this conversation was going somewhere. They sat on their bikes and Su waited to hear what the big man had to say.

'Have you mentioned anything about what we all get up to?' He didn't have to elaborate; the message was clear.

'We've had other things to talk about.'

Cerbarus thoughtfully rubbed his beard. 'It'll come up one of these days.'

'I'll know more about how he feels about things by then. I won't go mouthing off if that's what you're getting at.'

'Fair enough. Shall we leave you out of action for awhile? Might be a good idea.'

Su got off her bike and ran her fingers through her hair. 'You have something cooking?'

'The fight never stops. There maybe something in the wind. When the time comes, are you in or out?'

'I've never said no.'

'That was before you fell in love.'

'Who the hell said I was in love?'

Cerbarus laughed. 'Sunarmi. If *you* don't know you're in love, you're the only one. Might as well get it tattooed on your forehead.'

Su wasn't about to dignify that statement with a response. Instead she said, 'Anything in the planning stage?'

Cerbarus shrugged. 'Might be a little meeting about it tonight. You can sit in, but don't feel obligated to take part. Come on. I need a pint.'

When Su entered the bar, it was obvious the hardcore members were all present for the meeting. Cerbarus asked for and got the key to the back room from Phil Crowe and with his pint in one hand, he unlocked the door with the other, the rest following inside then he locked the door sat in his usual chair at the head of the table and the others sat, too.

Shadow was the first to speak. 'Cerbarus. Is it appropriate for Su to be in here tonight? No offence, Su.'

Su bristled but said nothing. Cerbarus did speak, however. 'I realise that ordinarily that question wouldn't have even been asked. Sunarmi and I have discussed certain developments, and I'm quite comfortable with her sitting in. Anyone object?' The use of her bikers name was significant; Cerbarus recognising the acceptance by him as the Revolting Animals motorcycle club leader for Su to sit in the meeting. There was an uncomfortable pause but nobody objected. 'Good. For the record, I have told Sunarmi she is under no obligation to be a part of our next operation but she is welcome to join us if she wants. Surf. For Sunarmi's benefit, explain what this is all about.'

Surf stood up and took a piece of paper from his pocket. 'Right. Sunarmi. So far you have been with us sorting out dog fighting, badger baiting, pigs in sow crates and a few other cases. I might skip over a certain chicken fiasco.' He looked pointedly at her, but she didn't flinch. 'All of those things are unfortunately still commonplace and I've no doubt we'll be involved in more of those. I imagine by now you are aware that it isn't just about pathetic little gangs killing badgers. Huge, multinational companies have been involved in practices of unnecessary animal abuse in the name of so called science but it's really all about making money.'

Su knew what he meant. 'Smoking beagles. Cosmetics on animals, that sort of thing.'

'That and a lot worse. Not fifty miles from where we are now, is an outfit we are targeting. It is actually a university research facility. The amount of testing on non-human primates in this country is unbelievable. You probably know that with most non human primates, we share at least ninety seven percent of our DNA with them. And yet even today, this is how we are treating them.' From his pocket he produced an envelope and placed it on the table. 'Everyone saw these photographs at the last meeting. They were taken three weeks ago by a concerned insider. Sunarmi. I have to warn you. This isn't nice.' Before passing them to Su, Surf looked at Cerbarus who nodded. Surf passed the envelope.

Su picked up the envelope and took a deep breath before opening it. The others looked away because they suspected what her reaction would be and didn't wish to add to her inevitable anguish. One by one, she took out the photographs and without expressing any emotions, carefully studied each of them.

'I'll be back in a minute.' She went to the door, unlocked it and went to the ladies toilet. Ten minutes later, after finishing throwing up and crying, she returned and locked the door.

'You swear to me this was three weeks ago?'

Cerbarus nodded. Su said, 'They cut the tops off the heads of monkeys while they were alive?' Cerbarus nodded again. 'They kept them alive like that?'

'Yes,' said Cerbarus. 'They were induced strokes. They were actually left like that overnight, without water, because the staff only worked nine to five.'

Tears were flowing again, and not just from Su. Like her, they were reliving their own emotional roller-coaster, and none were ashamed to do so.

Sunarmi wiped her eyes and stood up. 'If you lot don't let me come along and kick some ass, I swear to God I'll go and pull the bloody place down with my bare hands, brick by bloody brick.'

Cerbarus also wiped a tear away and forced a smile. 'In that case, you had better come along or there won't be any asses left for us to kick.'

Chapter 82

After throwing her full-face helmet into the ring, Su once again had to find a way to cope with humanities inhumanity. The following Sunday, she went off with Doc, ending up at Burton on the Water in the Cotswolds. It hadn't been planned, but it was where they ended up. It had been years since either had visited the quaint tourist spot, and they enjoyed the experience as if for the first time. To make use of the time available, they decided on two main attractions; the Cotswold Motor Museum and the Model Village. They decided on a fish and chip feed before they rambled and lay by the shallow river to eat them, throwing the few scraps to the ducks who had waited patiently.

Walking hand in hand to the museum, they enjoyed the old world charm of the Cotswold stone cottages, unchanged in over a century. There was a lot to see at the museum, with the old cars, caravans and the ever popular toy collection, but they were both felt like it was an almost religious experience at the old motorcycles. Doc being the most knowledgeable of the pair pointed out subtle details and Su was most impressed with how much he seemed to know about every machine.

Next came the model village which had delighted people since nineteen thirty seven. It seemed little had changed from their last visits, but they still marvelled at the detail and accuracy like the two churches with the singing congregations and the one ninth scale replica of the heart of the village even had the model village itself inside it. After that, they sampled a traditional cream tea with copious amounts of jam on their scones.

'I've really enjoyed today,' said Doc.

'Me too.'

Doc wiped the cream off his tash with his serviette. 'I can't help noticing how quiet you've been, though. Everything okay?'

'Sorry. Things on my mind.'

'Care to share?'

Deep down, she really did wish to share. Wasn't that what love was supposed to be all about? From the moment she had seen the photographs, she had thought of little else. Images of living monkeys with the top of their skulls removed, their dark brown, sad little eyes looking vacant after having strokes deliberately induced, left unattended and deprived of water for twenty two hours out of every twenty four lay heavily on her mind.

And yet she still had to keep these nightmare images to herself. She stared at him and wondered how he would react and cope if she told him what was realy on her mind, and more important what she and several others intended to do about it. As upsetting as it all was, she knew she had to keep her thoughts to herself.

She shook her head and held his hand, still sticky with strawberry jam. 'Nothing for you to worry about. Come on. Lets go home.'

Chapter 83

More than once Su found herself giving Doc excuses to not see him; like she was washing her hair or, the more ridiculous, had to work late, as if the Interglobal Insurance (Walsall Division) would have the pleasure of her company beyond ten seconds past five pm. Things had to be planned, debated and organised. Not everyone had the same ideas and all, including herself wanted to be heard.

Assumptions had to be made, such as after a successful raid on the research laboratory, even with the inside help, how did they intend to make their escape? If even one of them got caught, apprehension of all of them would inevitably follow. Clamming up wouldn't make any difference. Most of them had been arrested and a few even incarcerated for what they did. Arresting one could widen the net to catch the rest by association.

One entire meeting had been about what to do with the monkeys. Smiley said any in poor shape would be better using euthanasia and he was prepared to do it. Uncle Garf knew more than he let on about their activities, and should a simple stocktaking error mean certain items suddenly become unaccounted for, the old vet would no doubt mumble something about how important it was to maintain proper records. Smiley had no doubt that if Garf had more mobility and a good many less miles on his clock, he would be tilting at windmills like the rest of them.

Smiley absolutely refused to put to sleep any healthy animals, so they had to thrash out what to do with those, assuming they could be safely removed from the facility. At best they could perhaps liberate half a dozen animals, but what happened to them next? Setting them loose in some woodland area would be just a slow and hungry death for them. By the end of the meeting the practical issues of what to do with any rescued monkey had still not been resolved and without that, there would be no mission. It was at the PDSA clinic when Smiley approached Uncle Garf.

'Uncle Garf. Can I have a word?'

The old cripple smiled. 'About time. My office.'

Puzzled, Smiley followed the old bloke along the corridor, the tap tap tap of his cane resonating in its familiar way, and the painful and ungainly gait of the man that if he had been some animal may well have been put out of his misery. They entered Garf's office, and although there were just the two of them in the entire building, the vet locked the door, made his way awkwardly to his chair and with a noticeable wince of pain sat down. Smiley took the chair opposite him.

'Out with it,' said Garf, trying to get comfortable.

Smiley figured there was only one way to say what was on his mind. Straight out. 'Uncle Garf. If a monkey, perhaps an abused one, was in need of a home, where would you suggest?'

Ignoring his discomfort, Garf smiled, but the intensity of those faded blue green eyes chilled Smiley's bones like an Arctic blast.

'Only one monkey?'

Smiley found that his heart was beating faster than normal and his palms were sweating. His mouth dried up to the point where he couldn't speak, so Garf spoke for the two of them.

'You may possibly have noticed I sometimes limp a little.'

'I suppose I did, once or twice.'

'Do you know why I limp?'

'I always assumed it was arthritis.'

Garf nodded. 'A popular misconception. If I'd a mind to, I could show you the scars. One where the bullet went into my leg, and the scar where it came out.' Garf let that sink in. 'Once upon a time, I was young like you. All piss and vinegar. Like you, I too had seen a constantly moving conveyor belt of abused and mistreated animals. One day, it becomes more about prevention than cure. Stopping the abuse in its tracks.'

'Uncle Garf...'

'You should listen, because it won't be repeated. Not to you, not to anyone. I was what, thirty two, thirty three? I had heard of a puppy farm in Wales. Just on the border. Yorkshire terriers. Conditions you would not believe.' Garf seemed to go back in time and for a moment he didn't speak. 'I was of course still of the opinion I was bullet proof. How wrong I was. Like the impetuous fool I was, I went there with a van and in the shadow of darkness, set about rescuing as many dogs as I could. The pens were at the side of the house, out of sight from public scrutiny because it was shielded by a barn. The smell was unbelievable. I see a Yorkie today, that smell hits me like a truck.'

'Uncle Garf. Where is this going?'

'You'll see. Anyway, I left the back of the van open, sneaked up around the side of the barn armed with bolt cutters and good intentions, and started to attack the padlock. It wasn't a cheap one. I was still at it, reeling from the smell of urine and faeces when I heard the footsteps behind me. I turned and there he was with the rifle pointing at my heart. Believe me my heart almost packed in without being shot. We stared at each other for a moment, neither of us saying a word. I started to edge around the man, and all the time the end of the gun was no more from my body than you are from me this minute. Still saying nothing, I backed away from him, my arms in the air, sweat trickling down my spine. I reached the van, still facing him. I opened the cab door and was about to just get in and drive away. He lowered the gun from my heart and shot my leg.'

'Shit.'

'I think I said something like that myself. Smiley. Have you ever been shot?'

'No.'

'Good. I don't recommend it. The strange thing is, I didn't feel anything at all to begin with. Just a warm sticky feeling as my blood oozed out. A few seconds later, it was all red hot pokers and screaming agony. I went down, close to passing out with the pain. As I lay in the mud, I looked up and the end of the rifle was pressed against my head. I got hold of the cab door and heaved myself up. Expecting to be finished off at any minute, I somehow dragged myself up and into the drivers seat. You're asking yourself, how did I drive home all the way from the Welsh border with a shot leg. To be honest, I have no idea. All I remember is waking up at a friends place, a fellow vet, and the woman who saved my life that night.'

'That is the most amazing thing I ever heard. What happened to the man who shot you?'

Uncle Garf chuckled. 'Most curious, that. It took six weeks for me to be able to walk again. Apparently, one week later, the man who shot me met with a terrible accident and died most painfully.'

'Garf?'

'Not only that, all the dogs were rescued and found good homes. Probably just a coincidence. Smiley. All this has been an old man's way of saying you and I are very much alike. I understand you have had some inside information about some distasteful practices at one of our most prestigious academic establishments.'

'How the hell...'

'And you may possibly be considering some kind of...intervention. It would occur to a casual observer that one practical problem would be the rehousing of several rescued primates.'

'Garf. If you don't bloody tell me...'

Garf stopped him by raising a hand. 'A few years ago, it was my pleasure to teach a young man who to this day works in a prestigious academic establishment. And quite possibly he shares our mutual distaste for animal abuse. Quite possibly he called me for advice. Conceivably, I may have mentioned your telephone number to him.'

'You are something else.'

Garf smiled. 'I'll take compliments from anybody. But. It occurred to me the biggest obstacle would be finding new homes for our hairy cousins.' Garf took a hold of his stick and limped over to the door and unlocked it. 'It is quite possible that somewhere in my rats nest of a desk, perhaps the top right hand drawer, is a small brown envelope containing a telephone number. I do hope nobody takes that envelope while I go to the toilet.'

'Uncle Garf...'

'If I ever hear of this again, this will be our very last conversation.'

'Thank you.'

'For what?' Uncle Garf left his office and his cane tap tap tapped all along the corridor.

Chapter 84

Smiley was beaming with news he was eager to share with the others. In the locked back room of the Nagging Bladder, he held up a piece of paper.

'On here is a telephone number and an address. The couple who live there have a few acres where they run a sanctuary for exotic animals for when the rich and trendy brigade get bored with their fancy pets. They have actually been expecting a call.'

Cerbarus was shocked. 'Are you telling us they know what is going on?'

Smiley grinned. 'I could tell you the details, but I'd have to shoot you.'

'Smiley....?'

'Trust me. You don't need to know and I won't tell you anyway. We now have a safe place for any monkeys we can rescue. This means we can concentrate on the actual raid.'

Cerbarus still wasn't happy about it, but trusted Smiley to know what he was doing. 'Okay. We have two people on the inside to help us. The laboratory closes at five pm. One of our contacts has told us if we wear white lab coats, with official looking I D tags, nobody should bother us. We need to get in the place, hide somewhere for a couple of hours, do what we have to do and get the hell out of there.'

'I can borrow a few lab coats from work,' said Smiley.

'Good,' said Cerbarus. From his pocket he took out a plastic ID tag with a clip to attach it to a lapel. 'We all need one of these laminated tags. If we are not wearing one in that wing and somebody sees us, we'll be in trouble before we've done anything.'

Su picked up the tag and said, 'I think I can make something like this. It won't be exact, but close enough. I've access to printers, scanners and a laminating machine. I'll just need photographs to go with it.'

'I've a digital camera,' said Surf. 'I can do the mug shots. What about security alarms?'

Cerbarus said, 'One of our contacts will give us the code that opens the lab and the code for the internal alarms.'

Surf asked, 'Any CCTV cameras?'

'Yes. Because of the nature of their work, they have covered all bases. I know where the security control room is. Surf. Your job will be to immobilise that long enough for us to get the job done. I've been promised some info on all of that in the next day or so. I'm reliably informed that Friday night will be best because nobody hangs around that night. Apart from one security guard who patrols the whole uni. He has a set routine so we'll know exactly when to strike.'

Oddball said, 'This Friday then, Cerbarus?'

'If we can get everything organised, yes. We've a lot to do, people. We need to get busy.'

Chapter 85

'Is that it,' said Fran, propped up against her headboard. 'That's all I'm good for these days, covering your ass?'

'Fran. As soon as the news breaks, Mum and Mick will be looking straight at yours truly. I doubt very much if they'll believe I was here with you. Your mum and dad will tell them I wasn't here for sure. But they won't dob me in. You covering for me is for everyone else's benefit.'

'I'm glad I'm useful for something.'

'This job isn't for you. We'll be lucky if we get away with it.'

'So what's new, Su? There's a risk to all the jobs. What makes this one so special?'

'Security,' said Su. 'They're beefed up with it because of protesters, activists threatening to bomb the place, all kinds of shit. The badger baiters and dog fighters were caught by surprise. This lot are ready for anything.'

'So?' said Fran. 'You're going. Why can't I be involved?'

Su said, 'To be honest, they're only letting me tag along as a token female. That and the fact I said if they didn't let me go with them, I'd destroy the bloody place myself.'

'Yeah, you would, too.'

'Shall I tell you the real reason I don't want you going along?'

'Amaze me.'

'Because you're smart. Book smart. You're doing your A levels. You'll be going to uni. You'll have a great future. Me on the other hand has a dead end job going nowhere fast. This animal thing is a big part of my life, Fran. You have a future you need to take care of.'

Fran sighed. 'The annoying thing is that you're right of course. I just wanted to feel useful.'

'You are. For a start, you can help me get these damned clips stuck on these phony I D cards.'

Fran fiddled fixing the laminated card to the clip. 'This isn't a bad picture of Smiley. Who's driving the van?'

'Jimbo Smith. We're using his truck because we have no idea how many we'll get free. We might have to take the cages as well to keep them apart.'

'It sounds pretty exciting.'

Su said, 'This isn't fun and games, Fran. If you'd seen those photographs...I tell you it's a sick old world out there.'

'When are you going to tell Doc?'

'Certainly not until after this job. He'd drive me nuts trying to talk me out of it. Anyway, if the shit hits the fan, he'll find out soon enough.'

Fran shook her head. 'Don't talk like that. I'll be worried sick about you as it is. Isn't Doc expecting to see you in the Bladder?'

'I'll try to put him off going. But I he does go, just tell him I'll see him Saturday night.'

'Assuming you're not sharing a cell with a load of other bikers. Jeez. I wish I hadn't said that.'

'Me too,' said Su.

Chapter 86

Wednesday evenings in the Nagging Bladder tended to be quiet. Su was with the Doc and Fran was teasing Todd. He was starting to shave and had several razor nicks on his face which he naively thought made him look mature. To Fran he simply looked careless. He was somebody to practice flirting on, though.

'I was thinking of growing a moustache like Doc's,' he said as he sipped his orange juice.

Fran smiled and stroked his face. 'Oh, don't do that, Todd. You're irresistible enough as you are.'

Todd blushed. 'I suppose you're right. I'm not sure I could cope with girls throwing themselves at me.'

'I'd be so jealous if that happened. I mean, who would I dream about if not you?'

Todd's face lit up. 'You dream about me?'

'Constantly,' said Fran with a sly wink at Su.

Todd sipped his juice and said, 'You could do more than just dream about me, you know?'

'Oh, Todd. Leave me my fantasies. Let me worship you from afar.'

Todd sighed. 'Okay. But you only have yourself to blame if I get hooked by some woman.'

Fran placed her hand on her heart and rolled her eyes to the ceiling. 'Then I'll die a sad and lonely old woman never having known what it's like to have kissed a man.'

'Such a waste,' said Todd. 'I need to take a leak.'

As Todd walked off, Su said, 'You bloody tease. You'll break the lad's heart if you carry on like that.'

'I'm just warming up for when I meet the big boys. Anyway, Su. Isn't it your round?'

'Yeah, okay. A pint for you?'

Doc said, 'I thought you'd never ask.'

With Fran at the bar getting the drinks in, Doc leaned over to whisper to Fran. 'Do you think Su's seeing somebody else?'

'What a daft idea. Su isn't like that. Believe me, I'd know if she was fooling around.'

'So why is she fobbing me off all the time just lately? Have I done something wrong?'

Fran shook her head. 'You do everything right, from what she tells me.'

'I didn't mean...hang on. You've talked about, you know, what we get up to?'

Fran pouted and wiggled her eyebrows. 'In graphic detail,' she lied. 'Look. You have nothing to worry about. Cut her a little slack and trust her.'

Doc smiled and nodded. 'Fair enough. Thanks, Fran.'

Chapter 87

It was late Friday afternoon and Uncle Garf finished stitching up a mongrel's paw where it had been cut by broken glass and then applied the bandages. Without looking up at Smiley and Bumblebee, he said, 'Looks like being a big night, tonight.'

The nurses exchanged glances. 'Oh?' said Smiley.

'On television, I meant,' he said with a wry smile. 'One of my favourite old films. The Great Escape.'

'Steve McQueen,' said Bumblebee, picking up the doped dog and putting her into the cage to recover.

'That's the one,' said Garf. 'Of course I've seen it a dozen times already. I still never miss it when it comes on. That character was a biker too, as I recall. He got so close to the border on that motorbike then all those German soldiers were trying to kill him. So moving I reckon, where he makes a desperate bid for freedom, only to get caught up in all that barbed wire. Gets me every time. I always think he hadn't planned his escape well enough. Making sure about the escape plan. Very important, I think. Right. That's me done for the day.' He took off his lab coat and picked up his walking stick. He paused at the door and stared at the nurses. 'I'll see you Monday,' then added. 'I hope.'

As the stick tap tap tapped along the corridor to the front door, Smiley said, 'How the hell does he know we're doing it tonight?'

Bumblebee shook her head. 'That man is so strange.'

* * *

Everyone knew their places in the scheme of things. They had gone over the plan until each knew it word for word. The bikes had been parked up half a block away from the wing of university which housed the testing laboratory. Surf went in alone, leaving the others by their bikes. The lower half of his face was covered by a scarf and he had a baseball cap shielding his eyes. One man entering like that wouldn't arouse suspicion whereas a dozen people would have.

Knowing the positions and angles of the C C T V cameras, he turned his head away from them and entered the foyer and walked briskly to the gents toilets, pleased to find them empty. In a cubicle he took the lab coat which was rolled up and tucked under his leather jacket, slipped that over his day clothes, secured the I D badge to his lapel, removed his cap and stuffed that into his pocket. Twenty minutes past five, his watch said. He sat down on the toilet and waited.

Five minutes later, looking like one of the hundreds of members of staff, he left the toilets and with the directions memorised, he headed along the corridors. There was a quicker route to the small security room, but the way he was going would be away from the C C T V camera's that covered the labs and be missing the solitary security guard who would be off patrolling the corridors in the opposite direction. As Surf reached the final corner, he had to quickly double back as the guard was just leaving the security room. Surf counted slowly to ten and poked his head around the corner. He was alone.

From his pocket, he took out the latex gloves and snapped those on his hands, entered the security room and closed the door. The whole of one wall was a bank of monitors showing various parts of the university, including the entrance to the laboratory wing and the exterior. Using his expert technical experience he soon flicked the switches for the exterior cameras and two of the small monitors went blank. The clock on the wall told him he had timed it perfectly. The others would wait two minutes longer and then, already wearing their lab coats and I D badges, would calmly walk up the steps to the foyer.

Because of the inside information, Surf knew the guard wouldn't return for another forty-two minutes. With his heart hammering in his chest, Surf spent an tortuous ten minutes watching the clock, allowing plenty of time for the others to get inside the building. What seemed like hours later, he turned the camera's back on so the guard would be blissfully unaware.

Surf opened the door, glanced both ways down the corridor and went back the way he'd come but after a couple of turns, took a right instead of a left. Outside a storeroom door, he gently rapped out a signal and he was let inside and the door was locked behind him. All they had to do now, was wait.

Chapter 88

It was an uncomfortable two hours sitting on the cold hard floor in the cramped storeroom. Every five minutes one of them checked their watches.

'I don't know about you lot,' said Su, 'But if I don't get to the toilet in the next couple of minutes, it's going to get embarrassing.'

'Is it just a pee you need?' said Oddball.

'For now.'

'There's a bucket right there.'

'Oddball!'

'There's an old dust-sheet there,' said Smiley. 'We can corner off an area with that. I could do with a leak as well.'

Oddball was already busy with the sheet, tying two corners to some shelving. Then he placed the buckets behind it.

'Ladies first.'

'Disgusting,' said Su, disappearing behind the sheet. She emerged with a smile of relief on her face. One by one they all did the same. 'Jeez, that stinks. How much longer?'

'Just over ten minutes,' said Cerbarus. 'One last check. All wearing gloves? Good. I D tags? Good. Any last questions? No? Good.'

The adrenalin started to kick in and nobody spoke until the ten minutes were up. Surf was on his feet, ready to go. Again. It was his technical expertise to be put to good use first. He had five minutes to get back to the security room, and kill all the cameras, before the others could leave the storeroom.

'Good luck, everyone.'

'You too, Surf,' said Cerbarus.

A quick look out of the door and he was gone. The lights in the corridors were mostly off to save power through the night, leaving enough on for the security guards and in case of emergency. This time when Surf reached the security room, there was no sign of the guard. He turned off all the cameras and this time they were not going to be turned on again.

Leaving the room, he took a different direction than before, this time to the double doors of the massive animal testing facility. Knowing the others would be with him in minutes, he punched the numbers on the lock, opened the door and flicked the lights on. From the inside information he knew exactly where the alarm box was and with the memorised numbers, he turned it off. He had just finished doing that when the others piled in the room, Cerbarus closing the door behind them. They were mentally prepared for some upsetting scenes but the horrific sights stopped them in their tracks. It took a couple of minutes for them to focus and act.

Surf took out his digital camera and although he felt sick to his stomach, took picture after picture. Smiley, also feeling nauseous, assessed the health of the monkeys. He searched the lab for what he needed and amongst the instruments of torture were the needles and solutions to end the animals misery forever.

Going from cage to cage, he said, 'Healthy, healthy, maybe okay.' So the others could start collecting the cages of the animals that could be saved. These were placed on a wheeled trolley by the door, ready to take out.

A tiny rhesus monkey, strapped to a table, a myriad of electrodes embedded in her skull looked up at Smiley with dull brown eyes, wondering what new torture she was about to endure. Smiley wiped away tears so he could see properly, and loaded up the syringe. 'I am so sorry, sweetie. Forgive all of us. Goodnight.' He put the needle gently into her thin arm and injected her. Her eyes rolled to the heavens and she gasped one last breath and went on to a better place.

Everyone was busy, Surf photographing everything, Oddball pulling the chips out of computers and smashing them, Smiley putting to sleep monkey after monkey, the others still getting the cages onto two wheeled trolleys by the door. Su found a black felt tipped pen and on a wall wrote two words in large letters expressing what she thought of the lab workers questionable parentage.

Cerbarus checked his watch. 'Time to go.'

This time, they were heading straight for the front exit where that moment, Jimbo Smith would be reversing his truck with the lights off and the number-plates covered up, as close to the doors as possible. The trolleys with the doped up primates were pushed and pulled as fast as the bikers could go along the corridor. Cerbarus opened the front doors, relieved to find Jimbo Smith's truck there with the back open. Not bothering to take the cages off, the trolleys were lifted up and placed in the truck. Smiley and Oddball, the only two who had arrived on the backs of bikes, jumped in the truck and closed the door, then Jimbo Smith put the pedal to the metal and was gone in a cloud of black diesel exhaust smoke. Without waiting for instructions from Cerbarus, the others raced off to where their bikes were parked. Cerbarus was right behind them when suddenly he was grabbed from behind.

'No you don't, you bastard,' said the security guard.

The two men hit the the ground hard but the big biker tossed the man off his back like a bucking bronco. The guard still wasn't about to give up and grabbed Cerbarus's leg.

Cerabus said, 'Sorry mate. I've a previous engagement.'

The single punch ended the guards ambitions of detaining anyone that night. By the time Cerbarus reached his bike, the others had gone and he jumped on his motorcycle and kicked it off. His heart sank when he realised his I D tag had gone. He toed the gears into first and he was gone.

Chapter 89

Cerbarus sat down, folded his arms and stared. Amazingly, he kept his voice to a whisper.

'Are you certifiably insane? Don't answer that, because I already know you are. You were told, you were all told, do not visit me in here. When they told me I had a visitor, I should have known only you would be irresponsible enough to come here.'

'Nice to see you too, Cerbarus,' said Su Kane.

He pointed an angry finger at her. 'I won't even let Mandy come and see me. We all know the score. Apart from bloody Sunarmi, of course. You know why you stay away.'

'A month you've been banged up on remand. I had to see you.'

'No. No you didn't have to see me. The work goes on, Su. Me being in here is just an occupational hazard. I know the risks and I'm prepared to take the consequences. You on the other hand, *are* the bloody consequences.'

'Have you finished?'

'Finished? I haven't even started. I'm here on remand, waiting for my trial. This is the third time I've been banged up. This time for assault as well as criminal damage, and a list longer than both our arms. They got me, they have nothing but suspicions on everyone else, you included.'

'Do they let you watch television in here?'

'What?'

'A sort of box with moving pictures. Voices and everything, these days.'

'You need help, you do.'

Su got up to leave. 'You need it more. Watch the evening news.'

* * *

It was a communal lounge in the low security remand centre. Only a handful was gathered around the television. The news came on and it was all the usual Middle East, Far East, the state of the economy, the latest OPEC meeting. Cerbarus was about to give it up as a bad job, when he heard his name mentioned.

'...latest on the break in of the university animal testing laboratory. We go live to our reporter, Gail Mandrake at the scene. Gail. What can you tell us?'

'Simon. I hope you can hear me outside the university. As you can see, we have a procession of motorcycles, some estimations say as many as two thousand, going round and round the entire university. We have an estimated three thousand animal rights campaigners also marching round carrying placards protesting against the animal testing that's been going on here. Many are also carrying placards in support of the man who goes by the name of Cerbarus, who is now on remand awaiting trial.'

'Gail. I understand you have a lawyer there acting on behalf of this Cerbarus character?'

'Indeed we do, Simon. He is actually a top barrister who has donated his time and expertise completely free. He is Sir Giles Sinclair, Q. C. Sir Giles. What has prompted you to not only represent your client, but to do it for free?'

'Gail. Thank you for this opportunity. I was approached by a young lady, sorry, I'm not at liberty to divulge her name, who, not to put too fine a point on it, stormed past my secretary and barged into my office.'

Cerbarus laughed. 'I wonder who the hell that was.'

'I was of course, about to call the police, when she threw some photographs on my desk. I'll admit to being fifty seven years old and I have to tell you, these were some of the most sickening images I ever saw in my life. Furthermore, I was incensed to learn that those very photographs were taken just over a month ago in this very establishment behind us. I was also deeply ashamed because it was at this establishment where I attained my law degree. That is why I intend to give whatever help I can to one of those who risked everything to bring this atrocity to public attention.'

'I see. And do you think there will be a positive outcome for the incarcerated man?'

'Gail. I have faith in the British legal system and also the British people, many thousands of whom have gathered here to show their indignation at the barbaric practices that have been carried out here in the name of so called science. Incidentally, it was I believe, that same young lady who stormed into my office who has worked non-stop to organise this protest from groups from all over the British Isles.'

'Sir Giles. It looks like a spokesman for the university is about to make a statement.'

'Really? Then I am very eager to hear it.'

A dozen television cameras and reporters gathered around the nervous looking middle aged man who was standing on the steps. It took a moment, but word went out and two thousand motorcyclists turned off their engines and three thousand on foot became silent.

'Hrmm. Ladies and gentlemen. It befalls me, Gerard Fuller, head of public relations at this university to make the following announcement. To take effect immediately, the head and deputy head of the laboratories have resigned their posts.'

There was a huge cheer from the crowd but that died down when there was obviously more revelations to come.

'Furthermore, also effective immediately, the principle and vice principle have also resigned their posts.'

An even bigger cheer from the crowd.

'That concludes this official statement. No questions will be answered at this time. Thank you.' With that said, the man raced back into the perceived sanctuary of the university.

'Sir Giles. Do you have any comments?'

'Gail. I'm both speechless and delighted.'

'Thank you, Sir Giles Sinclair. This is Gail Mandrake from unprecedented scenes, live outside the university. Back to Simon in the studio.'

Chapter 90
Five months later

It was standing room only in the Nagging Bladder. "Welcome home Cerbarus" banners hung everywhere. Phil Crowe had taken on three extra bar-staff to cope with the numbers. When Cerbarus and Mandy finally arrived, the cheer that went up was apparently heard in the next town. Carol, Todd, Bluesdog, Fran and Su were already on stage and if Hendrix ever played "for he's a jolly good fellow" the band did a very acceptable cover version of it. That done, Su jumped down, kissed the Doc and went over to Cerbarus.

'Still mad at me?' Sunarmi asked.

'Hell, yeah. Come and give me a hug.'

'Glad to have you home,' said Su.

'Bloody glad to be home. So. What's going down?'

'Nothing much. Maybe a little visit to company breeding animals for vivisection. Are you in?'

'Hell, yeah,' said Cebarus with a laugh. 'Bring it on. This is one war that's never going to end.'

Three nights later, Su astride her Tiger, Doc on his Ducati and Cerbarus on his Yamaha were side by side, fifteen other bikers ready to follow.

Sunarmi looked over at Cerbarus. 'Ready to kick some ass, old timer?' she said with a grin.

Cerbarus poked her shoulder with his finger. 'Yours if you're not careful. Let's roll.'

The bikers roared off, ready once again to tilt at windmills. As they disappeared out of sight, hidden in the shadows, a solitary figure shook his head and sighed.

'Bloody young idiots.'

He turned and walked slowly away, his cane going tap tap tap on the pavement.

That's all, folks. Uncle Garf

Hi. Many thanks for buying this book. All earnings from the sales will go to the PDSA which is the Peoples Dispensary for Sick Animals. This is an organisation dedicated to treating sick and injured pets of people without the funds to go to a regular veterinary clinic. The PDSA rely totally on donations from the public, so you have contributed to them by purchasing this book.

The reason I wrote it is because I was inspired by the Bike Doc and Su Kane, (she's the one on the cover by the way) and the Revolting Animals Motorcycle Club, led by the amazing Cerbarus. They are actively involved in rescuing abused animals and finding new homes for them as well as raising money for the PDSA. The chapter about the kitten and Cerbarus is very much a case based on true events.

Cosmetic and toiletries testing on animals. Thankfully, in the UK and across the EU countries this is now banned. HOWEVER, these products are still on sale in the UK imported from other countries still testing on animals. I leave it to you to research to find out names and make informed decisions about supporting those companies with YOUR money.

There is concern that the EU are considering back peddling on its **2013** banning of sales and importing of animal tested cosmetics which could set things back up to ten years. You can sign a petition of protest at the following site. **Let your voice be heard**. www.nocruelcosmetics.org supported by Sir Paul McCartney, Ricky Gervais, Joanna Lumley, Chrissie Hynde, Joss Stone and many others.

This book is fiction, but based on real events and situations, that actually occurred. Sadly, many of the situations still go on today, such as dog fighting, badger baiting, laboratory testing and sow crates for pigs. A sow crate measures six feet six inches long by two feet wide. The pregnant sow is kept in this for months on end and impregnated again very soon after having her litter. Sow crates have been banned in the UK since 1999 but it still goes on in many other countries, including, I'm ashamed to say, here in

New Zealand until 2015. You may wish to investigate this disgusting practice and decide where you buy your pork products from. Well done McDonalds for working with farmers to phase out sow crates and using non sow crate raised pork as much as possible, BUT will seek to only use non sow crate raised pork from 2017. That is still another 5 years of suffering.

The testing on the monkeys as described was done in the late nineties by one of the biggest universities in the UK. A quick search should reveal which one it was.

Badger baiting and dog fighting is illegal in the UK, but it still goes on.

Finally. I like to think the book is an entertaining read and worth your $2.99 US in its own right. If however, you have been encouraged to research some of the above, even better. I make no apologies if some details have disturbed you. It was certainly an education and an emotional roller-coaster for me. It has been a privilege to be a small part in the war against animal abuse and cruelty.

Thank you. Gary Weston.

Please look out for other books by Gary Weston. One Man's Dream out now and The fabulous Abigail Jones will be telling the story of her life, just in time for Christmas!!!!

ABOUT THE AUTHOR

Lives in New Zealand and writes a bit.

Printed in Great Britain
by Amazon.co.uk, Ltd.,
Marston Gate.